WF (Bill) Roberts

W.F. Roberts

AN INVESTMENT OF LIES

Cover photo by the author

Photo enhancement and cover design by Amy Roberts

www.wfroberts.com

ACKNOWLEDGEMENT

Lots of people helped me overcome my reluctance to publish this book but Nancy, Betsy, Sallie and Ben deserve special recognition. If there is any goodness in this work it is due to their encouragement and assistance.

As with all things, this is for Maddie.

An INVESTMENT of LIES

PROLOGUE

The thin man was exhausted, but he kept moving. If he stopped, it would be disastrous. He was accustomed to working in an office, manipulating numbers, keeping balance sheets up-to-date and confirming purchase orders, not being pursued by a boorish overweight man his former friends called upon to "deal with" people who got out of line.

Although he kept moving on the crowded street, the fat man was always behind him, waiting for the perfect opportunity to make a move. He rode a small motor scooter that allowed him to weave in and out of the traffic and keep a safe distance behind.

A broken water line had traffic clogged and the sidewalk was blocked by repair equipment, so the thin man turned onto a side street that was only slightly less crowded. He pulled a silk handkerchief, elaborately monogrammed with a "W" from the breast pocket of his jacket and wiped the sweat from his face. He haphazardly crammed the handkerchief back into his pocket and glanced behind him. The fat man was still there, sitting on his little motor scooter in the midst of the clogged traffic. His bulk hung over the seat of the small machine like stuffed saddlebags on an over-loaded pack mule.

The thin man maneuvered through the traffic to the other side of the street and half walked, half stumbled through the rock archway into Gallivan Park. He was willing to lose the safety of the crowd for the winding pathways of a public park where he expected to find a place to hide. If he could rest for a couple of minutes, his body might recuperate and he could continue. With just a little luck, he could hide from the fat man and then get to her house where she would keep him safe. She knew how to deal with these people much better than he did.

The fat man watched his quarry enter the park. He licked his dry lips with his tongue and a slimy smile crept onto his face. He could not believe his luck. The fool he was chasing had made a blunder. The park was the perfect place to overtake the wealthy bastard and complete his assignment. He glanced at his watch. It was early afternoon. If he were lucky he could be home in time to watch the Maury Povich Show.

He gunned the throttle of the scooter and the engine struggled to move his bulk. Weaving through the work crew on the road and the gridlocked traffic, he forced the machine to pick up speed. The protesting motor sounded like the scream of a terrified animal. He leaned and turned the scooter into the main entrance to the park. He was familiar with the park and knew the path the thin man took. It was just a matter of time now.

The side entrance to the park led into a rose garden. It was meticulously maintained and the roses were in full bloom, but there were no people viewing them. Immediately, the thin man realized he had made a mistake. He was alone and there was no place to hide in the open garden area. There was a single path winding through the rose bushes. If he had turned around and returned to the side street, he might have eluded the fat man, but he wasn't thinking clearly.

Instead of escaping, he started down the pathway, frantically looked for a hiding place. He saw the motor scooter with its monstrous load, stop at the opposite end of the path. Realizing that he could neither hide nor flee, he shrugged his shoulders and sat on one of the park benches, like a zoo animal reluctantly accepting the limits of its cage.

The fat man waddled down the path and stopped in front of the bench. He looked down at the pitiful man. Although, the thin man didn't look up, the fat man sensed his fear. He allowed himself a small smile of satisfaction. 'Godamned rich son of a bitch,' the fat man thought. He felt contempt for the other man with his expensive clothes and condescending attitude, but he suppressed his feelings. He had a job to do.

He had been told not to talk with the man. His instructions were to just deliver their message and leave.

"Look at me you little prick," he said, ignoring his orders.

"You don't have to hurt me. I won't talk. Hell, I'm just an accountant. Accountants know how to keep their mouths shut." The thin man slowly raised his head as he talked. When he was looking into the fat man's face, he asked, "Why are you doing this?" His voice cracked on the words. He sniffed and wiped wetness from his nose with the sleeve of his jacket.

"Don't go playing dumb. You know why." The fat man hit him on the side of his face. He held his hand open-palmed, but with his fingers curled into his hand, so the hit was more than a slap, but less than a full fisted slam. The thin man fell over the bench and rolled into the rose bushes. The hit bore into his head with an intense hot pain that made him ignore the thorns that tore into his hands and snagged his clothes. The fat man grabbed him by his jacket and jerked him over the bench and back into a standing position.

"Not again. Please, don't hit me again. I told them I wouldn't talk," he said. "I can pay you more than they're paying you. How much do you want? Just tell me. I'll give you anything you want." He tried to reach into his pocket, but the fat man grabbed his arm.

"Money won't do you no good," the fat man said. "You rich sons-a-bitches think your money'll buy anything."

"I can make you a rich man. You'll never have to work a day for the rest of your life."

"Nope, ain't gonna risk what I got," the fat man replied hastily. Then he rammed the heel of his palm into the other man's right side just below his rib cage. Breath shot from the thin man's mouth. The pain was sharper than the hit to his face and it worked its way deeper into his body. Nausea grew from his stomach and he had to fight to keep from vomiting. All of his muscles seemed useless. He tried to fall but the fat man held him up and rammed a palm into his left side.

Then the fat man let him fall. "Ain't gonna do you no good to act so innocent. You're just as guilty as the rest of them." He paused, but kept staring at the thin man. "You rich bastards make me sick to my stomach. Think you're so much better than me. Well you ain't! Guess you know that now."

He turned abruptly and walked away a few steps, then turned around. "You got off easy. Next time they send me, I'll kill you." That said he pivoted and walked away, leaving the thin man huddled in a fetal position.

In a way the group's plan had worked. The thin man no longer had a desire to change the group. He no longer cared. Surviving was all that mattered and to survive he knew what he had to do. He had to talk with her. She would know what to do. But if she didn't, he had heard of someone who could help him.

---One---

Delia held my hand tightly and pulled me toward the dreaded roller coaster that some public relations genius had named, *The Great American Scream Machine.* I had promised my little nine year old angel that we would ride the terrifying machine together if she were tall enough to qualify.

Our weekends together were special and I tried to pack as many kid-friendly activities as possible into each of them. Friday, we had gone to Stone Mountain, where we had a nice picnic on the lawn and watched the laser light show. Then on Saturday we attended the Atlanta Kennel Club's agility competition and watched dogs navigate obstacle courses. Delia claimed that both activities had been her favorite thing but I knew she was waiting for the amusement park, so today we were at Six Flags over Georgia.

We had ridden most of the other rides, but she was beside herself with excitement about the roller coaster. I was hoping for a long line, but there were only a few people waiting to ride the coaster.

"I know I'm tall enough, Daddy. I measure myself everyday," she said seriously and then proudly added. "I'm forty three and one half inches tall."

"That's great sweetheart," I said dreading the swooping track before us.

Delia strutted to the measuring station and jumped with excitement that she had grown enough to ride.

An attendant strapped us into the torture machine. Just before it started, Delia worked her hand under the big metal restraint designed to keep us from being thrown from our seats to crash into the ground. She patted my leg and said, "It'll be fun, Daddy. Lots of fun. You'll see."

This was just enough to let me know that she understood.

I smiled at her. If riding this awful machine

would make her happy, I was willing to do it, but it wouldn't be fun. Not for me.

The ride was every bit as awful as I had expected it to be, but I managed to keep my lunch down and hide my discomfort from Delia. As we exited the ride she grabbed my hand, pulled me down and whispered in my ear.

"Thank you Daddy," she said.

***

That evening I drove to her mother's house. Delia knew the drill. She didn't ask me to come in and she didn't prolong our good byes. When I opened the passenger side door, she kissed me, got out of the car and skipped up the walk. Her mother opened the door to let her into the house. She gave me a perfunctory wave. I returned it and drove away.

Delia's mother, Annie Hamilton and I had lived together for many years. At one time we were both convinced that we would be together forever, but when she became pregnant things changed and she began the transformation from a supporting partner into a protective mother.

She claimed that the life I lived was too dangerous and that she couldn't imagine raising a child while I was associated with thieves and murderers. Our relationship deteriorated, until she announced that she was leaving me to live with a viola player with the Atlanta Symphony.

Delia's mother now spent her time trying to convince the Family Court that my occupation was inappropriate for frequent visitation by a young and impressionable girl. She told the court that I made reckless decisions which attracted the kind of violence that could impact our daughter's safety.

---Two---

A couple of days later, Atlanta police Lieutenant Ed Vigodsky came strolling into my office with a Krispy Kreme doughnut bag in his hand.

"The coffee ready?" he asked, as if we met every day at this time.

He was wearing one of his trademark all-weather coats over a wrinkled blue shirt and permanent pressed trousers that had long ago lost any permanence. Although his hair was combed, it was way too-long and scraggly to be called neat and the scuffed boots he wore would fit in on a farm much better than an over-crowded city. All in all, Ed Vigodsky didn't look like a homicide detective, but he was one of the best cops in the city.

"Yep, coffee's ready. Come on in," I said.

He stopped and gave the office a once over inspection. "Could use some art on the wall. Maybe a potted plant by the window," he said.

"Yeah, and you could use a good tailor." I said.

Although we've known each other for a long time, this was the first time he'd been in my office. In high school, Ed had been my brother's best friend and I had been an annoying tag-along. Ed barely tolerated me back then, but when my brother died, we ended up growing close enough to support each other. It would be stretching things to say we were close friends, but over the years we had developed a relationship that was occasionally civil.

"I brought doughnuts," he said, taking a seat in one of the visitor's chairs in front of my desk.

"Sloppy clothes and doughnuts. If you had a stub of a cigar in your mouth, you'd be the perfect cop," I said.

"Shut up, you smart ass." Vigodsky grabbed one of the doughnuts from the bag. "Hey, they're warm too." He placed the bag on my desk.

Showing a remarkable amount of restraint, I poured coffee into a mug and handed it to him before taking one of the doughnuts and biting into it. "This'll cost me an extra thirty minutes on the treadmill," I said as the warm sugary pastry melted in my mouth.

"You could use a little exercise. Get rid of some of that flab around your middle." I ignored the insult, but I did take a breath and suck in my gut. Vigodsky blew on the steaming coffee and took a sip. "Not too bad. 'Course it's not as good as Johnny's, but it'll do." He was comparing my coffee to that served at Chez Monde, a local restaurant that specialized in freshly cooked beignets and custom brewed coffee. Johnny was one of the owners of the restaurant. Ed and I met at Chez Monde for coffee and beignets some Saturday nights.

"Hard to beat Johnny's brew," I said trying to keep my end of the banter going.

"Got any sugar?" he asked.

I handed him the sugar container and he put two heaping spoonfuls into the cup, turning my custom brewed beverage into coffee syrup.

"What brings you out this morning?" I asked.

"Not much. They gave me a new partner."

"What happened to Elliott?" I asked. Harold Elliott and Ed had been partners for more than ten years.

"Got himself promoted."

"That's nice." I waited for him to tell me more

about his new partner but there was something else on his mind.

"Yeah, it's nice," he said. Then he took a slow slurping sip of his coffee concoction, swallowed it and sucked in a deep breath. A look of guilt crept over his face as if I'd caught him stealing from the orphans' fund. "Uh...uh!" He struggled to select his words and a few drops of sweat collected on his forehead.

Since I couldn't tell if he was nervous or angry, I braced myself for an onslaught. Ed and I had almost come to blows last month while I was working on the Halbrook kidnapping case. Vigodsky was convinced that I was withholding information that could help him with the case. When I rescued the kid and returned him to his parents, Ed got furious, cussed me out and called me an interfering publicity seeker.

He stammered a couple more times, took another deep breath and said, "We're retiring Colvin." From all the time and struggle it took for him to say those words, I was expecting an animated enthusiastic proclamation. Instead, he spoke the words matter-of-factly as if discussing the retirement of police personnel was as common as reviewing the score of last night's Braves game.

"It's about time, y'all sent him packing," I replied, relieved that he wasn't angry at me. "The man's a dinosaur. He's a racist and a remnant of the south tha's 'Gone with the Wind'." I exaggerated my accent; then continued talking regularly. "Someone like Colvin makes the whole department look bad. He's a disgrace to the fine folks who serve on the force."

Sergeant Brian Colvin and I have a long and troubled history. When he was a beat cop and I was a student at Georgia State University, some of my college friends and I were protesting something at one of the banks in the Five Points area.

To be honest, I can't remember what it was that sparked our activism, but at the time we thought it was terribly important. It was probably something like the World Bank neglecting hungry children in the third world or some cosmetic company that was testing its products on live animals.

When the cops discovered that we didn't have a permit, they ordered us to leave the area. Our little group gathered to talk about what to do. All the cops waited for us to decide to comply, except Officer Colvin, who came crashing into our group and shoving people out of his way. When he got to me, I stood in front of him and without giving any warning, he clubbed me. He hit me hard and I feel to the ground. It hurt like hell and as I lay on the ground my anger grew.

Colvin stared me in the eye while rhythmically pounding his billy club in the palm of his hand. "Come on big boy," he taunted.

I jumped up and headed for him but a group of friends who were more level headed than I restrained me. They carried me away before I could pay him back. I still considered that he owes me a debt and one day I expect to collect.

"Come on, this is serious," Ed said while taking another doughnut from the bag.

"What's serious is how a pig like Colvin stayed on the force as long as he did. Y'all should've sent him away years ago. If you had, he wouldn't be retiring. He would be entering his prime as a security guard working on the third shift at a department store and getting his kicks from feeling up the mannequins."

Ed flicked his tongue and knocked a piece of sugar coating from this lip. "Come on Art, he's not all bad."

"The hell you say, but what's his retiring got to do with me?"

Ed got that 'cat who ate the canary' look on his

face. "He wants you to speak at his retirement party." He spoke the words with sincerity.

I, however, couldn't hold back laughter. "Yeah, and I want to win the lottery. Ain't neither one likely to happen," I said between chuckles.

"It's important to him," Ed said attempting to be serious but allowing a smile to creep onto his face.

"This is insane Ed. It just doesn't make any sense. Colvin and I have never had a civil conversation in all the time we've known each other. So why the hell would he want me to speak at his retirement party."

"I think all the bad blood between the two of you has been eating at him all these years and he's trying to make things right with you before he leaves the force."

"Bullshit. All he has to do is pick up the phone, call me and say I'm sorry for being a son of a bitch and it's all over."

"Quit being so stubborn! Just think it over."

"Why do you care?" I asked.

"To tell the truth I don't, but the Captain wants him gone about as much as you do. He's ordered me to put together a first rate going into retirement party for the Sergeant and that's what I'm going to do. Colvin really wants you. I don't understand why, but it's my job to convince you to do it and I'm going to do my job."

"Be a lot easier to convince me to stick my dick into a yellow jacket nest." I said.

He smiled. "That's vulgar, even for you. But if you decide to do it, I'll pay to watch."

"What the hell," I said. "Give me a damned doughnut." I grabbed for the bag but he moved it out of my reach.

"Just think about it. We'll talk some more later." He looked into the Krispy Kreme bag. "Only one left. Last one's yours. See you later, chump." He handed me the bag and turned to leave.

"I hate it when you call me chump."

"I know! By the way, it's a luncheon and it's next Monday. Noon at the Riverdale Center. See you there."

"That's not much notice," I said.

"I know," he said again as he walked out the door.

After Ed left I ate the last doughnut and straightened up the office. Then I killed some time solving the crossword puzzle in the paper and pondering Sergeant Colvin's request. By lunch time I hadn't finished the puzzle or thought of a reason why Colvin would even want me to attend his party, much less be a speaker.

For lunch I walked the ten blocks to Amos.' It is an out of the way restaurant one block off Piedmont Road behind a warehouse. It has been an Atlanta institution for as long as I could remember. There are no signs on the building and they don't advertise. The only people who eat at Amos' are people who have been introduced to it by someone else and the place is always packed for lunch. Amos' is famous for their meat and three vegetables special, featuring either fried chicken or chicken fried chicken – on Fridays it is fried fish or country fried steak. Their food is prepared from scratch each day. The meats are fried in pure lard and the vegetables are mostly starches, but the food is so good you'd gladly risk high cholesterol levels and clogged arteries.

It was a strange group that crowded into the place for lunch. I found a seat at the counter between two guys. One of them wore a dirty pair of jeans and a blue tee shirt. He looked like he had spent the morning picking up aluminum cans to pay for his meal. The other was decked out in a tailored business suit that probably cost more than anything in my closet. He complemented his fancy outfit with a pair of suspenders that he wore as a fashion statement not to keep his pants in place.

I skipped the special in favor of one of Lucille's hamburgers. Lucille, who may have been Amos' wife or sister or daughter – I never knew which – hand patted the meat and fried the patties on a flat top grill that was reserved for her burgers. During the lunch rush the grill would be full of sizzling burgers and Lucille would be hustling to keep up with the orders.

I had a burger with lettuce, tomatoes, onions and mayonnaise and a side of potatoes that they cut and fried on site. They had a few bottles of ketchup scattered around the limited seating area and lots of bottles of malt vinegar. I sprinkled the fries with a generous amount of malt vinegar and ate them with my fingers, like you're supposed to. The whole meal was so good it erased the resentment I felt for Sergeant Colvin.

---Three---

Back in the office, I opened my center desk drawer and pulled out a check. It was my fee for getting some dirt on Marjorie Sanderson's husband. I had been holding the check since last week hoping I could wait long enough to feel better about making an almost obscene amount of money for stalking Mr. Sanderson and taking photos of him with another woman.

Waiting didn't help much. I still felt that the check was the kind of dirty money you'd get from selling drugs at a middle school or running a telemarketing scam to bilk money from old folks. However, my bank account was dangerously low and I had a child support payment to make, so I decided the best thing to do with dirty money was deposit it into my bank account. A side benefit would be another opportunity to talk with Betty Lou, my favorite bank teller. I locked the office and walked to the bank. It was only a couple of blocks away but it required crossing both Peachtree and West Peachtree. Three drivers honked their horns and motioned me to hurry even though I was crossing with the light. Atlanta drivers consider pedestrians a nuisance.

At the bank, I had to wait in a short line for Betty Lou, but it was worth the extra time.

"Good afternoon Mr. Gaines. How may I help you?" Betty Lou asked when I walked up to her window. It was a professional greeting, but her eyes revealed a deeper message. *"Hello you good-looking hunk of masculinity."*

I flushed at the compliment her eyes conveyed.

"You're the most beautiful teller on the planet," I said.

"You're much too kind, Mr. Gaines," she said as she took my deposit slip and the Sanderson check. She smiled when she noticed the amount of the check. "I'll have this processed for you in a moment," she said turning to the computer screen to process the deposit.

She worked quickly. "There you go. All done. Is there anything else I can do for you, Mr. Gaines?"

"Marry me."

"I'm still waiting for a ring from the last time you proposed." She winked at me. "Next in line please," she said looking over my shoulder to the customer behind me.

Betty Lou had been fighting the urge to rip off all her clothes and throw herself at me, but she once again managed to control herself. Betty Lou is a strong woman.

Now that my money was safely in the bank, I decided to call it a day and head for home. There is a new convenience store near my house that is more like a mini-mart. They have a nice selection of frozen meat, some seasonal fresh vegetables plus a decent selection of other necessities in addition to beer, cigarettes and lottery tickets. I picked up a few groceries before heading down Peachtree Street and joining the early afternoon rush of people trying to get ahead of the five o'clock traffic snarl that would paralyze the city for at least two hours.

My house was off Peachtree Street on Blossom Lane. At one time the area had been a thriving neighborhood of upscale homes. In its prime, it had been far enough from downtown that middle-income families could raise their children and feel safe, yet close enough to allow them to participate in all the cultural events the city provided. Now it had been absorbed into what was called mid-town and it was no longer a neighborhood. Developers had lured most of the long-time residents away, leaving only me and Thomas Grainger, my next-door neighbor as the remnants of our once proud community.

When I pulled into my driveway, Mr. Grainger was working in his rose garden. There was a basket of cut flowers on the ground which meant he was preparing for a visit from Miss Agnes who had been his gal-pal for the last seventeen years. He always had fresh flowers for her.

He motioned for me to wait while he worked his way out of the rose garden and over to where I stood beside my car. For a seventy-two year old man he moved fast, but a wound he received in World War II made his gait look like a shuffle.

In addition to being a neighbor and a friend, Mr. Grainger was also my official pet-sitter. I had a dog named Gort and a cat named Chester. Gort is an AKC registered Pug who had belonged to my brother before his death. Chester is a black and white tabby cat with no pedigree. He was the remnant of my relationship with

Annie Hamilton. When she got pregnant and left me she moved in with a geek who played the viola with the Symphony Orchestra. He claimed he was allergic to cats. I lost the woman and gained the cat. Not a very fair trade: Annie got a classical musician and I got a cat for whom I was nothing more than an unimportant irritant that provided food and cleaned the litter box.

"They made me another offer today," Mr. Granger said, leaning his arm against the top of my car. He was referring to the Newton Development Company. They were the most aggressive company seeking to turn our little two-house community into a parking tower. "This land's becoming too valuable. Won't be long till it's worth enough that the damned greedy developers will stop waiting for me to die and start trying to find a faster way to get my land. Hell, this place might become so valuable that one of my kids will knock me off just so they can sell it and get the money."

"You're not thinking of selling are you?" I asked.

"Hell no! They'll have to kill me to get me to sell. So if you find my dead body one day, I'm counting on you to get the bastard that took me out."

"You can count on me. Justice for geezers is my motto."

He gave a chuckle and headed back into his yard.

"You tell Miss Agnes hello for me," I yelled after him.

"She'll be angry that you called me a geezer. She thinks I'm a stallion"

"Go for it Man-O-War!"

"Damn right I will," he said. He scurried away, but stopped in mid stride and turned to me. He paused and took a deep breath. "Time you had a woman in your life too. You been moping around too long." He paused, but he had that look that says he wanted to say something else. "You think on it."

I shrugged my shoulders and left.

***

Chester was waiting for me at the door. He gave me one of his hurry up looks and marched to his food bowl. For Chester, nothing took precedence over getting new food in his bowl. Naturally, I placed my groceries on the counter and went to feed the damn cat. Chester had trained me well.

While Chester sniffed the food to determine if I had given him something worthy of his discriminating pallet, I went to the rear door, opened it and called for Gort who strutted from behind the oak tree at the rear corner of my property and headed for the open door. Some dogs take on the attributes of their owner. Gort was one of those dogs. He carried his short, muscular body proudly and defiantly, just as my brother had.

Gort and I went inside. He danced around while I placed dog food into his bowl. He gulped it down, and then licked the bowl on the chance that he might have missed an edible morsel. Gort doesn't have a very discriminating palate. He will eat anything except my almost famous hot dog chili.

***

Later that evening, I was sitting at the kitchen counter with the morning paper and a cup of coffee. Although Atlanta had given up publishing an evening paper many years ago, I hadn't given up the habit of reading the paper in the evening. In the mornings, I scanned the headlines, checked the scores, if the Braves were playing, and read the comics, but in the evening I really studied the newspaper.

Around seven o'clock, I had finished both the newspaper and the coffee, so I began preparing a batch of hot dog chili. One of my goals in life is to create a chili that's better than what is served at the Varsity Drive-in and I was close, very close. The management of the

Varsity should call an executive meeting soon to discuss the threat my culinary skill poses to their supremacy as the hot dog vendor of the South. I can't tell you all of the ingredients, but tomato sauce and beer are included in my recipe.

A couple of hours later, I finished eating a second hot dog. The chili was one of the best batches yet. There was a little left on my plate and when I placed it on the floor for Chester, he gave the chili high marks, by only sniffing it once before lapping it up. Chester had developed a fine appreciation for gourmet hot dog chili. He meowed for more. The scrapings from the bottom of the pan also met with his approval. Gort never showed the slightest interest in my chili, but he did snarf down a wiener.

I was cleaning the dishes when Gort's claws clicked as he sought for traction on the ceramic tiled kitchen floor. He shot from the kitchen to the living room. Seconds later there was a loud pounding on the front door. Gort was already standing guard at the front door, growling and ready to take on whatever threat that might be outside. The pounding on the door was followed by the noise of the doorbell being quickly and repeatedly pushed, then more pounding. Whoever was at the door wasn't a salesman. Salesmen are persistent but they rarely bang on your door. It might have been some religious zealot who had heard about me and felt an urgency to save my soul. But most likely it was someone in trouble. See how fast a professional detective can size things up?

I dried my hands and casually walked into the living room and towards the front door. The room was dark and as I flicked the light switch, three gunshots rang out. Splinters from the front door exploded into the room. One bullet whizzed by my head and hit the plaster wall behind me with a dull thump, creating a plume of white plaster dust. I dove to the floor in front of the sofa and crawled to the front window.

Gort was beside me with his teeth bared and the fur on his neck stiff and upright. He planted himself between me and the door. I rubbed his head but that didn't lessen his determination to protect me and his home.

I moved to the side window. It was dark outside, but with the street lights and all the illumination from the office building, I could clearly see a large dark sedan speed away, its tires squalling as it rounded the corner in front of the professional building beside Mr. Grainger's house. From my vantage point, it wasn't possible to read the license plate or to determine the make of the car but it had the size and shape of a large luxury car like a Cadillac or a Lincoln or maybe a Mercedes.

With the car gone, it was probably safe to open the door, but the graveyard is full of folks who did something they thought was safe. Carefully I pushed myself back from the window so I could see the front door. There was some splintering on the door and light from outside was shining through the bullet holes in it. A moaning sound penetrated through the door and hauntingly echoed in the room as it would in a large empty space. I crouched beside the door and opened it slightly. In the event the shooter had not been in the car and was standing outside, I was ready to drop to the floor. Gort was beside me staring at the door. A rumbling growl vibrated from his stout little body.

I opened the door slowly and let the weight of the body leaning against it force it fully open. The body of a man slid down and fell towards me. I caught him and eased him onto the floor. Gort pushed around me and jumped over the body. He planted himself firmly on the corner of the porch where he could watch the whole yard.

I turned the body over and felt a weak pulse at the

carotid artery. Two of the bullets fired had hit him: one in his chest and one in his stomach. Blood was flowing from him and it was obvious he would bleed out quickly. You didn't need a medical degree to see that his wounds were terminal. His eyes were closed. He turned his head toward me and without opening his eyes he smiled and reached his hand up to me. I took his hand. He opened his eyes and pulled me closer. In a weak, near-death voice, he said. "We weren't evil, but we set it in motion and it got out of control." He paused trying to get enough air to continue, but he couldn't. Then he uttered what sounded like "Key....." and frowned at his inability to force more words from his mouth.

Panic covered his face for a few seconds before the blank stare of death calmed his expression.

I pried his hand loose and gently laid him on the floor so I could grab a pen from my shirt pocket and index cards from my rear trouser pocket. I would have to work fast. By now hundreds of people had heard the gunshots and called nine-one-one.

I reached into his inside coat pocket, grabbed his wallet and a leather business card case. His clothes were expensive and rich folks usually carry their wallet in their inside jacket pocket. We working stiffs carry ours in our rear pocket.

It was unlikely that the police would dust the wallet for fingerprints, but if they did, having my fingerprints on the wallet wouldn't make things any worse that they would already be.

His name was Berry Smythe Wellington. His address, off West Paces Ferry Road, not only indicated money; it indicated old Atlanta money and lots of it. I recorded the name and address, plus his driver's license number on an index card and replaced the wallet. The leather business card holder contained two different cards. On one side were his personal business cards from Wilfield Importers and Distributors and on the other side were cards that showed a collection of five flags. The center flag was the Confederate flag, but I didn't recognize any of the other flags. In the bottom right corner of the card was '*Our Heritage, Inc.*' and a phone number. I took one of the flag cards and one of his business cards and put them into my pocket before replacing the case.

I patted down his pockets until I found a set of keys. His dying word might have been "key" or it might have been the start of another word whose first syllable sounded like key. In either case having his keys might be useful so I pulled the keys out and quickly placed them into my pocket.

This man had come to me for help and someone had killed him on my front steps. That pissed me off. "Alright Mr. Wellington," I said to the body, "I'll find the bastard who killed you." Corpse or not, Berry Wellington was my client. I could afford to be a little generous with my time since the Sanderson divorce money was safely collecting interest in my bank account.

The sound of sirens cut through the silence. Gort turned toward the sound and let out a soft rumbling growl. The police were on the way and I had very little time left. I took a quick look at the body. Berry Wellington was a nice looking man. His face was long, narrow and cleanly shaved. He had eyebrows that had been plucked and shaped and hair that had been cut and styled. There was a bruise on his right cheek and a swelling under his left eye. Even with the bruises his face was boyish and I would have guessed his age to be around twenty-five or twenty-six. His driver's license, however, revealed that he was thirty-seven years old. He wore a dark suit with light stripping. It was tailored and had never seen a rack in a retail store. His trousers were covered with pick marks as if something had pulled individual threads from the material. His shirt was a custom-tailored, heavily starched white shirt with the letters BSW embroidered on the cuff. The color of the letters matched a silk pocket handkerchief that was half in and half out of his front suit pocket.

I placed the index card in my rear pocket and prepared for the onslaught of the Atlanta Police Department. Don't get me wrong about this, I think Atlanta has one of the best police departments in the country, but the combination of a dead body and a private investigator was certain to bring out hostility and loads of bureaucracy. As the first police car arrived, Gort jumped over Berry Wellington into the room and took a protective stance beside me. Gort barred his teeth ready to take on any threat.

As I waited for the cops, I noticed there were no cars parked in front of my house. I wondered how Berry Wellington had gotten here. He wasn't the kind of guy who would have ridden either MARTA or the bus. Was it possible that Mr. Wellington had been a passenger in the car with his murderer? Stranger things had happened.

The first cop on the scene arrived with a drawn pistol. "Hands where I can see them!" he ordered.

Gort gave a quiet growl. I motioned the dog to

heel as I complied with the cop's order without an argument or a snide comment. Being a cop is dangerous work. A cop never knows when one of the kooks he has to deal with will do something that could end up with the cop lying on a morgue stretcher with a tag tied to his big toe. It was natural for the cop to determine if I was one of those dangerous kooks. Plus, anyone at a murder scene is automatically a suspect.

"Stand up and move away slowly!" he said.

I backed into the living room. Gort stayed with me and matched my steps. The cop followed both of us. By this time the cop's partner had arrived and was kneeling to inspect the corpse. The cop guarding me motioned me to the far wall. Gort continued with his low growl and the cop kept cutting his eyes to the dog, unsure which of us posed the most immediate threat.

"Easy Gort," I said and the dog fell silent.

"Turn around," the cop said. It was an order and I complied. He started patting me down.

"I have a gun, but it is in the kitchen." It's always best to give cops information about a weapon quickly.

"Your name?" he asked as he kept searching my body for a weapon. He ignored the keys in my pocket and the index card. They weren't weapons.

"Art Gaines," I replied to his question. I started to turn around, but he stopped me with his hand.

"Stay where you are! You live here?"

"Yes."

"I've heard of you. You're the guy who's friends with Vigodsky?" he said.

"Vigodsky's got no friends," I said. "Hell there's only ten guys in the whole city who can stand him. I happen to be one of the ten."

"He said you had a mouth on you."

"You can't believe anything that man says. He's just upset because he's not as good looking as me." I was trying to add a little light chatter to the situation.

"Yeah, sure. OK, you can turn around." The cop had no sense of humor and he kept his gun pointed at me. "Now, who is the dead guy?" he asked.

"I never saw him before tonight," I said, carefully avoiding having to lie to the police.

"What you mean?" He spoke so the phrase sounded like a single long word and instead of 'you' he said 'chew.' The word he spoke was 'whachewmean'.

"I mean exactly what I said. Until he got shot on my front stoop, I had never seen the guy."

Our conversation was interrupted by a

commotion. The officer at the front door was saying, "You can't go in there."

My next door neighbor, Mr. Grainger was undeterred. "Be damned I can't," he stated as he stepped over my client's body and entered the room.

The cop questioning me moved to block Mr. Grainger, but my neighbor just brushed him aside. "I'm going to check on my friend." It's amazing what an assertive old man can get by with. The cop watched dumbfounded as Mr. Granger limped past him.

"What happened Art?" Mr. Grainger asked.

Gort stood on his hind legs and placed his muzzle on Mr. Grainger's leg. Mr. Granger reached down and rubbed the dog's head.

"That guy was banging on my door. Somebody shot him before I could open it," I said.

"Yeah, we heard the shots. You aren't hurt are you?"

"No, I'm fine."

We both turned at yet another commotion and saw Miss Agnes holding her dress hem up and gently stepping over Mr. Wellington's body. The cop at the door tried to stop her, too. "Ma'am this is a crime scene. You can't come in here."

Miss Agnes calmly replied, "Young man, this may be a place where a tragic crime has occurred, but it is also my friend's home. Do not forget that."

After that neither cop tried to stop her. She came over and stopped in front of me. "Arthur!" She gasped in horror. "Get to your bathroom immediately and wash that man's blood off your hands and arms. Change your clothes too and put those stained clothes in the washing machine," she ordered.

"Excuse me ma'am. There is a police investigation going on here." One of the policemen said to her.

"Young man!" she replied, "conducting an investigation does not empower you to endanger the life of my friend and having him stand around with someone else's blood on him does just that. Now you run along and investigate somewhere else. Mr. Gaines will not be leaving his house, but he will be taking care of his health and well being." She then turned to me. "Hurry up Arthur." She started to grab my arm and move me along, but stopped herself. "Get yourself cleaned up and be careful doing it. Then hurry back, so these policemen can complete their work."

I felt like a grammar school boy being ordered around by a teacher, but I followed her instructions. It took about fifteen minutes to clean up. When I returned to the living room it was almost ten o'clock. The group of cops had grown. At least a dozen of them crawled around my house, generally making a mess of things.

The questioning and the investigation continued past midnight. Mr. Grainger and Miss Agnes stayed with me for the whole ordeal and paid close attention to what was going on. When Miss Agnes disapproved of one of the cop' attitude, she immediately corrected him. "There is no need for that tone. You are a guest in my friend's home." When her reprimand didn't correct their language, she said, "Young man you may not use that tone. This is not a barroom. I expect you to act like a gentleman while you are here." I'm embarrassed to report this, but once she had to correct me. She said, "Arthur, sarcasm is not appropriate in this situation."

When she said this, Mr. Grainger jumped in and told the cops. "Sometimes he can be a smart ass."

To which Miss Agnes said in a disapproving tone. "Thomas, there is no need for vulgar language."

It was after two o'clock in the morning before the police finally left. It took an additional half hour to convince Mr. Grainger and Miss Agnes that I was safe and that I would lock the door securely behind them.

That night when I opened the rear door, Gort refused to go outside. Instead, he stationed himself beside my bed alert to any danger. I fell asleep before Gort relaxed enough to lie down.

---Four---

The next morning I woke at six o'clock. Gort was on the floor beside my bed gently snoring. When he realized I was awake, he bolted upright and scurried around the bedroom sniffing in all the corners and potential hiding places. When he was convinced it was safe, he trotted off to be certain no one had slipped into the house while he was snoozing.

I shuffled to the kitchen, because it's difficult to lift your feet and walk when you've had less than four hours of sleep. Gort finished his security inspection and sat beside the rear door. I let him out, set some coffee to brew and placed a couple of eggs in a pot of water on the stove If everything worked like it should, by the time I showered, shaved and got dressed, the eggs would be a perfectly cooked, with a hard white and a firm but not completely solid yolk.

I returned squeaky clean and neatly groomed and went to the front door to collect the newspaper and see what it said about the murder of Berry Smythe Wellington. On the way through the living room, I made mental notes of the supplies it would take to repair the damage on the wall and the front door.

Back in the kitchen, I poured a cup of coffee, fixed the eggs with some butter and grabbed a piece of toast. The newspaper carried an article about Berry Wellington's murder on the front page above the fold.

The paper gave me just a bit more information. Mr. Wellington had been the accountant for Wilfield Importers and Distributors, a locally owned, multi-national company with estimated sales of seventy five million. The company had recently gone public and was now listed on NASDAQ. Their initial public offering had raised over fifty million dollars and the company's stock price had risen twenty four percent since its listing. The company was involved in importing and distributing novelty items, coin operating vending machines and packaging materials. Their product lines didn't seem to fit together very well. But what did I know about big business?

Some eager reporter had spoken with Horace Wilfield, the President of the company. Mr. Wilfield praised the deceased:

> *Berry Wellington was a vital part of the management team here at Wilfield importers. We counted on his competence, knowledge and work ethics to maintain the history of financial excellence for which our company is so rightly proud. Mr. Wellington could be counted on to complete his assignments on time and with accuracy. His creativity will be missed and it will be difficult to find anyone who can replace him.*

His statement sounded like the kind of institutional sincerity you get from the Public Relations Office or a company attorney, but what else would you expect from a quote given to a reporter who called in the middle of the night to ask about an employee who had been murdered.

The newspaper mentioned my name; they identified me as the brother of the famous Harold Gaines.

The article's writer called me a "prominent investigator who had successfully brought the man who murdered his brother to justice."

I patted myself on the back. The article also mentioned that I had solved the Anderson Finance embezzlement, the Mathew kidnapping and the Yomatogoma Industrial patent cases. I was glad they didn't know about Marjorie Sanderson and her husband. If they had known I did that kind of work they would have called me notorious instead of prominent. The paper didn't mention my winning personality, nor did it mention that I was irresistible to women. That omission was just another example of biased reporting by the media.

I folded the page from the paper and stashed it in the bottom drawer of a file cabinet in the spare bedroom where my brother had spent the last few months of his life. Who knows? One day I might need a newspaper story to include in an advertising brochure.

***

By nine fifteen, I was ready to start some serious investigating for my dead client. Unfortunately that was also the time an Atlanta Police Department car pulled up in front of my house. The day shift was on and ready to hit me with a whole new round of the same questions they had asked last night.

I considered the options and decided that the police would have to wait. I slipped out the rear door, patted Gort on the head, hopped the fence, jumped the creek and climbed a steep bank that led to Peachtree Street, just a block from Merrideth Brothers Hardware store. The Merrideth Brothers had died years ago and now Joe Hansen, a nephew of the brothers, owned the store. Joe was determined to keep the store open and I was determined to do everything I could to support him. However, both of us realized that no amount of determination could overcome the store's limited parking, the escalating value of the store's property and the unrelenting growth of the mega stores that were popping up all over the metropolitan area. It was only a matter of time before the 'march of progress' would trample this reminder of the slower and gentler Atlanta. Just the thought of having to buy a package of nails from a wall rack at the mega store instead of a hand full from the nail barrel at Joe's store sent a cold shiver over my body. Some things, although inevitable, are just too unpleasant to consider.

I picked up the few items I would need to repair

W.F. Roberts

the door and walls, and then waited near the key machine while Joe finished with a customer.

"Read about you in the paper this morning," he said when he came over to assist me.

"I'm a big celebrity. They'll be so many women throwing themselves at me that I might need to hire someone to keep them in line. You interested in the job?"

"Can I pick up some of your culls?" he said playing along with the joke.

"All you want, big boy," I quipped.

"Sounds like the perfect job for me, but I could never give up selling nuts and bolts. It's in my bones."

"If you change your mind, just let me know."

"I read about that guy getting shot at your place," he said, trying to bait me into telling him about the event.

"Always good to read the paper," I replied.

"Yeah, yeah, yeah. Don't change the subject on me. What's the story?"

We talked about the shooting and I answered his questions. That's another thing about a small neighborhood business. When you shop you have to be prepared to exchange a little gossip and listen to some local news. You won't get that from a mega store clerk whose main interests are break and quitting times. The

46

story of a man being shot just blocks from the hardware store would be the main topic of discussion at the hardware store for at least a week. Joe's business would improve, when people discovered that he had some inside information. Of course he really didn't, but just saying I came into the store for the supplies to repair the gun shot damage to my house would have sterling, maybe even platinum, gossip value.

I handed Joe the keys I had 'borrowed' from Berry Smythe Wellington's pocket. As we talked about the murder, Joe duplicated each of them, including the one that said 'do not duplicate.' That wouldn't happen at the mega store either. Just thinking about that sent another cold shiver over my body.

Joe tallied my bill on a hand held calculator, and wrote a receipt on a pad. I paid, grabbed the bag with my supplies and headed back to my house. During the trip back, I carefully wiped the original keys with my shirttail and placed them in my pocket. That might have been destroying evidence, but I wasn't going to let the cops find Joe's fingerprints on the keys. I paused at the bus stop on the corner and sat inside the enclosure that protected waiting riders from the weather, where I slipped the duplicate keys into my shoe. This would make walking a little uncomfortable but it was unlikely the cops would make me take off my shoes.

As expected, crews of Atlanta's finest were at my house. There were three police cars, two marked and one unmarked, parked haphazardly along the curb. The unmarked car meant police detectives were on the case. That was good. A gaggle of cops can dig up a lot of information and if I played my cards right they might just drop some clues into my lap. Never turn down that kind of help.

Even from a block away, I recognized Ed Vigodsky standing on the front sidewalk with a female plain clothed officer I had never seen before. She wore a navy duster over a light blue pants suit and a white blouse. The duster blew open and she looked heroic as she stood with both hands on her hips watching four uniformed cops inspect my yard as if it were a minefield.

Ed saw me walking down the sidewalk. There was a distinct look of contempt on his face as he watched me approach. He threw the cigarette he was smoking onto the sidewalk and crushed it into oblivion with his boot. He only smoked when he was angry or before going into family court to face one of his former wives.

"Nasty habit." I said.

"Go to hell Gaines. Just tell me what happened here and let us inside your house so I can see the crime scene. And where the hell have you been?"

He took a step toward me as he talked. Ed liked to intimidate people. We stared at each other for a few seconds, before I broke away and turned towards the female officer. "I'm Art Gaines, according to this morning's newspaper, I'm a prominent investigator." I extending my hand and she took it with a firm grasp. "I apologize for Lieutenant Vigodsky. He's old and ugly and sometimes forgetful. He neglected to introduce us. You must be his new partner," I said.

Up close, she was more than attractive; she was stunning with a look that let you know she could be vulnerable if she wanted to be but she would always be able to take care of herself. Her hair was light brown with lighter highlights and it was cut just above her shoulders and her hazel colored eyes were intent, but soft and gentle.

She let my hand go. "You were right," she said to Ed.

"About what?" I asked.

"The lieutenant said you would try to hit on me," she said.

"Who could blame me?"

"The lieutenant said I could shoot you if I wanted to. He promised to testify that you attacked me and I had to shoot in self-defense."

"Are you going to shoot me?"

"Maybe," she smiled at me. A feeling of warmth spread through my body. It made me feel uncomfortable. I wasn't ready to have 'warm' feelings about another woman, after my unfortunate experience with Annie Hamilton.

Ed Vigodsky jumped into the conversation. "Don't ever say maybe to him. He can keep going for years on a maybe." He was joking with me now, so I assumed his initial anger was lessening.

"Yeah, he looks the type," she replied.

"That's me, persistent."

"That's you! A pain in the ass," Vigodsky said as he grabbed the bag from my hands.

"Got a warrant to look at the supplies I need to repair the damage the murderer did to my house and to clean up the mess your henchmen on the third shift left when they were investigating."

"Oh shut up. Just checking to see if you have tootsie rolls in the bag. Everyone knows I have a weakness for tootsie rolls." He patted his stomach which didn't have any extra ounce of fat and handed the bag back to me.

"Let's have a look inside your house, Mr. Gaines," the female officer said.

"Wait! What's your name?"

She winked at me but didn't answer the question.

I reached to take her arm, but she had turned away and was marching ahead, leading us towards the house. At the front steps, she gave the lead to me and I unlocked the door, and then stepped aside to let Ed and his partner enter. After confirming that the uniformed police weren't looking, I quickly pulled the keys I had 'borrowed' from Berry Wellington out of my pocket and dropped them into one of the Burford holly bushes beside the steps.

While Ed and his un-named partner inspected my front door and living room, I went to the kitchen, unloaded the supplies I had purchased at the hardware store and found a hiding place for the duplicates of Berry Wellington's keys under the flour canister.

I made some fresh coffee and collected cups, sugar and cream, then toted it all to the living room. Chester followed me, on a mission to inspect the new group of people messing around in his territory.

"Help yourself to coffee Vigodsky." I said while pouring a cup for his partner. "Cream and sugar?" I asked her.

"No thanks, black will be fine." She took a sip. "Very nice. It tastes like French roast." She took another sip. "Is it Kona?" she asked.

"Mysterious, beautiful and knows her coffee. I think I'm in love," I replied.

"Oh brother!" Ed Vigodsky said as he poured himself a cup of coffee. He doctored it up with a generous amount of cream and a couple of heaping spoonfuls of sugar. He took a sip and frowned, and then he added more sugar and sampled the coffee again. This time he smiled and slurped some of the concoction he had created into his mouth.

Chester was rubbing against Ed's leg. Ed bent down and rubbed the cat, who immediately rolled over inviting Vigodsky to rub his stomach. The damned cat even cut his eyes to be certain that I was seeing this shameless behavior.

We were interrupted by one of the yard cops, who came in carrying a small plastic bag with Berry Wellington's keys inside. "We found some keys,

Lieutenant."

Vigodsky stopped petting the cat and stood up making a grunting sound. He took the bag and inspected it. "Where?" he asked the yard cop and he took another loud slurp of this coffee concoction.

"In the middle of one of those holly bushes," the cop replied.

"The ones by the front door?" he asked but didn't wait for an answer. "Didn't you look there before?"

"Yes sir. Must have overlooked them the first time."

"These your keys Gaines?" he asked turning his attention from the cop to me.

"Nope!" I answered. You have to deal with the police, just like you deal with attorneys. Answer the question, but don't volunteer any information. Vigodsky took the bag with the keys and sent the cop back to the yard.

"What do you think Amanda?" Vigodsky said.

"Amanda! What a beautiful name," I said.

"Shut up Gaines," Vigodsky angrily barked to me. Then to Amanda he asked. "Well?"

"Your buddy here planted the keys," she said pointing to me. I looked at her, but kept quiet.

"That he did. That he did," Ed said while staring at me.

"More coffee, anyone?" I asked attempting to discharge some of the tension that was building between Ed and me.

"You've gone too far this time, Art. This is tampering with evidence. What did you hope to accomplish?" Vigodsky was annoyed, but he wasn't angry yet.

"I told you they weren't my keys."

"Go to hell, Art. Did you make copies?"

"I'm shocked you would ask such a thing," I protested.

"Bull shit. The keys won't do you any good. We'll find what they unlock long before you even have a chance to snoop around and get in the way." He was starting to show his anger now.

"More coffee?" I asked again

Ed turned around and yelled at me. "Just shut your mouth you smart ass. I ought to run you in and lock your butt in a cell." He chugged the rest of his coffee and placed his empty cup on the table beside the entrance and marched out of the house.

Amanda watched him storm across the lawn. She

gulped down the last of her coffee and placed the empty cup on the tray. "Nice brew." She smiled at me. "I wouldn't piss him off if I were you."

Chester was sitting beside the door. He hissed at Amanda as she passed.

"Bad cat," I said as I followed Amanda to the door. "What's your last name?" I asked.

"Thought you were a detective, Mr. Arthur Harrison Gaines." About half way to the car, she turned and said, "We'll be back." It was a respectable imitation of Arnold Schwarzenegger's Terminator. The smile she flashed at me had an intensity that shot into the core of my being. I don't really know what it meant but I was certain that it held a wonderful promise. Somehow a flippant response seemed inappropriate, so I just returned her smile.

I picked up Chester. "Didn't like her, did you?" The cat didn't answer the question but he watched Amanda until he was certain she was in the police car and leaving his property. Then he started fidgeting. I placed him on the floor and he strutted around my feet, proud that his snarl and hiss had driven the evil woman away. "Well, I might as well go to the garage and get some exercise now that I have the cops gathering facts for me,"

I said to Chester.

I spent the next two hours in the part of the garage I had turned into an exercise area and a workshop. The activity made me feel as if I had gotten a full night's sleep.

---Five---

Back in the house, my cell phone was buzzing. I hate the thing and more often than not I forget to carry it and leave it plugged in to its charger on the counter. The phone's display indicated that I had missed five calls and had two messages. They had to be from Annie Hamilton and it didn't take a detective to know what she wanted. I decided to postpone listening to the messages or returning the calls and placed the phone back on the counter. It immediately started buzzing. The display announced it was Annie Hamilton.

I took a deep breath, pressed the talk button and said, "Hello."

"Why the hell haven't you returned my calls?" she

said, but before I could answer she continued. "Do you honestly think I can allow my daughter to be anywhere near you?"

"She's my daughter too," I said.

"Go to hell, Art. You're a dangerous man. Do you think Delia would be safe near you?"

"What do you want me to say Annie?"

"I want you to say that you'll stay away form my daughter. That's what I want you to say," she said.

"I would never let anything happen to Delia and you know that," I said.

"How can you say that? A man was just killed at your house. What would have happened if Delia had been staying over?"

"I would never let anything hurt her."

"How can you say that. Wherever you go there's killing. First, your brother was gunned down and then Art, you killed a man yourself. I saw you do it, Art. I saw you kill a man."

"You know I either had to shoot him or he would have shot me and you too."

"I'm an adult Art. I knew the kind of man you were. I knew how dangerous your life could be. Hell, Art at one time I thought it was exciting. I even wanted to help you. But now I have Delia and I have to think of her. She is just a child. She deserves to have a safe environment to grow up in."

"And you don't think I can be part of a safe environment?"

"No, I don't. I know how you work. You poke around and stir things up. You goad people. You make things happen. That's why you're so damned good at what you do, but that means that trouble seeks you out."

It took me a moment to respond. "Don't you think you're being a little melodramatic?" I said.

"Listen to me Art. Did you know that man was coming to your house?" When I didn't respond quickly she added, "Well, did you?"

"No," I said.

"Do you know who shot him? Again, when I didn't immediately respond, "Well, did you?"

"No."

"Could you have stopped the murder? Could you have kept that man safe?"

"No, damn it I couldn't, but that doesn't mean I couldn't keep Delia safe."

"Oh, Art you're impossible."

"I love Delia," I said.

"I know you do and she loves you too. That's what makes this so difficult." She clicked off.

I held the phone to my ear and played the conversation over in my head. Eventually, I clicked the 'END' button, re-attached the charger to the phone and placed it back on the counter.

Annie had a point, but I knew I would never let anything hurt Delia.

---Six---

My brother always advised me to stay out of the way and let the police do their job. It was good advice. "The cops have a lot more resources than you and they're better at finding things and collecting facts," he had said. "If you're lucky, you can use what they uncover to do what you do best and that is be persistent and use logic. Cops can rarely be persistent; they have to move on to the next crime and logic tends to elude them."

By now the police would be interviewing everyone who might be remotely connected to Berry Wellington. Ed Vigodsky would have a legion of cops assigned to finding what the keys recovered from Berry Wellington's body opened. My best course of action was to follow

Buddy's advice and do nothing for the time being and see what the police stirred up.

I headed for my office to check the mail and be near the business phone. Being at the office would also give me an opportunity to do some internet research on Berry Wellington and his employer, Wilfield Importers and Distributors. As a side benefit, some new business might drop into my lap – you never know.

My office is located at the intersection of Peachtree and West Peachtree streets in one of the older high rise office building. It was pretentiously named the Century Center Tower. I pulled into the parking garage and maneuvered my car to the space marked 'Reserved – Mr. Gaines.' and rode the elevator to the seventeenth floor. As the elevator door opened I noticed some grass clippings on the hallway carpet.

A strange feeling that something was wrong jarred me into alertness. In this business you learn to trust your feelings and I instinctively moved to the side of the elevator car and pressed the button for the top floor. I got off the elevator and went to the stairway and walked down to the seventeenth floor.

It was rare that I carried a gun. I had four guns; one at the house, two inside my office and one in the car.

Now I regretted not having one with me.

The stairway door had a panic bar that couldn't be opened silently. I tried anyway, but the noise of the latch releasing rumbled in the empty hallway like the thunder of an approaching September storm. I peeked into the hallway toward my office. The hallway was empty and my office door was closed, but there were grass clippings, pieces of leaves and other yard debris trailing from the elevator to my office door.

The lock to my office door is one of those that can be opened from the inside even when the door is locked. It's really a nuisance because if you have your door locked and you have to run to the bathroom you find yourself locked out when you return. Since I would have to use the key to get into the office, and since the noise from opening the stairway door could have been heard by anyone in the office, I opted for the direct approach and walked straight for the office door. I fumbled with the keys making an extraordinary amount of noise before unlocking the door. I was gambling that whoever was in the office would hide instead of standing his ground and preparing to shoot me.

The office has an outer waiting area with a secretarial desk that has never been used and four armchairs that were only rarely needed. The same kind of yard debris was all over the floor of the outer office. If the intruder was still here, he wasn't a professional. He was probably just some joker whose main claim to fame was being a graduate of the Acme School of Lock Picking.

I was alert, but unprepared for what happened. The door to my inner office flew open. It slammed into the wall, the floor shook and vibrated as the silhouette of a monster sized man moved out of the office towards me.

This guy was over six feet tall and weighed at least three hundred and fifty pounds. When he got into the light of the outer office I could see that his bulk was from fat not muscle. He had a mop of red hair on his head that was badly in need of a barber. He wore a wrinkled pair of loose fitting jeans with an elastic waist band and a worn and aged tan jacket over a white shirt. He lumbered toward me and with each step his whole body quivered and flapped as the fat on his chest and under his chin flopped from side to side.

As he came near, he swept his massive arm in my direction and swiped me aside. I anticipated his action and was moving away before the full force of his arm hit me. I had enough control over my fall to land at the side of the door and ram my leg in front of his foot to trip him.

He crashed into the hallway floor sending vibrations over the whole area. The fall stunned him. He attempted to get up and made it part of the way before he fell to the floor again. This time he landed on his huge stomach, shaking the floor once again.

With him on the floor, I noticed the work shoes he wore still had some grass clippings and yard trash in their treads. They were those light brown boots you see on sale at discount stores. They have deep treads on the bottom. I jumped up and threw myself onto the heap of a man. I formed a fist with my right hand, and brought it around so the back of my hand smashed into his jaw. If you need to really hurt a guy, that's the best way to do it rather than hitting him with your knuckles. It hurts your hand less too.

With Goliath dazed, I patted him down and found a small incredibly light pistol in the front pocket of his jacket. It was one of those new polymer body pistols, I had read about them in magazines, but this was the first one I had seen. It was an expensive pistol that certainly didn't go with the discount store boots and factory outlet clothes this too-tall, too-fat thug wore. I continued patting him down and felt something strange in his front pants pocket. I worked it out. It was a small pocket knife with a corporate logo and an engraved message - Wilfield Importers – Our 30th Year.   I placed the knife in my shirt pocket then pushed the monster on his side and retrieved a wallet from his rear pocket. The first thing I saw was an official looking badge, which read 'Security Specialist' on the top and 'Captain' on the bottom. Big deal. Ten dollars and ninety five cents at a novelty store.

Eric Lynch has the office beside mine. He peddles disability and cancer insurance.   When he heard the commotion, he stepped into the hallway. "How's it going Art?" he asked matter of factly, as if finding me sitting on top of a mountain of a man searching his pockets was an everyday occurrence.

"Everything's under control. Just some insurance salesman who got pissed when I told him I only bought from you."

"Yell, if you need anything," Eric smiled and returned to his office.

The monster beneath me started to come around so I placed the little gun against his forehead and continue looking at the wallet with my other hand. His drivers' license said his name was James Andrews and that he lived at 417D Jonesville Highway MHP. I knew the area. It wasn't a mobile home park, it was nothing more than a run-down trailer camp. He had the usual compliment of credit cards and a corporate American Express Card on the account of Wilfield Importers and Distributors. He also carried an employee ID card from Wilfield Importers and Distributors. It was one of those magnetic cards that allowed access to various areas of a building. I placed the card into my shirt pocket along with the anniversary knife, and then stuffed the wallet back into James Andrews' pocket. He groaned. I stood up and allowed him to roll over onto his back. When he opened his eyes I showed him the gun.

"Up, big boy, but do it slowly," I said, as if he could get his bulk from the floor quickly.

I followed his efforts and while he strained to comply with my order I kept the pistol pressed under his chin or behind his ear. As he struggled to move his bulk from the floor, there were a couple of times when a normal sized man could have knocked me away but he was so heavy he needed both hands to keep himself balanced as he got upright.

"Into the office," I motioned the way with his expensive little gun.

He took a couple of steps and lost his balance. Fortunately, I had stepped back so he had room to brace himself against the wall to keep from falling again.

He said, "You broke my jaw. I need a doctor," while he rubbed his face and tried to stand without holding onto the wall.

I slapped him behind his right ear. "You damned, big candy ass. Don't go breaking into my office and then cry for medical help when you get caught. Now get into the office before we attract more attention." Actually we already had. Mr. Emerson, the property insurance investigator who has an office on the other side of mine, was watching us. He nodded at me and stepped back into his office. We had worked on a couple of small projects together. I knew he would be listening at the wall in the event I needed assistance.

When the giant and I got into my inner office I ordered him to kneel in front of my desk. He struggled to comply but couldn't support his weight enough to keep from slamming his knee onto the floor. He grimaced with pain.

"Give me a name," I ordered.

"What you mean? You done hurt me. You better just let me go and forget about all this. Go easier on you in the end."

I slapped him behind his left ear with the back of

my hand. "Just a word of advice. You don't need to worry about me. What you need to spend your time worrying about is whether I will break your leg or maybe even put a bullet from this cute little gun into your pea-sized brain. Now give me the name!"

"James Andrews," he replied.

"Not your name ass hole. I know who you are."

"What name? I don't know what you're talking about."

"Who do you work for?"

"None of your damned business," he said defiantly. Then he added, "I'll kill you for this 'fore it's over." As if he could regain some of his dignity by issuing the threat.

I swung the heel of my hand into his side near where his kidneys should be. I didn't hold back on the punch and I would have probably caused some internal damage to a normal sized man, but to a guy his size the blow would just cause a lot of pain. He screamed and fell to the floor.

"Get yourself back up on the desk, Dumbo."

He gasped for breath. "Can't."

"You best find a way to."

"OK! OK! Just give me a minute."

I grabbed the collar of his shirt and helped him back to a knelling position.

"Name!" I ordered.

"I work for the Wilfields. Well really I work for Andy Wilfield."

"What does this Andy do?"

"Boss's son," he replied.

"Is that his job title?"

"How the hell should I know? Don't matter none what his title is, he's still the boss's son."

I came around to the front of the desk, sat down and propped my arm on the desk and pointed the pistol at his head.

"Give me his number," I said as I picked up the phone.

"Come on man. Cut me some slack. I'm just a guy trying to make a living. Ain't many jobs out there for people like me," he pleaded.

"Give me the number or you'll be looking for your next job without any teeth."

He hesitated, but when I held the telephone receiver like a club he gave me the number.

I dialed it.

"Good morning. Wilfield Importers and

Distributors." It was a beautiful voice. If I hadn't been hard at work I might have fallen in love sight unseen. Someone with that kind of voice would have to be beautiful, sexy and able to mix a perfect martini.

"Let me speak with Andy Wilfield," I said, trying to sound masculine and debonair.

"May I tell him who's calling?" she said in a very professional tone.

"You may. My name is Art Gaines."

"And may I tell him who you are with Mr. Gaines."

"He'll know," I lied.

She placed me on hold for less than a minute. "I'm sorry Mr. Gaines, but Mr. Wilfield is in a meeting." She was now speaking with her I-knew-he-didn't-know-you tone of voice.

"I'm sure he is, but you must get a message to him immediately. Tell him I need to ask his advice. I have one of his employees here with me in my office. His name is James Andrews. I can't decide whether to turn him in to the police or to just shoot him with the expensive little gun he was carrying when he trespassed and broke into my office."

"I beg your pardon?" she asked.

"Just tell him," I said sharply.

She placed me back on hold. I smiled at James Andrews. "Well Jimmy, it looks like they're voting. I really hope they vote to turn you in to the cops. I just had the carpet cleaned and I'd hate to have to shoot you. Blood stains are so hard to get out."

He stared at me with contempt. I ignored him.

We waited for close to five minutes before the line was picked up again. "Mr. Gaines, my name is Horace Wilfield."

"Hello Horace. Actually I was calling for Andy Wilfield."

"Andy is my son. Whatever you have to say to him you may say to me. I'm a very busy man. What can I do for you?"

"Well Horace, I have a problem," I paused and cleared my throat. "James Andrews, your son's goon, has broken into my office. Do you have any idea why your little boy Andy and his trained gorilla would have an interest in the contents of my meager little office?"

"Mr. Gaines, I don't...."

I interrupted him, "Horace, when you order someone like big, bad James to break into a man's personal office that establishes an intimate relationship. Now that we have become intimate you may call me Art."

He ignored me. "Mr. Gaines. I apologize for my son's enthusiasm, but there are some unusual circumstances involved that might have clouded his judgment."

"And just what are these unusual circumstances?" I asked.

He paused and took a deep breath. "Prior to his ... ah... unfortunate death at your home, Mr. Wellington took some valuable property from our company. It was natural for my son and me to assume he might have involved you in his, shall we say, nefarious activities. So you see..."

I interrupted him, "Just slow down. Exactly what kind of valuable property did Mr. Wellington take from your company and what are the nefarious activities you claim he was involving me in?"

"Does that mean that you didn't receive any papers or documents from Mr. Wellington?"

"Horace, Horace, Horace. You can't answer an investigator's question with a question of your own. And don't you know that any detective worth his modest fee would never reveal that kind of information?"

"Mr. Gaines, we are very interested in recovering our missing documents. We would like to ...

I interrupted him, again. "Oh Horace, you've been watching too many TV detective shows. What are you going to do, offer me a job finding these mysterious missing papers you claim dead Berry Wellington took?"

"As a matter of fact, that is exactly what I was going to do. How does fifteen hundred a day plus expenses sound to you."

"Sounds like a nice number. It's about right for a daily fee but it's way too low for a bribe. Horace, let me ask you a question. Assuming I believe that Berry Wellington took something of value from you or your company, why would you send Godzilla to break into my office to look for it? Do you think I would have let Mr. Wellington hide anything in my office where your security agent could just pick it up and bring it back to you?"

"That was a mistake. My son should have never authorized the break in of your office. And as for Mr. Andrews, not only is he personally embarrassing but he is inept as well. You may deal with him however you wish. However, I would like to meet you and discuss my concerns with you. Please come to my office this afternoon so we can talk about all of this face to face."

I glanced at my watch. "How about three

o'clock?"

"Fine," he answered before slamming the phone into its cradle.

"Well Jimmy it's just you and me again." I said gently hanging up my phone.

He grunted and glared angrily, but he didn't say anything.

"Your employer doesn't seem to give a damn about you. He says I can do what I want with you. My new buddy, Horace Wilfield, didn't seem to care when I told him I might shoot you. The way it looks, I don't think you'll be getting the "Employee of the Month" award anytime soon. It's a shame James, after all those years of loyal service to the company they just don't give a damn." I paused and shook my head. "Listen Jimmy, I'm feeling charitable today. Why don't you just jump on up and waddle out of here? If I was you I'd use the time to take a bath and get some clean clothes before starting a search for a new job. You might want to pick up an iron while you're at it. You don't want to go on a job interview with wrinkled clothes."

He didn't respond but he started the process of moving his bulk from a kneeling to a standing position. I heard his knee joint pop as he tried to get upright.

"Can I have my gun back?" he asked.

"Afraid not. You break into my office; you lose your gun. That's the rule."

"It ain't my gun."

"Whose gun is it?" I asked.

"Andy's," he replied.

"Well don't you worry, he'll never miss it. Now run along. Go buy yourself a candy bar. It might make you feel better."

"You somabitch!" He backed out of the office, then turned and ambled toward the elevator.

That's what I like about this business. Sometimes you don't really have to do a lot of investigating. Sometimes the clues just come to you.

***

I looked around the office and didn't see any damage. The desk drawers had been opened and the contents shuffled about and the few things on my desk had been re arranged, but otherwise every thing was in its proper place. I sat down behind the desk and pulled the *Our Heritage, Inc.* card I had taken from Berry Wellington's body and dialed the number on it. It was a long shot, but what the hell.

"May I help you?" A cheerful voice answered after the third ring.

"I'd like to speak with someone about your organization."

"Mr. Estes is not available. Would you like to leave a message?"

"Perhaps you could tell me about your organization."

"We're just an answering service, sir. You'll have to speak with Mr. Estes."

"When are you expecting him?"

"Sir I do have other lines to answer. Would you like for me to take a message for Mr. Estes?"

"Please have him call." I gave her my office number. "Tell him Berry Wellington suggested I call him."

She hung up with out getting my name, acknowledging that she heard the message or saying good bye. Talking with her made me thankful for my reliable, old- fashioned answering machine.

---Seven---

It was getting close to lunchtime so I locked the office and headed uptown on West Peachtree where there was a nice little Mexican restaurant called El Bromista. The place is hard to find and has limited parking, but it is always packed for lunch. Fortunately, it was too early for the lunch crowd so there were a few empty tables. A waitress brought a glass of water and took my order for the Hot-lanta Special - a cheese, a chicken and a beef enchilada with refried beans and sweet ice tea, brewed from real tea leaves and sweetened with real cane sugar. It was a treat. Da nada, y'all!

I didn't have a newspaper or anything else to read, so I passed the time rating the women in the place.

Starting with my waitress who was an 8.67 and ending with lady standing in the kitchen behind a swinging door operating a tortilla press. She was a 2.42. After the meal, the 8.67 gave me a check for the food and smiled so nicely, that I raised her to an 8.9 and left her a big tip.

My next stop was two doors down at Hillary's Beanery. An after lunch latte - two shots of espresso with steamed whole milk – is always a good idea. Then to prove I was brave, I jaywalked across West Peachtree Road. It was worth the risk to get to Pam's Pie Pavilion. Pam claims to bake the best pies in the South. It's a bold claim, but if Pam says it is raining inside a building, you should open your umbrella before entering, because Pam doesn't lie.

After the pie and the latte, I hopped on a MARTA train and thirty three minutes later I hopped off at the West End Station. Wilfield Importers was less than a half-mile from the station, a brisk walk through an area of antique shops, used bookstores and collector boutiques, before you get to the industrial district.

Wilfield Importers occupied what looked like a nineteen fifty's warehouse, to which an extension had been added to house its administrative functions. There was a fence with razor wire surrounding the place with an ominous guard shack beside the only entrance. As I approached, the shack door opened and an armed, uniformed guard stepped out. The guard was the exact opposite of James Andrews. This guard was five feet five inches or maybe five feet six inches tall. To call him skinny would have been an exaggeration. His waist couldn't have been more than twenty six inches. His trousers were too big for him so they were folded and gathered and held in place by a belt cinched tightly around his waist. The wide belt holding his holster and gun didn't have buckle holes in the right place, so someone had punched crude holes to make the belt fit. The extra leather was too thick to dangle; instead it stood straight out and swung back and forth as he moved.

"Yeah!" he said as a greeting, proving that he had missed the courtesy lesson during the security guard training program.

He wore an identification badge that said Melvin.

I extended my hand and said, "Good afternoon Melvin, it's my pleasure to meet you," trying to model courteous behavior.

He ignored my offer to shake hands. "Yeah, nice to meet you too. What you want?" he said, oblivious to my lesson in courtesy.

"Mr. Wilfield is expecting me. I'm a little early, but I'm certain he won't object." It was two thirty and my appointment was at three o'clock.

"Name?" he asked.

"Art Gaines."

The tiny man smiled, "You the guy that beat up Andrews?"

"My reputation precedes me."

A smile broke out on Melvin's face. He kept smiling while he handed me a visitor badge and pointed to the main entrance. "Receptionist name's Emily. She don't like James Andrews much neither." Melvin disappeared into his shack and left me alone. As I headed off to meet Emily, I swear I heard laughter coming from the guard shack.

He must have called ahead because Emily was waiting at the front door. She held the door for me. "Mr. Gaines," she said, with a large smile, "May I bring you a cup of coffee?"

"No thanks," I replied. Office coffee is almost always an under brewed and over heated concoction that only imitates real coffee so I usually pass on it. Also, I like cream in my coffee and that powered chemical stuff they call lightener is awful. I'm convinced that the hottest place in hell will be reserved for those people who put sugar in corn bread and the guy who invented powdered creamer.

"I've notified Mr. Wilfield that you're here. He'll be with you soon." She returned to the reception desk but kept smiling at me. I could tell by the look in her eyes that she wanted to take me home with her and make me her personal sex toy. I thought about it for a while, but I'm an experienced professional whose training and professionalism require me to resist such temptations.

The phone buzzed and she answered it. After hanging up, she said, "Mr. Wilfield will see you now. It's the last office at the end of the hallway." She directed me to a door and as I walked toward it I heard the click that unlocked the door. Ah, corporate security. It makes you feel warm all over to know that these business geniuses were safe behind electronic locks controlled by a push buttons at a receptionist's desk

A man came from the end office and walked toward me. He was fortyish and about six feet tall. He worked out and it showed, but the whole effect was wasted by a full head of hair that was a deep jet black color you can get only from a bottle of dye. He extended his hand. I took it and we gave each other a firm squeeze.

"I'm Andy Wilfield. Thank you for coming." He turned around before I could reply and led me into the end office where an older man stood behind a massive oak desk

Andy said, "Mr. Gaines, may I introduce my father, Mr. Horace Wilfield, the Chairman of the Board and Chief Executive Officer of our company."

"Pleased to meet you," I said and extended my hand.

Old Horace however, didn't extend his hand in return. Instead he motioned to an overstuffed leather chair in front of his desk. I sat in the chair and Andy went to a straight back chair beside his father. He pulled out a writing shelf from the side of the desk and placed a legal pad on it. His chair was lower than his father's and he looked like a dutiful student waiting for the teacher to speak.

Horace Wilfield looked at me for a few moments. I kept eye contact. "Have you a card, Mr. Gaines?" he asked.

I fumbled in my pocket, pulled out my card case and extracted a card. My business card is nothing fancy. The simple card had my name and CONFIDENTIAL INVESTIGATION centered on the card with my office address and phone number in small letters on the bottom. No cell phone number and no e-mail address. I have all these things but don't advertise them. I'm still an analog guy reluctantly living in a digital world. Each year it becomes more and more difficult to fight off technology, but I keep struggling to hold back the inevitable. By the time I withdrew the card from the case, Andy had left his seat and was standing beside me. He took the card and rushed around the desk to give it to his father.

Horace studied the card for what seemed like a long time, before asking, "Your card says 'confidential investigation.' Just how confidential are you Mr. Gaines?"

"As confidential as I need to be."

"Will you lie, Mr. Gaines?"

"If I need to."

"If I hire you will you do what I ask you to do?"

"I might or I might not," I quickly replied.

"I beg your pardon," he exclaimed, sounding as if he was unaccustomed to anyone challenging him.

"I'm not very good at taking orders and I'm a little bit picky about what I will or won't do. That's why I work for myself. However, if I agree to do something, I will do it."

He paused for a few seconds, "That's more than most people can say." He cut his eyes to his son, who sat dutifully hunched over the writing shelf jotting notes on his legal pad. Andy didn't look up, but it was apparent that he knew his father was looking at him.

Horace Wilfield returned his attention to me. "As I mentioned on the phone Mr. Gaines, I would like to retain your services to recover certain missing papers and documents and to return those papers and documents to me personally and to no one else." Again, he turned an accusatory glace towards his son.

"I do seem to recall that discussion. Exactly what 'papers and documents' are missing?" I spoke the words paper and documents sarcastically, but Horace didn't seem to notice.

"It will not be necessary for you to have that specific information in order to complete your assignment. In fact, I am willing to pay for the return of any and all papers and documents you find that relate to Wilfield Importers, myself or my son."

"Sorry that's not the way I work."

"What the hell do you mean? You work the way your employer tells you to work."

"Nope!" I wasn't trying to be arrogant, but I didn't want him to treat me like some mid-level manager forced into compliance by years of thankless work and a generous pension plan. "I only work for clients who are truthful with me. The nice thing about being good is I have enough business that I can be picky." I exaggerated a little, but what the hell, I was dealing with big business where exaggeration was common place.

"Don't be smug with me in my own office. I can buy over a thousand like you any day of the week."

"Yeah, isn't free enterprise wonderful? It's the only system in the world that gives you so many choices. Have you noticed the cereal aisle in the food store? Lots of choices in cereal, too."

"Shut up!" he snapped.

I started to get up from my seat. Usually when someone yells 'shut up,' it's time to go.

"Just keep your seat. We will return," he ordered. He had heavily emphasized the word will. I sat down and he stood up. "Andy!" he snapped and his son jumped to attention. The two of them marched to a door on the sidewall. Andy opened the door and they went into what appeared to be a small conference room. Horace closed the door behind them with more force than was necessary.

Less than two minutes passed before the door re-opened and Horace led the way out with Andy following. Old Horace walked proudly, but Andy was dejected and sweat was visible on his forehead. I hoped his hair coloring was permanent. I would have hated to see the sweat dilute the dye and make it run onto his expensive shirt.

After the duo was seated Horace turned to me. "Very well, Mr. Gaines, we have decided to give you some additional information." He paused as if he were waiting for me to say thank you or something. I smiled at him and he cleared his throat and started talking.

He wasn't stingy with the details. As Harold talked, Andy kept his head bowed. I couldn't tell whether it was from embarrassment or anger. Harold spoke unemotionally and matter-of-factly as he relayed the information.

Some years earlier Andy had found a tract of ocean-front land on one of the Georgia barrier islands that he wanted to buy. Unfortunately, he didn't have enough money for the purchase so he drafted Berry Wellington to help him buy the land with company funds and to hide the transactions from his controlling father and a meddlesome Board of Directors composed of jealous relatives and their attorneys. Berry and Andy had become friends and Berry was willing to help his pal embezzle the money from the company to purchase the land. He devised a series of contracts and lease back agreements that effectively hid the purchase. His creative accounting fooled the auditors and the Board, but Horace uncovered the scheme. At first the old man was angry, but he was so impressed with Berry's ability to manipulate data that he decided to join the deception by using company funds to purchase a beachfront condominium in Hilton Head, South Carolina. Once again, Berry played the accounting shell game and hid the debt in the bowels of the corporate books. To insure that Berry would keep quiet about the purchase, Horace offered Berry the opportunity to purchase some expensive beachfront property for himself.

"It's just good business to be certain that people who have damaging information about you are in a position where it will cost them a great deal to reveal the information," Horace said in explanation for his deal with Berry Wellington.

"They teach that at the Harvard Business School?" I asked.

He ignored my comment and continued with his story. It seems Berry Wellington had no use for beach property, but he did want to purchase a little cabin on Lake Alatoona. So once again, Berry turned up the heat and cooked the books some more. A couple of years passed and no accountant or Board member uncovered the deception. But then Horace decided to retire from the day-to-day operations of the company. He planned to take the privately held corporation public and have the stock listed on the NASDAQ. This would accomplish two things: first, it would put a large amount of money into Horace's personal bank account and secondly, it would allow Horace to leave Andy as Company President under the control of a Board of Directors, composed of business people, not relatives, with himself as Chairman of the Board. Horace realized that the scam they had successfully shielded from local accountants might not fool corporate accountants under the scrutiny of the Security and Exchange Commission.

At this point in his narrative I interrupted and asked, "Do you really think Berry Wellington's deception might fool world class SEC auditors?"

"It was possible. We did receive a clean audit report conducted in preparation to our stock being listed on the exchange and unless the auditors suspect accounting irregularities, it would be unlikely that they would delve into our accounting history. But, I'm a very careful man and I am unwilling to take unnecessary risks."

"Always a good policy to be careful." I said. Then I changed to subject, "I assume the papers and documents Berry Wellington took related to these accounting manipulations."

"Yes, they did," he said.

"Why did Berry feel it was necessary to hide sensitive document?"

"He only hid copies of the documents."

"That still doesn't answer my question. Did he feel threatened?"

"What do you mean?"

"Usually when one crook hides stuff from another crook, it's because the first crook feels threatened."

"I have no idea what he felt, but at that time the future of this company was at risk. If any questionable accounting practices had been exposed, I could have lost control of the company."

"So you threatened Mr. Wellington?"

"Yes, Mr. Gaines, I did."

"So, Berry took copies of documents that could prove you were a party to the embezzlement of company funds."

Horace interrupted me. "Mr. Gaines, what we did was not classified as embezzlement."

"I bet a jury would disagree with you, but what the hell do I know? I'm just a small business person who uses a little old lady to keep my books and fill out my tax return. I don't really know about you corporate tycoons and your corps of accountants."

Old Horace made a 'hump' sound, but otherwise remained silent.

"I assume then that Berry took the documents and let you know that if you carried through with the threat he would provide the documents to the police or the SEC."

Horace did not speak but he nodded his agreement. Andy also looked up and gave a slight nod.

The rest of the story was simple: After Horace was awaked by the pesky reporter who told him that Berry Wellington had been murdered; he drove to the company's headquarters building and started a search of Berry's office hoping to find the files and keep control of the paper trail for the property transactions. When he found no documentation he had Andy send James Andrews to search my office. They assumed that since Berry was shot at my house he and I knew each other.

"Then you knew your son was sending James Andrews to my office."

"Yes, Mr. Gaines. Very little goes on around my business that I do not know about."

"So you lied to me."

Horace shrugged his shoulders.

"Well, at least now I know," I said.

I asked a few more questions before agreeing to take the assignment. I agreed to search for and return any documents I discovered that related to Wilfield Importers, particularly any documents that related to the land swindle.

"What is your fee for these services?" Horace asked.

I quoted a daily rate that was higher than he had offered on the phone and much higher than I normally charged. "That's more than I would normally charge, because I'm charging you my special pain in the ass rate."

Andy looked offended but Horace didn't show any reaction. He had been called worse.

"And if you send Jimmy Andrews or any other

thug to interfere with my investigation, I'll double my fee."

Horace nodded. "When can we expect a report on your progress?" he asked.

"When I have something to report I'll let you know."

"That is unacceptable. You will report each Friday."

"Nope! There are plenty of guys that are willing to do things like that. Be glad to give you a referral."

"Oh shut up." he ordered, "If you don't give reports how do I know that you are working on this assignment? How will I know that when you send a bill it is an accurate reflection on the effort you placed on finding our missing documents?"

"Because I do what I say I'm going to do and because I'm honest in my billing practices. I don't know what you big business guys call that but in the Private Investigation business we call it integrity."

"Bull shit," he said.

I asked for and received a retainer that was twice as much as I would ask from a normal client, but I was dealing with corporate America and I needed the extra protection. Who knows, Horace and his Board of

Directors could go on a cost cutting campaign and decide to downsize me.

On my way out Emily the receptionist hardly noticed me. She was too busy flirting with a salesman. Obviously after realizing she couldn't have me, she rebounded to the first available guy. I wished her luck as I left the building.

---Eight---

It was close to four o'clock when I got back to the MARTA station and joined the small group of people waiting for the train. There would be a mad rush of people fleeing Atlanta, but only a few trying to get back into the city. I sat down on a secluded seat on the rear wall, pulled out my cell phone and turned it on. There was a strong signal so I made some calls and in less than ten minutes I had the information I needed to prove my investigating skills to policewoman Amanda.

The train came and our little group got on. I found a seat and settled down for a boring ride. The trip took way too long and by the time I walked to the parking garage at my office building to get my car, the nightly traffic was in bedlam, with drivers maneuvering cars from lane to lane in a quest for the one mythical lane that would move faster than the others. I yelled at a couple of drivers and made some insulting remarks about their mothers, but that didn't improve their driving. A couple even yelled at me. One even shot me the bird. Their admonitions did nothing to improve the way I was driving either.

Around Piedmont Hospital the traffic was completely clogged. I inched my car along for close to twenty minutes, just enough time to watch the 'Atlanta Population Now' sign add a bunch more people to the already bloated population of the city.

***

Later that evening, after taking care of Chester and Gort, I put on my jogging outfit and placed a change of clothes into a backpack and set off on a jog to Vuitton Gym where I planned to work out for an hour or so and goggle at the ladies in spandex. You just can't get a full work out like that at a home gym.

My plan for was to take a quick shower after my workout and have a late dinner at Angelo's, an absolutely wonderful restaurant three blocks from the gym. After dinner, I'd jog back home to counteract the extra helping of Angelo's meat sauce I would order. It was a good plan, but like many plans, changing circumstances would ruin it.

About a mile from my house, the road narrows to two lanes with no parking area on the either side. At the same time the sidewalk moves close to the road so there is no planting area between the sidewalk and the street. Atlanta, like many Southern cities, grew without strong zoning and no one made plans for the peaceful co-existence of cars and pedestrians to peaceably co-exist. As I entered that area, a car slowed behind me. If I wanted to shoot someone from a moving car this was the place I would choose. It might be paranoia, but less than a day had passed since a guy had been shot on my doorstep and less time than that since a monster thug had broken into my office. I was understandably nervous and decided that being overly cautious was better than overly dead. So I went on the offensive. As a side benefit, this would be a good way to use the experience from my high school days on the wrestling team. I stopped instantly, much faster than the driver of the car could react so the car following me kept moving after I had stopped. By the time the driver slammed on brakes, the passenger door was beside me. I jerked it open, hoping that the door would be unlocked and I would have surprise on my side.

Lady Luck was smiling and the door flew open when I pulled the handle. I reached in, grabbed the driver by his shirt and yanked him part way into the passenger's seat. This pulled his feet off the brake pedal and the car kept rolling; I reached over and threw the gearshift lever into park. The car stopped with enough force to throw the driver into the floor.

That was when I recognized Sergeant Brian Colvin.

"Get the hell off me, you god damned freak," he yelled

I got up by placing my elbow just below his shoulder blade and putting my weight on it.

"That hurts, damn it." He sat up and slid back behind the steering wheel. "You did that on purpose," he said.

"Now Sarge, you know I wouldn't do anything to hurt one of the finest, most tolerant men to wear the blue uniform."

"Don't wear no blue. I'm a detective," he snarled massaging his aching elbow.

"And criminals quake with that knowledge."

"Shut up," he said.

"Yes sir. Now why the hell were you following me like some drive-by shooter?" I said.

"I was doing my job you turd."

"If your job's harassing the public, you ought to get a raise"

"Just what this damned city needs – more of your smart assed mouth."

I slid out of the seat. "Nice talking to you!" I slammed the door with enough force to release some of my anger. I started jogging away from him, but stopped and strolled back to his car. I opened the door. "Alright, why me?" I asked.

"How should I know? The Lieutenant said to find you and get you to call him. I don't know what he wants or why he wants to talk with you. I'm just doing my job."

"That's not what I'm talking about, you buffoon! Why do you want me to speak at your retirement luncheon next week?"

"I just do," he relied.

"Look Colvin, I've always thought you were a racist pig and you've always thought I was an arrogant prick. So...."

"Just a minute," he interrupted, "I never thought

you were just an arrogant prick. I thought you were an overrated, smart-mouthed, egotistical, arrogant prick."

"Glad you cleared that up."

"Anything to help," he said.

"But the point is we've never liked each other." I paused and added, "And just what do you expect me to say?"

"I don't care; you can say whatever you want to."

"It doesn't make any sense. I don't know anything about you." I paused and looked him in the eye.

"You don't need to. Anyway, it's not about me. It's about you."

"What the hell are you talking about?"

"My relationship coach says I need to find a way to let you release your anger."

"Your relationship coach?" I asked.

"Sure."

"You have a relationship coach?"

"Naturally, don't you?"

I turned away, threw both hands into the air and exclaimed, "Jeez damn, now I've heard everything. What's next, a quilting circle at police headquarters?"

He ignored my insult. "My relationship coach says I can't let go of my hatred of you until I enable you to forgive me."

"I've never heard such a bunch of psychobabble crap before. Do you pay this relationship coach money for this advice?"

"Don't make fun of my coach," he protested. "She's helped me a lot."

"Oh my god," I said, throwing my hands in the air again. Then I turned back to Colvin and asked, "How does your coach think my speaking at your retirement dinner will help either one of us?"

"She says that preparing your remarks will help you release your pent up emotions and allow you to confront the hostility you feel towards me."

"That's a bunch of hooey. Why didn't your relationship coach tell you to apologize to me?"

"What for, I was only doing my job."

"Bull shit. Since when did it become a cop's job to beat up college kids?"

"I didn't beat up college kids. I made an example of the leader of a group of unruly college punks."

"Punks? Nobody uses that word anymore."

"I do."

I laughed and said, "And you think I was the group's leader?"

"Damn right."

"Why did you think that?"

"Because I'm a damned good cop and I used common sense. When we ordered your group to move on, instead of responding most of the people in the group turned to you for instructions and on top of that, you were the only one who kept eye contact with me. You weren't afraid. I gave you a reason to fear me."

"I wasn't the group's leader. I was only there to impress Amy Henderson, who, I might add, was the best looking gal at George State University."

"You mean you were protesting and being a nuisance just for a piece of ass?"

"I wouldn't put it that way," I paused to think things over, "But, yes I guess I was."

"Well I'll be damned," he stated and leaned back in his seat. He gave a huge belly laugh and between gasps for breath he said, "You be sure and call the Lieutenant. See you next week."

I don't think his relationship coach would approve, but I could hear his outrageous laughing until his car disappeared around a curve.

---Nine---

An hour later I was walking on one of the second row treadmills cooling down after a thirty-minute workout in the weight room. Actually I wasn't cooling down very much. Originally, Sid Vuitton, the owner of the gym, had the stair step machines on the front row so the exerciser would be facing into the gym. This resulted in a large crowd gathering at the front window to ogle at the near perfect rear ends of the young women struggling to develop truly perfect fannies. After protests from the ladies, the owner turned the machines around so the girls now faced the window. This meant the view from the second row became a line of cute little butts stuffed into too tight spandex. The crowd that had previously collected at the front window was disappointed, but we dues paying regulars who quickly filled the second row of treadmills were pleased.

Luck was on my side when I found an open treadmill behind a girl with a 9.987 rear end. Just watching her gave my cardio vascular system an additional workout. I resolved to come to the gym more often. A guy needs to keep in shape.

My exercising was interrupted by the unmistakable clang of street shoes on the highly polished floors of the gym. Only a klutz would risk damaging the floors. I stopped the machine and turned to give the offender a lecture on gym etiquette and saw Ed Vigodsky walking towards me, staring at the stair step girls.

"You're breaking the rules. No street shoes allowed," I said as he walked up.

He shrugged his shoulders. "I'm the law and I'm here on official police business," he said never taking his eyes from the 9.987 fanny in front of us. "I need to see about a guest membership."

"You're a dirty old man," I replied.

"I resent that. I'm not that old."

"Then quit gawking," I said. One of the stair step girls heard us talking and turned around. She smiled at us before turning back and increasing the speed of her exercise.

"Damn that makes you glad to be alive," he said. His eyes stayed focused on the fanny line in front of us.

"Go away you horny old fart, I need to finish my work out."

"Can't do that. Come. Take a break. Walk with me. We need to talk." When he talks in staccato sentences he has something important to say. Vigodsky turned and walked away, certain that I would follow him. I did.

He led us outside and propped himself against the rock wall on the side of the front entrance. "Berry Smythe Wellington, the guy that got himself shot at your front entrance?" He said the statement as a question.

"Yes!" I replied.

"He was HIV positive."

"Oh shit," I said in reflex to the announcement.

"You need to get yourself checked out. The police report said you had his blood all over you"

"Yeah, thanks for letting me know." Although I was initially shocked by the news, I wasn't too concerned about contracting AIDS. I would, however, check with my doctor. There was no reason to be reckless. "I assume he didn't get the disease from sharing a needle with a junkie?" I added.

"At this point it doesn't look that way. It seems that he got the disease the old fashioned way."

"What else do you know about him?" I asked.

"We talked to one guy who said that Berry liked to collect dirty pictures. Seems like he might have been involved on the fringes of the pornography industry."

"You mean buying and selling."

"Maybe, we really don't know yet."

"Ah, capitalism," I quipped.

"What have you found out?" Vigodsky asked, letting me know we were playing a game of tit for tat.

"Not much, but he was also involved in corporate financial schemes."

"Legal or illegal?"

"Hard to tell. Seems to be one of those get rich quick schemes that starts out legal but as soon as the lawmakers find out about it they will pass a law to make it illegal." I was trying to minimize the illegal land purchases, at least for the time being.

"Then the damned media boys will jump all over the cops for not moving fast to stop it." Ed was still angry about some negative reporting he received while investigating the death of a wealthy socialite. I wasn't personally involved in the case, but Ed took a lot of heat from the local press when he didn't immediately arrest the husband. Ed was right and he proved it when he got a confession from a jealous friend, but he still held a grudge with the press. The newspaper's favorable comments about me probably added to his prejudice against the media.

"That's about the size of it," I said.

"So before Barry Smythe Wellington became a corpse on your doorstep he danced on the legal side but let his toes cross the border occasionally," Vigodsky summarized.

"That seems to be accurate."

"People like that almost always know a whole bunch of folks that dance on the illegal side. You think he got in over his head and attracted the wrong kind of attention?"

"Could be, but I doubt it." I said, not wanting it to seem like I had enough information to form an opinion.

"I don't know. Seems like a good working theory to me. You dance around with financial hanky panky and pornography and you're going to get to know a lot of bad guys."

"Maybe, but knowing bad guys doesn't mean much. Hell, cops know a bunch of bad guys too," I added.

"But cops don't dance."

"I know a few who tried."

"There's always a few that try. A few of you private guys try to dance on the dark side too, but it don't work for you guys either."

"Maybe," I said.

"You got anything else on Mr. Wellington?"

"Nothing definite. Hell, between us, we haven't got much. So far all we know is that he liked porno and he pulled off shady accounting tricks. He might have been involved in some state's right group or something like that."

"What makes you say that?" he asked.

"Just guessing," I replied.

"Sure. We saw the card in his pocket too." He shrugged his shoulders. "You'll tell me as soon as you have anything?" he asked.

"Ed, I can't believe you would have to ask the question."

"Bullshit!" he said. Then his facial expression changed to serious. "There's one more thing." He paused and took a deep breath. "The cops who answered the call reported that you had lots of his blood on you."

"Yeah, guess I did."

"Ought to get it checked out," he said.

I shrugged my shoulders and he turned and walked off.

At the end of the sidewalk he turned around. "Get your smart ass to a Doc. Don't take any chances with your health."

"Thanks and by the way, are you coming to the game tomorrow?" I asked. It was time for our monthly poker night. This month we were meeting at my house.

"Wouldn't miss it. I need the money I win from you to supplement my pension fund," he replied. Although I hate to admit it, he usually did win my money and that of the other guys too. Ed claims he wins because of his skill. I claim it's luck. Those of you who don't play hold-em won't understand this and those of you who do won't believe it, but last month I went all-in against him. I was holding two pair – aces and kings. He called me with pocket fours and got the third four on the river.

I yelled at his back, "Gambling is illegal in the State of Georgia, you know?"

He stopped and turned around. "Lots of things are illegal. See you tomorrow."

I walked back to the gym and headed for the shower. Vigodsky's visit left me pondering all the unanswered questions concerning Berry Wellington. The main one being, why would a man from a wealthy family spend his time orchestrating fraudulent accounting schemes and handling pornography?

---Ten---

The next morning I got up early, fed the animals and headed out to find Barry Wellington's property on Lake Altoona. The lake is not that large, but its shoreline meanders into more than one county. If you want to find who owns property you can look it up on the internet unless the property is in a small rural county, then you just go to the county courthouse and ask. I decided to start with Bartow County because I knew how to get to that county's courthouse. If I didn't have any success there I could get directions to the next county and keep digging from county to county until I found the information I needed.

I turned right onto Peachtree Road and headed

for the infamous Atlanta Perimeter Highway. As usual, the traffic was backed up on the entrance ramp, but it moved steadily and soon I was among of the throng fighting for space on the twelve lanes that circled the city. I poked along at 80 miles per hour and ignored the angry looks from the drivers who zoomed past me.

About an hour later I pulled into Cartersville, Georgia, the county seat of Bartow County, to begin my search of real estate records. One of the truisms of life is that the same county employees who are rude and obnoxious when you have a problem are charming and efficient when you need public information. A second truism is that county employees are more enthusiastic when given an incentive. Usually my charming personality was incentive enough, but today I needed fast results, so I had stopped along the way at a Krispy Kreme shop with its "Hot Doughnut Now" sign brightly proclaiming the availability of their delicacies. I ordered fourteen freshly cooked and glazed doughnuts – a dozen for the records clerks and two for me to nibble on while driving to the courthouse. If Krispy Kreme ever realizes that their product is such valuable currency in the favors market they might raise their prices. I don't plan to let them know.

As expected, the doughnuts worked and within an hour I had the information I needed. Berry Wellington owned three pieces of property in the county, one on Lake Alatoona and two in the rural areas near the lake. One of the clerks gave me a map and directions to the lake property.

It was near lunch, so I picked up a half dozen Krystal burgers and a large Coke to eat in the car while I drove to the lake property.

Getting to the property required four turns off the main highway and with each turn the quality of the road diminished. The third turn was onto an uneven gravel road full of bumps and ruts. The road into Berry Wellington's property was an even narrower driveway with heavy growth that formed a canopy turning the entrance into a dark, almost threatening tunnel. The bushes and shrubs on each side of the drive were so close that they scraped the sides of the car. The driveway ended in a large parking area with a panoramic view of the lake. A small cabin with a large single pane picture window sat on a rise above the lake.

The forest and the deep undergrowth enclosed half of the cabin, isolating it from the sprawl of week-end cabins and giving the illusion that the wildness of nature was trying to absorb this little symbol of civilization.

A black SUV, one of those expensive ones that's about the size of a tank, was parked at the end of the drive partially blocking the entry to the property. I pulled around the vehicle, did a 180-degree turn and parked facing the drive.

I wasn't expecting any trouble, but since I didn't know who was in the cabin I retrieved my pistol from the center console and placed it inside my belt. As I opened the car door a massive figure came from inside the cabin. It was James Andrews moving toward the SUV as fast as someone his size can move.

I reached behind the front seat of my car and pulled a baseball bat from under the seat. I had carried the bat for over two years in anticipation of such an emergency. It always pays to be prepared.

When you have a mountain of a man coming at you, you need direct action and it's best to do something unexpected. So, I started running towards James Andrews.

He stopped, uncertain how to react, before firmly planting his feet and slightly hunkering down as if he expected me to try and tackle him.

Instead, I stepped to the side and slugged him in

the gut with the bat as I passed him. He crumbled to the ground, rolled onto his side and pulled himself into a fetal position while he tried to breathe. As he gasped for air, he tried to form words but he couldn't.

"Jimmy, Jimmy, Jimmy. You're such a slow learner," I said.

This gave him enough time to gain some control of his respiration but he still was unable to form complete words. "Ga dam so bit," he managed to sputter.

It wasn't too difficult to figure out what he was trying to say.

"Now Jimmy, that's not the way to talk to a co-worker. Since we both now work for the Wilfield family, I was hoping we could become friends. I realize we could never be close buddies. I would never invite you to my home for dinner or anything like that, but we might be business friends. Maybe we could pair up for the three-legged race at the company picnic. That sounds like fun to me."

"Shut up, you prick. I'm gonna kill you." He spat the words out between gasps for air.

"I thought we had gone over that before," I grabbed his shirt collar and jerked.

"Stand up!" I ordered. "And stop threatening me.

You might be big enough but you're nowhere near mean enough to scare me."

"Go to hell," he replied.

I pulled my gun and placed it beside his ear and pushed off the safety. "I'm tired of you Jimmy. I just took the safety off. This is a little 22-caliber pistol. Not even half as nice as the pistol you carried when you broke into my office. This little gun isn't fit for much except shooting rats at the dump or maybe putting a slug into that thick skull of yours. Now get to your feet."

"All right. I'm moving," he said as he struggled to raise his bulk.

When he was about half way up exhaustion hit him and he paused. "Move it Jimmy. You can rest later," I said.

He inhaled deeply and finally stood up. "Ain't nothing in there." He pointed to the cabin. "I done looked. Looked damned good too. You ain't gonna find nothing in there," he boasted.

"Is that what they pay you to do big boy?" I tried to put a surprised look on my face. "But wait! Isn't that what they pay me to do too?" I paused, took a deep breath and scratched my head. "You know Jimmy, the company doesn't need to pay both of us to do the same job. I hate to see the company waste money. It might cut into our Christmas bonus. What do you think Jimmy?"

"What do I think about what?" he asked.

"Pay attention Jimmy. Do you think they need us both working on the same project? You see, if both of us keep on like this we'll probably just get into each other's way. Looks like one of us ought to leave and since I've got a gun and a baseball bat, you're the one who has to go." I motioned toward his car. "Get your big butt back to the bus-like thing you're driving." We moved together. As we came beside the SUV, I said. "Wait! Don't get in; just sit down on the ground beside the car."

"I ain't sitting on no ground," he said.

I aimed the gun and fired a round. The bullet whizzed by his ear and landed in a tree behind him. A few wood chips sprayed the area. James changed his mind and sat beside the SUV. I walked around him, opened the door and quickly found a gun hidden behind the owner's manual in the glove box under the passenger's side front seat.

"You're going to lose another gun Jimmy." I checked the clip on the gun and cocked a shell into the chamber. "Whose car is this?"

"Old man Wilfield's"

"I thought so. Hold your ears big guy." I emptied the clip, 15 shots in all, into the side and rear doors of the car, then I removed the clip and threw it and then the gun into the lake. "Hop in Jimmy and get your fat ass back to the Wilfield's. Be sure and show them the car."

"You're crazy."

"So I've been told."

"Mr. Wilfield and Andy won't like this at all."

"I wouldn't either if I were them. Get in and get out of here and what ever you do, don't come back and don't get in my way again."

"The door won't open," he said after trying the knob. "You broke it shooting it like you did. It's a damned new car, too"

"Get in on the passenger side then."

He plodded around the car; crawled into the passenger's seat and then maneuvered himself over the center console and squeezed his tonnage behind the steering wheel. He started the car and pulled forward slowly. As he started turning the vehicle around, I picked up the baseball bat and motioned for him to stop.

I opened the passenger side door. "Give me your cell phone," I said. He started to say something but decided not to. He reached into his pocket and pulled out one of those mini flip phones.

"You are one crazy mother," he said as he handed me the phone.

I flung the phone into the lake. "You'll have to tell the Wilfields what happened in person. And while you're at it, tell Horace that I'm charging him double for having to deal with you again. I got out of the car, but left the passenger side door open. "Don't move," I ordered. I walked to the front of the car and smashed both headlights with the bat. I returned to the open door, leaned in and said, "Now Jimmy, you drive carefully. There are a lot of crazy people out on the roads and I wouldn't want anything to happen to you before you report to Horace and Andy." I closed the door and motioned James towards the driveway. As he drove away, the sound of the bushes scraping on the sides of the oversized SUV were as sweet as a Streisand song.

I pushed the safety on the pistol, placed it under my belt, and then walked to the front of the cabin. I didn't need the duplicate keys because the door had been kicked free of the jam and torn loose from two of its hinges.

The interior of the cabin was sparse. On the right side there was a small kitchen, with pans dangling from nails driven into the wall. An old-fashioned porcelain enamel kitchen table and four slightly rusty chrome chairs with worn plastic seats sat in the far corner of the room. There were two refrigerators on the far wall of the little kitchen. The first was stocked with a selection of beers and soft drinks and the second one was filled with liqueurs, mixers and bottled water.

On the left was a larger room that served as both a living room and a bedroom. An overstuffed sofa sat in front of the window and a heavy wooden bed with a bare mattress filled occupied the rear wall. An empty open-front wardrobe was centered on the far wall. The walls were freshly painted and there were no pictures hanging from them. One side wall was covered with a modern entertainment unit containing a large television, a DVD player and a tape player. It also contained a shelf with video cameras.

The cabin was a mess. Obviously, James had emptied all the drawers turned over some of the furniture and up ended the mattress. "Damned amateur," I said under my breath. He'd also left two empty bottles of Killian's red beer he'd snitched from the refrigerator. I'd misjudged him. I had him pegged as a Pabst Blue Ribbon kind of guy.

James Andrew's search of the cabin had been sloppy but thorough. There was little to be gained by going over what he already had tossed. If there was anything hidden in the cabin it would have to be in a place James hadn't looked. He had knocked over a nightstand during his search. I stooped over to stand it back up and inspect it more closely.

As I did, the distinctive odor of a damp crawl space became obvious. I felt around and found loose boards and started removing them to reveal a square opening into the crawl space under the cabin. I wasn't going to stick my hand into the dark space, so I went to the car and got a flashlight.

In the space under the bedroom was a fireproof box. I reached for its handle and maneuvered the box through the hole in the floor. I moved the flashlight around and found three more fire safe boxes in the same general area. One had a cottonmouth moccasin resting on its lid. The snake didn't want to move, but a gentle nudge from the baseball bat convinced him that I wanted the box more than he did. The snake crawled away without hissing. It learned faster than James Andrews.

I lugged the boxes two at a time to my car and loaded them into the trunk and started trying to open them with Berry Wellington's keys. One fit the lock, but didn't open it. I tried the key on the second box with no success, but it easily opened the third box. There was a set of keys taped to the bottom of the box with duct tape and these keys opened the other boxes.

One of the boxes contained the documents regarding the Wilfield's land swindle. These were the papers the Wilfields had hired me to find. I did some fast arithmetic with my doubled fee and smiled. Another trip to visit Betty Lou at the bank was in the bag. The boxes also contained incorporation papers for a Limited Liability Corporation called Keystone Land Development. A guy named Sammy Estes was president, Berry Wellington was listed as vice president. Randall Kingsmore was secretary and Bob Macek was treasurer. I recognized Macek's name, but couldn't make a connection. I did however realize that some of the pieces were falling into place.

Now I had to get busy and turn them into a picture.

Two of the other boxes were filled with video tapes and photographs. I scanned them quickly. Most were of young men and women in provocative poses, but some were of two, or sometimes more, people in various sexual situations. I'd had my fill of pornographic pictures with the Sanderson divorce affair, but these pictures struck me more as desperation and aloneness than eroticism.

The photographs didn't add too much to the investigation but I did recognize one of the participants. It took me a moment before I realized it was Bob Macek, a city councilman. Now I knew why the name was familiar.

I placed everything back in the boxes and I confirmed that each of them was securely locked before closing the trunk of the car. If you want to get technical, I was tampering with evidence, but the local media was already scratching for crumbs of information about Berry Wellington. If they discovered that his murder also involved politicians and pornography they would go into a feeding frenzy. I didn't want that.

I returned to the cabin and replaced the boards and put the night stand back in place. There was no reason to make it easy for someone else to find the opening.

---Eleven---

My house was set up for the monthly poker game. Although the front door was still splinted and the plaster on the wall was damaged, the front room was neat and clean. Edna Hamilton, the lady who cleans my house once a week, put in an extra day and gave the room a thorough cleaning.

Cleaning up from the murder was easy, but cleaning up after the cops was a challenge. Anytime cops are involved, they leave a terrible mess behind themselves. Their claim was that they were looking for evidence, such as bullets and bullet fragments, but they had picked up everything in the area, inspected it and carelessly replaced it. They had moved all the furniture, looked under the rugs and re-arranged the cushions on the sofa.

Before Edna cleaned there was dark smudges on most of the items in the room from the cops' ridiculous search for fingerprints, as if the killer would have come into the house and touched the candy bowl, the cigar lighter and all the lamps.

I set up two tables for poker: a large one for Texas hold-em and a smaller table for draw and stud games. There were some guys who didn't like hold-em, but the main function of the smaller table was to give the guys who got knocked out of the hold-em game something to do. I stocked the refrigerator with a generous supply of beer and set up a bar with the hard stuff.

The membership of our poker group had changed little since we started playing, but the number of members who attended varied. This night there were only nine: me, Ed, Mr. Grainger, Tim Mangram, Gene McCoy, Peggy Fulton, Edward Witherill, Andrew McCraw and Eric Lynch, the guy with an office next to mine. Mr. Grainger only got to attend when Ms. Agnes was out of town. She did not approve of gambling.

Gort enjoyed poker night almost as much as I did. He'd meet people at the door, bark a couple of times, sniff a little then beg to be petted. As each member arrived, they had to deal with Gort before asking about the details of the murder.

Fortunately, Mr. Grainger assumed the role of narrator and tour guide. He patiently showed where each bullet went and recounted the events of the Wellington murder. With each re-telling, his role increased and by the time the last person arrived, Mr. Grainger was directing the murder investigation.

While most of the group was inspecting my damaged front door and living room wall, Tim Mangram caught my attention and nodded his head in the direction of the sunroom. Tim is my personal attorney and I have paid him way too much money to represent me in family court. I followed him.

Tim has a tendency to over react. He looked around the room as if there could be people hidden behind the plants trying desperately to overhear what he was about to tell me. When he finally spoke, his voice was barely above a whisper.

"I got a letter from Annie Hamilton's attorney. She's petitioning the court to restrict your visitation rights," he said.

"Can she do that?" I said.

He rolled his eyes up and to the right while he considered his response. "It's hard to say. It all depends on which judge is assigned the case."

"What about the law? What does the law say?"

"Come off it Art. You've been in family court before. You should know how it works. Family courts don't just deal with black and white issues of law and family court judges have lots of leeway."

"That's a crock of ....."

"Don't get upset," he said interrupting me. "We just need to wait and see what happens. Annie is claiming your home is an unsafe environment for Delia and that your visitation should be restricted to public places with no overnights, meals, parties or gatherings at your house." He pointed to the bullet damaged front door and the holes in the wall. "We might have our hands full with this one Art. I'll keep your posted." He turned around and walked into the living room.

***

Around ten o'clock the hold-em table was down to me; Ed; Gene McCoy, a defense attorney; and Peggy Fulton, a feature writer for the *Journal-Constitution* newspaper. I'd just won a big pot on a cold bluff, which is dangerous when you are playing with people who rely on luck to fill out a bad hand.

After raking in my chips, I threw the business card with the confederate flags onto the table. "Anyone know anything about this?" I asked. Ed sliced his eyes to me and gave me a cold angry stare, but he couldn't hold it and started smiling.

"This got anything to do with the guy who got himself whacked at your door the other night?" Gene McCoy asked.

"Nobody uses the word 'whacked' except characters on television," I quipped.

"Says who?" he replied playfully.

Our little verbal sparring match was interrupted by Peggy Fulton. "I know about this group," she said picking the card up and studying it. "This card is from one of those wacko groups," she paused and looked at me. "Can I say wacko?"

"A good looking woman like you can say anything she wants to, except whacked," I jokingly replied.

"Did the card belong to the guy who got himself murdered?" she asked.

I nodded and said, "Yeah, he was the one."

"And he was a member of this *Our Heritage* group?"

"Might be. What can you tell me about the group?"

Vigodsky snorted, but he stayed silent.

"A rich socialite involved with that group. Could be an interesting angle," she commented.

"Cool it Peg, don't get your reporter instincts stirred up. There's not a story here," I said.

"Would you tell me if there were?"

"Naturally. I could never keep secrets from a beautiful woman like you."

"Yeah, I'll bet. Anyway, I did a piece on this group for the newspaper. I remember them well."

Ed winked at Peggy. "Always good to remember things," he said.

"I'll always remember you," she replied to Ed, with only a hint of joking in her tone of voice.

"Go on," I nudged her to continue.

"Well this is a group that calls for the South to secede from the Union. There are similar groups popping up over the South and some of them claim to have Northern members." Everyone who was sitting at the table and those who were standing around watching snickered. "No, they're serious," she said. The group grew quiet. "Where have you guys been? Don't you read my articles?" she rebuked us.

"Sweetheart, I read everything you write," I joked.

"It won't do you any good to flirt with me. I'm saving myself for Vigodsky over there. I want to be his next trophy wife."

Vigodsky's face turned red. "Just tell us what you know about this group," he said, trying to act offended, but not fooling anyone.

"He's interested, but trying to hide it from you guys," she said to the table. Then she winked at Ed and continued with her story. "As I said, there are lots of groups out there that want their state or the whole South to be a separate country. Most of the other groups were either established by, or co-opted by,...How do you say it?...kooks."

"Kooks, wackos! You're a professional journalist. What kind of a vocabulary is that?" I asked.

"I got it hanging around with this bunch of illiterates." she said gesturing to the group. "Anyway, the run-of-the-mill wackos that are into Southern separatism are also into what they call family values. They believe that the man is to be the head of the family and that woman must be subservient and all that kind of stuff. They're what we gals call the 'keep her barefoot and pregnant' crowd." She looked around at the group and started laughing when she saw none of us were. "Anyway, these types of kooks care about all that bull shit. They are convinced that their religion is under attack and that morality must be forced on a morally corrupt citizenry. They want a new South to install their brand of religion and government. You get the picture?" She paused long enough to allow us to nod our understanding. "This *Our Heritage* group of kooks is a little different. They have a bunch of members who don't have traditional families and many of their members do not live a traditional life style."

I watched the faces in the room as they realized what she was saying. "You mean they are homosexuals." The speaker was Edward Witherill. He spoke slowly, with a deep southern accent and he pronounced each syllable carefully. If you didn't know better you'd classify him as a hillbilly, but he was a real estate broker who deals exclusively with condominiums just outside the city. He's one of the most intelligent deal makers in the Southeast and he was the wealthiest person in the room.

"You got it," Peggy replied.

"Will someone deal the damned cards?" Ed Vidogsky barked.

Peggy had the dealer button so she picked up the cards, confirmed the blind bets and dealt. "Funny thing about the *Our Heritage* group," she said as she dealt. "They have lots of members who aren't gay. This group's main concern is that the government has gotten too big and doesn't care about individual liberty. They believe if they can form what they refer to as a free and independent Southern Republic, that it will protect individual liberties and freedoms. They're part of the less government is more crowd. Seems like there are a bunch of folks interested in what they are doing who didn't want to hang around with the kooks in similar organizations."

I had an ace and a king, its called 'big slick' in poker slang and it's a nice starting hand. Additionally I had decent table position so I raised the bet hoping to get some action. It didn't work and I only won a small pot because everyone folded.

The conversation moved on to other topics and I picked up the *Our Heritage* card and tucked it back into my pocket. I had learned enough to know that I needed to follow the trail of this group a little deeper into the tangled jungle this case was turning into.

Around ten thirty, the hold-em table was down to a heads up match between Ed Vigodsky and Peggy

Fulton. Ed had gone all in and Peggy had called. This could possibly be the last hand of the night so everyone gathered around to watch. The table showed two tens and two jacks. Peggy turned over a ten and a queen. Ed turned over a Jack and a three.

"Damn luckiest man on the face of the earth," Peggy said as Ed raked in the pot.

"I keep telling you guys it's skill, not luck," Ed replied.

"What the hell," Peggy said, "It's time for me to go anyway. I've stayed out too late and drank too much and Art's starting to look good to me."

"I grow on people," I said.

The game had ended much earlier than normal and although Peggy had claimed to be ready to leave she didn't get up from the table after she saw that Ed wasn't ready to leave. In fact, no one was particularly eager to be the first to leave. People were looking for an excuse to have one more beer and another handful of peanuts. Ed Vigodsky gave it to them when he boasted that he had won over a thousand bucks. Naturally no one believed him, but his claim started a lively discussion as the rest of the group added up their individual loses to determine if Ed was being truthful. I doubted his calculations because

I was up one hundred and twenty five dollars. That was more than enough to pay for the booze and the snacks the group had consumed, so I kept quiet.

The group finally broke up around eleven-thirty. Ed and Peggy Fulton hung around after the others had left to help me straighten the room. Or rather, Ed stayed to help and Peggy stayed to be with Ed. It took less than ten minutes to put things back in order.

"Want to pick up a cup of coffee before we call it an evening?" Ed asked.

"I'd love to," Peggy said, replying much too quickly.

"How about you Art?" Ed asked.

"No. I think I'll call it a night," I replied, not wanting to be the third person.

"Are you gonna replace that door?" Ed asked when I opened the door for them. He was referring to the damage from the bullets fired at Berry Wellington.

"Oh, no. The door is much too nice, I'm going to fix it," I replied.

"Are you that good with wood work?" Peggy asked.

Not wanting to brag, I just shrugged my shoulders.

Ed started down the front steps with Peggy right behind him. She stopped at the bottom of the stairs, turned around and then she took a deep breath and said, "By the way, I saw Annie Hamilton last week."

"That's great," I said, trying to act nonchalant. "How is she doing?" I asked.

"She seems to be doing fine. I heard she was taking you back to court to limit your visitation rights. Is she really doing that?" Peggy said. Both she and Vigodsky were looking intently at me.

"Sorta," I said not wanting to discuss my family court problems with either of them.

"You seeing Delia very often," Ed said.

"Not as often as I'd like," I said.

"Doesn't seem fair," Peggy said.

"It was the best deal I could get. Fairness very seldom makes the docket at family court."

Peggy was shifting her weight from foot to foot and Ed was staring at her avoiding eye contact with me. "Okay, what's going on?" I said.

Instead of answering, Peggy said. "You and Annie ever talk with each other?"

I decided to stop playing whatever game we were involved with and just shrugged my shoulders.

"She's getting married," Peggy said.

"Had to happen sooner or later," I replied straining to keep my voice from cracking.

"I guess so," she said, "But we always thought it would be you and Annie."

"Too many bad things have happened between us," I said.

"That happens. I should know." Ed said. Ed had been married and divorced three times.

"When?" I asked.

"Next month."

"Is she marrying that viola player?"

"Sure. Annie says he makes her very happy."

"I'll bet," I replied.

Peggy came back up the stairs, gave me a quick hug, and then she and Ed walked off.

---Twelve---

The house felt unnaturally lonely, but I ignored the feeling and poured some scotch into a glass. I added some ice and took a short sip to see if it was worth drinking. It was. I took the drink and walked to the sun room, stopping by the desktop humidor to pull out a Garmirian corona and cutting its end. The sun room has a small round table with two chairs. Mr. Grainger keeps it full of plants. He says I need a place to relax and he needs a place to put some of his plants.

I sat in one of the chairs and slid over to give Gort room to join me. He jumped up and lay beside me. The darkness seemed to cover the sun room. Clouds had moved in and blocked the moon and stars and even the garish lights of the businesses crowding in on the house were muted. I lit the cigar and tried to blow a smoke ring then tipped the glass of scotch and let about quarter of it flow into my mouth. I held it for a few seconds then let it trickle down my throat and enjoyed the warmth that spread through my body.

I was determined not to think about Annie Hamilton, but I couldn't control where my mind wandered. Memories of a two-week road trip through Alabama, Mississippi and ending at Jazz Fest in New Orleans, Louisiana, flashed by, followed quickly by glimpses of water skiing on Lake Hartwell and tubing down the Chattahoochee River. For just a brief moment my hand tingled with the memories of touching her body, but the memory that lingered clearest in my mind was having her with me on the worst day of my life.

***

The phone rang around three o'clock. I bolted up in the bed. Annie and her cat, Chester, were sleeping soundly beside me. Annie merely grunted and grimaced before turning over and jerking the covers up to her neck without missing a wink of sleep. That wasn't unusual because she slept more soundly than I could imagine. Chester on the other hand woke quickly, but never happily. He looked at me convinced that I had made the phone ring to disturb his nap. The damned cat gave me a look that said; 'If this happens again, I'll claw your face off,' before curling up and pushing tightly beside Annie's back.

I grabbed the phone quickly, trying to stop a second ring, but my cheerful greeting was met by the silence of a dead line on the other end. I replaced the headset into its cradle and fell back onto my pillow, annoyed that some prankster had bothered my sleep. I tossed and turned seeking that perfect position and had just found it when the phone rang again. This time I didn't try to answer cheerfully.

"What!" I barked into the receiver.

"Mr. Arthur Gaines?"

"Yes! To whom am I speaking?" I turned on a bit of culture to smooth over my rudeness. You never know when it might help.

"My name is Marge Haynes. Mr. Gaines, do you have a brother by the name of Harold Gaines?"

"Yes I do. Has something happened to my brother?"

"I'm afraid he has been shot and involved in a rather serious automobile accident."

"Is he alive?"

"Yes he is, but both the gun shot wound and the injuries he sustained in the automobile accident are life threatening. We would like for you to come down to Eastside Hospital."

"What happened?"

"Mr. Gaines, we understand your concern, but if you will just come to the hospital everything can be handled much easier."

"I'll be right there." She was starting another sentence, as I hung up the phone. In all probability she wanted information about my brother's health insurance coverage.

I shook Annie into semi-consciousness.

"Buddy's been in an accident. I have to get to the hospital." My brother's name was Harold Gaines, but I called him by his boyhood nickname of Buddy

Annie sat up in the bed and gently moved Chester to a place on the floor. "I'll go with you," she said.

"That's alright," I replied. It wasn't that I didn't what her to go with me but I didn't have time to wait for her. I couldn't remember her dressing in less than an hour and that was into a tennis outfit.

"I'll hurry," she said.

She dressed in record time and in less than fifteen minutes we walked out the front door into one of those rare cold snaps Atlanta has every few years. It was nineteen degrees. The wind was blowing between ten and fifteen miles per hour and the cold cut through your clothes effectively stripping them away and making you feel like you were facing it in the nude. In the south we consider anything below forty-five degrees as being unfit for human habitation.

Annie and I ran to the car. Inside the car it was just as cold as outside, but the wind wasn't blowing and it felt almost tropical by comparison.

Normally when it's cold, I let the engine run for a minute or two before driving, but as soon as the engine started, I put the car into reverse, backed out of the driveway and headed for the highway. Traffic was light and we made the forty minute trip to the hospital in less than twenty minutes.

***

Annie and I stood on either side of Buddy's hospital bed. Before they allowed us into his room, the medical staff warned us that his injuries were serious and life threatening. No amount of explanation prepared us for his appearance. There was virtually no place on his body that wasn't bruised, bandaged or stitched. Needles and tubes were all over his body, either sending things into him or draining things out of him.

There were two doctors and corps of other medical personnel attending my brother. The doctors stood beside us with serious looks on their faces, while the other personnel buzzed around the room. There was not a chart, needle, tube or item of supply that escaped being picked up, examined or studied by one of the staff hustling around the room.

The two doctors introduced themselves. Later, I discovered that they were almost as famous as my brother was. Dr George Ormeyer, an orthopedic surgeon, was in such demand that he had his own jet to fly from city to city performing surgery other doctors considered impossible. Dr. Shelia Underwood, a world famous plastic and reconstructive surgeon, had a steady stream of starlets flying into the city for her services, but her real talent was correcting disfiguring birth defects and reconstructing the appearance of accident victim.

All the medical personnel hustling around Buddy's room came to a complete stop when a man in a white doctor's coat came in the door. He was Dr. Henry Thomas, the preeminent neurosurgeon in Atlanta and the

Chief of Staff at the Hospital. Dr. Thomas was a very skinny man with a mop of black and grey hair that hadn't been combed recently and bounced erratically as he walked. His face was wrinkled and red and frozen in a frown.

If you or I had been shot and involved in a serious automobile accident, we would not have had this level of medical care, but then we weren't the guy who recovered the missing Jade Pheasant when it was stolen from the Atlanta Museum or who rescued the governor's wife and daughter from a group of kidnappers. This was one of those times when Buddy's celebrity was desirable.

Dr. Thomas had a presence in the room that commanded respect and fear. With his arrival the non-physician personnel had faded into the back of the room.

"Mr. Gaines?" He spoke in a booming voice that was a contrast to his slight build. He extended his hand and we greeted each other. Then he turned to Annie. "Mrs. Gaines?" he asked.

"Annie Hamilton," she replied, with a mild rebuke in her voice.

Dr. Thomas turned back to me, unaware or more likely not caring, that he might have offended Annie. "Your brother was involved in an accident earlier this evening. He sustained a bullet wound of his shoulder that we believe caused him to loose control of his vehicle. The car left the road and ran some distance into the forest area before crashing into a tree. He received significant blunt impact injury to his chest. We estimate that this happened early in the evening and that approximately two hours transpired between the accident and the time your brother was discovered. This amount of time in sub freezing weather exacerbated his condition. When he finally reached our emergency room, our ER staff recognized the severity of his condition and after identifying him, they called me. I requested that Dr. Ormeyer and Dr. Underwood join me. Your brother was in trauma care and surgery for over three hours. Frankly, he would not be alive at all had he received a lesser level of care." Dr. Thomas certainly didn't lack an ego. "We are all in agreement that your brother has only a slight chance of surviving but if he does he will be paralyzed from his waist down and he will probably not have the use of his left arm."

The words, "Oh my God," erupted spontaneously from Annie.

Dr. Thomas gave a reassuring nod in her direction and continued talking to me. His tone was authoritative and assertive. You could tell he had experience delivering similar reports. "Your brother will require a number of additional surgeries, but we can do no more until he regains some strength, which, as I have already told you, may be unlikely." This genius surgeon must have flunked the course on bedside manners. "We will keep him heavily sedated for a while longer. It may be possible for you and Ms. Ah...."

"Hamilton," Annie added.

"Thank you. You and Ms. Hamilton may be able to visit with your brother briefly tomorrow, but it will be a few more days before you can talk with him. We will of course have therapists standing by to begin working with him in the event there is an improvement in his condition. Do you have any questions?" Although his tone of voice sounded sincere and caring, he did not pause long enough to allow questions. "Very well. We will talk later," he said, as if he had answered all our questions. He turned and left the room

After he left the room, you could almost feel the relief from the medical personnel. Dr. Ormeyer then came over and calmly explained the orthopedic procedures he had performed and Dr. Underwood explained the reconstructive work she was planning if

Buddy's condition improved. Now that Dr. Thomas's enormous ego had left the room, we were able to discuss Buddy's situation in more detail; however all the discussion didn't change the prognosis. If he lived at all, Buddy would be confined to a wheel care and have almost no function in this left arm.

We left the hospital later that evening and went to Buddy's house, a bungalow behind one of the Ashford Park mansions. He rented the place from a man he had cleared of a wrongful embezzlement charge. We picked up his dog, Gort, and brought him to my place and began the preparations to move my brother in with us when he was released from the hospital.

***

Reliving that awful day had lessened my depression over Annie's upcoming wedding. I fixed a second scotch and tried my damnedest to think of nothing at all. For a while I continued trying to blow smoke rings. I failed at that too.

---Thirteen---

So far, detecting by poking around and stirring things up was paying off. I hoped this technique continued to work for me the following day at Berry Wellington's funeral. It was held at a small but elegant chapel on the grounds of the Northside Memory Gardens. I arrived thirty minutes early and took a parking space away from the chapel. A black sedan with ugly black tires and no trim was parked on the other side of the chapel. With a car that ugly, it had to be cops - probably it was Ed Vigodsky and Amanda. If it was, they were here for the same reason I was, to see who showed up. I took a seat in a rear pew where I could see the mourners as they entered the chapel and by looking through the panels on each side of the main door, I could see part of what was happening outside.

Three people were already in the chapel. A man and two women sat on the second row at the front of the chapel near the huge assortment of flowers that was arranged to cover the front wall. The women were dressed in appropriately stylish black dresses and the man was decked out in a tailored grey stripped suit. When I opened the door to the chapel, they turned to see who had entered and started whispering to each other as I slipped into the rear pew. Occasionally, one or the other of the women would sneak a glance at me.

A hearse followed closely by a black and grey Rolls Royce pulled up outside the chapel. When the car stopped, the driver of the Rolls hopped out and rushed to the rear door and opened it. The solitary occupant of the expensive car was an older lady dressed in the type of clothes you would expect from a matron in a chauffeured Rolls. I recognized her from a picture in the newspaper as Berry Wellington's mother. One of the funeral attendants reached for Mrs. Wellington's arm but she shooed him away and marched unattended into the chapel. She took a seat in the front pew, then turned slightly and stared at the group in the second row. They immediately got up. The women took seats on each side of Mrs. Wellington and the man took a seat beside one of the women. The women both hugged Mrs. Wellington and began whispering in her ear. She listened to them for a moment before jerking free and turning to face me. Her look was cold and determined. She turned back and issued an order to one of the young women, who immediately got up and walked towards me.

"You're Art Gaines, aren't you?" she asked.

"The one and only," I replied.

"Mrs. Wellington would like to speak with you. Will you follow me?"

I flashed my best smile and said, "I'd follow you anywhere."

She returned the smile and led the way back to Mrs. Wellington. "Mother, this is Mr. Art Gaines."

Mrs. Wellington extended her hand. I shook it. "You have my deepest sympathy," I said, but she dismissed my gesture without any acknowledgement.

"Mr. Gaines, I am Elizabeth Smythe Wellington. This is my eldest daughter Harriett Meyers Wellington Tucker and the young lady who delivered you to me is my youngest daughter Margaret Eddings Wellington." There was a hint of enthusiasm in her voice when she introduced Harriett but none for Margaret.

"Margaret is not yet married," she added as if being an unattached adult Wellington woman was such a reprehensible situation it needed to be explained to strangers. She did not bother to introduce the man who quietly sat beside the older daughter. "Did you know my son?" she asked.

"No I didn't."

"Why was he at your house, Mr. Gaines?" Obviously she thought that only those who lived at an exclusive address like hers could have a home.

"I don't know why he came to my home, Mrs. Wellington," I replied emphasizing the word 'home' and hoping she would recognize my sarcasm.

"I was given to understand that you are a private investigator. Is that correct?" she continued, unaffected by my cynicism.

"It is," I answered.

"Be at my home this evening at seven thirty sharp. We will have dinner and then discuss this matter in more detail." She spoke slowly and enunciated each word, but she was unable to make her statement sound like anything less than an order.

I didn't want to be disrespectful to a mother

attending her son's funeral, but I also didn't want her to think that she could boss me around like a house servant. "No thank you," I said. Both daughters gasped for air simultaneously; obviously they were accustomed to obeying their mother and were shocked when her orders weren't immediately followed.

"I beg your pardon," she replied in a tone that let me know we were into a power struggle.

"I might be interested in having dinner with you, especially if your lovely daughters will be there, but I am not interested in following orders from anyone, Mrs. Wellington, yourself included."

"I plan on making you a very lucrative offer, Mr. Gaines. Doesn't the prospect of earning a great deal of money make it easier for you to humor an old lady who has just lost the most precious thing in her life?"

"You certainly have my sympathy, but not my obedience."

"Are you a wealthy man, Mr. Gaines?"

"No ma'am, I'm not."

"Understandable." She paused in disgust and took a deep breath. When she continued she added a touch of levity into the tone of her voice. "Very well, Mr. Gaines. My daughters and I would be honored if you would join us for dinner and a discussion of the circumstances of my son's murder."

I reached into my inside jacket pocket, withdrew a small note pad and flipped a few pages, pretending to check my social calendar. "As it happens, I'm free this evening. Seven-thirty would be convenient for me. Is that a good time for you?"

"Yes, Mr. Gaines. Seven-thirty would be convenient." Her words dripped with contempt. She held eye contact longer than necessary then turned from me and looked toward the front of the chapel; clearly communicating the conversation was over. Her disdain lingered.

"Ladies," I said, "I look forward to seeing you tonight." I nodded to the man beside Harriett Wellington and returned to my seat.

While Mrs. Wellington and I had been arguing over dinner arrangements a couple of people had entered the chapel. I looked them over on my way back to the rear pew. They appeared to be bankers or stockbrokers who were probably more interested in being certain Mrs. Wellington knew they were in attendance than in paying respect to Berry Wellington.

I returned to the rear pew and, as I sat down, two

funeral attendants opened the chapel's double doors and pushed a bier with the coffin into the room. A double line of men, serving as pallbearers, followed them, three on each side of the coffin. They wheeled the coffin to the front of the chapel and positioned it among the flowers. The attendants efficiently withdrew leaving the pallbearers formed into a single line. They passed by Mrs. Wellington and her daughters. Everyone shook everyone else's hand and then the pallbearers filed into the third row of pews and quietly sat down as a group.

I turned toward the chapel door in response to a commotion. Four ladies were entering the chapel and making an excessive amount of noise. Three of them were supporting the fourth, who was so involved in crying she couldn't be relied upon to walk unattended. The three sympathy givers were completely occupied with chanting soothing words to the distraught forth member of their group, loudly enough that everyone could hear them.

The group chose a middle pew and entered after some shuffling and pushing to determine who should sit on either side of the main mourner. The lady who lost the contest for the two primary support positions leaned over and handed the crying lady a nice lace handkerchief, then sat back and, not to be outdone, began to sniffle quietly.

Mrs. Wellington turned around to chastise the noise makers, but the anger on her face turned to a slight, very slight, smile and she nodded to the group.

Horace and Andy Wilfield entered next. Horace gave me a look of contempt, and then turned away. He must be holding a grudge about the car I shot and beat with a bat. Andy however smiled and nodded a greeting, probably because it was his father's car not his. They walked to the front pew and gave their condolences to the family. As they walked by the third row, the pallbearer sitting on the end made a slight movement toward Andy and Andy responded with a quick smile before following his father to an empty pew. I made a mental note to get a good look at that pallbearer before leaving.

About twelve more people came in before a robed minister walked through the door and to the front of the chapel. He quickly arranged his notes, and invited us to bow our heads. As he began reciting a prayer, the chapel door slowly opened and a young man slipped quietly into the room. He took a seat on the rear pew opposite from where I was sitting. He slid down into the bench making himself as inconspicuous as possible. His eyes were red and he held a wadded tissue in his hand that he used to blot tears as they formed in his eyes.

The service was remarkably short. In less than ten minutes the minister invited us to adjourn from the chapel and reconvene at the graveside. He motioned the congregation to stand while the pallbearers took their places beside the coffin. When everyone was in their proper place, the minister invited us to pray once again. As most of us were bowing our head, my pew mate slipped from the pew and out of the chapel.

I paid close attention to the pallbearers as they escorted the coffin from the chapel. I wasn't the only one watching them. Andy Wilfield's eyes never left the curly haired pallbearer who had reflexively reached for him.

They loaded the coffin into the pale gray hearse and then the pallbearers and the other mourners walked behind the hearse for the short distance to the gravesite. I trailed behind the group and noticed the young man who had shared a pew with me standing beside a tree to the right of the gravesite. He was silently crying and although most of the mourners saw him, no one made an effort to communicate with him or to bring him into the group. The curly haired pallbearer stayed with his group beside the hearse. The cluster of ladies who had sobbed all during the service walked beside the casket. Each of them placed a rose on the casket. The one who was most upset bent down and kissed the metal casket, and then her friends escorted her to a seat under the tent protecting the grave area.

I found a tree about a hundred feet away and stationed myself where I could watch the goings on. When all were settled, the minister read some scripture, said a few words and called for another prayer. The graveside service was shorter than the chapel service and in less than five minutes the small group of mourners started wandering from under the tent and moving toward their vehicles. The curly haired pallbearer left in one of the funeral home's cars and my pew mate walked to a new Mercedes sedan parked far away from the other cars. The four ladies got into a luxury SUV. The one who had been most upset during the service, had lit a cigarette while walking to the car. She took a couple of deep drags, and then threw the half used butt to the ground before getting into the car. When they had all gone, I wandered back to my car.

Two familiar people stood beside my car. I ignored Lt. Vigodsky and directed my attention to his assistant. "Good afternoon Miss Amanda Jean Halsell."

"I'm impressed. You discovered my name."

"You must have been the most beautiful graduate of Sandhills High School in Fairfield County, South Carolina."

"Maybe he is a detective after all," she said to Ed Vigodsky.

"Just a lucky guess," Vigodsky said.

"I never guess. This leads to my first question. What are you two doing here?" I paused and winked at Amanda then turned to Vigodsky. "Wait a minute I know why Amanda is here. She just wants to be near me, but why are you here Vigodsky?" I asked him.

Vigodsky smiled at Amanda. "See, I told you. Here we stand in a cemetery and he doesn't know how to be serious."

"I should have listened to you," she replied. They were talking as if I weren't present.

"A valuable lesson learned," Vigodsky quipped then he turned to me, "Now Art, back to you. We are here because the tax payers of this community pay us to find criminals and bring them to justice."

"And you think there is a criminal among this group of mourners."

"Oh yes, probably more than one. Don't you agree?"

"Probably," I replied.

"Okay, what have you got?" he asked.

Amanda took a pad from her purse and prepared to take notes.

I began reciting the few facts I had learned, omitting the parts that I needed to keep confidential since they might lead me to a fee. "Not much. The dearly departed owns a cabin on Lake Alatoona."

He turned to Amanda. "That must the Weiser lock key on Mr. Wellington's key chain?" He turned to me. "Did you find the cabin?"

"Yes."

"And how did you get into the cabin?"

"Someone beat me to the place and kicked down the door then ransacked the place before I got there."

"Yeah, I'll bet. And exactly what did you find in the cabin?"

I knew I needed to give them something so I said. "Nothing, the place had been torn apart by the guy who got there before me. There was something strange however."

"Well go on tell us," Vigodsky said.

"Well it might not mean anything, but I thought it was odd. There were two refrigerators in the kitchen of the cabin. One was stocked with beer and soft drinks and the other had any kind of booze and mixer you might want."

"Sounds like you discovered someone's party place," Amanda said.

I winked at her and she smiled at me. "That's what I think too," I said.

"What about a fire safe storage box? There was a key to an Ajax Fire Safe box on Wellington's key ring. Did you find the fire safe box?" Vigodsky asked.

"What are you talking about?" I asked, trying to avoid a direct lie.

"As I said, Berry Wellington had a key that opens one of the Ajax Fire Safe Company boxes." Then he turned to Amanda and said, "Go ahead Amanda, tell him."

"To be exact, the key fits a model AJ 406 Fire Proof Lock Box sold exclusively at the Your Home Center chain of stores," she replied, "Would you be interested in the serial numbers of the box the key opens?"

"Damn. Ya'll are good," I drawled in an exaggerated southern accent. Then in a normal voice continued. "The cabin is just two rooms and a bathroom. There are not a lot of places to hide anything in the cabin.

If there ever was a box inside the cabin it was gone by the time I got there." I knew I was stretching the truth, but the boxes hadn't technically been inside the cabin. "Do you guys know where this box might be?" I asked.

Vigodsky just smiled at me and said, "We don't know, but I think you do."

"What would make you think I know where the box is?" I asked.

"He's good at playing dumb. I think he knows. What do you think?" Vigodsky said to Amanda.

She looked at me. It was a piercing look, like she wanted to peel away my clothes and sneak a peak at my naked body. I tried to match her look, but she was better at it than I. "He knows," she said.

I continued to look at Amanda. "Years from now when our children are grown and we are sitting side by side in front of the fireplace telling stories about the good old days and sipping our prune juice. I'll remind you that you once doubted my truthfulness."

"Has he always been like this?" she asked Ed.

"I'm afraid so. What do you think we should do with him?" Vigodsky asked his partner.

"I think we should just leave him in this cemetery while you and I get on out there and solve this crime."

To Amanda, Vigodsky said, "I agree!" Then to me he said, "You will let us know if you find anything." He said the sentence as a statement more than a question. They turned and headed for their city issued car.

"Of course I will," I replied. "Wait a minute. I need to ask you a question."

"You need help from us?" Amanda asked sarcastically.

"Yes. Who was that man who slipped in late for the funeral and stood behind that tree during the graveside service? And who was the young lady who was so racked with grief that she needed three of her friends for support?"

"Just when I was beginning to think you might be a competent investigator. Should we tell him Amanda?"

"If we tell him, do you think it will slow down his imagination?"

"I doubt it."

"Then don't tell him a thing. After all the Atlanta newspaper called him a competent investigator. Surely a competent investigator could find out on his own."

Vigodsky paused as if in deep thought. "You're right, but I'm going to tell him anyway. It'll be fun watching his embarrassment. The crying man's name is

Randall Kingsmore. He was Berry Wellington's special friend, partner or lover, we're not sure which."

"Maybe all of the above." I stated.

"Could be. Anyway, Mrs. Wellington believes that Kingsmore gave her son AIDS."

"What about the crying lady?"

"We don't know for certain, but we believe she was Abigail Patrick. She was engaged to Berry Wellington."

"Wait a minute! Berry Wellington was gay," I commented.

"Go figure," Vigodsky added.

"What about the curly haired pallbearer?"

"You should turn in your investigator license. Do you want us to do all the work for you?"

"Why not?" I replied.

They turned and walked away. Their car was parked of to the side. They got in and as they drove by me Vigodsky rolled down his window. "We don't know anything about the curly haired pallbearer," he paused then added, "Yet!"

"Thanks." I leaned into the window and spoke to Amanda. "I make one of the best London Broils and the very best Fettuccini Alfredo that's available east of the

Mississippi. How about Friday at seven thirty?"

"Is he harmless?" she asked Vigodsky.

"Completely, but you might need antacids if you eat his cooking."

"Not true, not true. Never trust advice from a man who thinks frozen dinners are gourmet fare," I quipped.

"I'm tempted. Maybe next time. Who knows what the future might bring." she smiled at me.

"Then how about dinner at a restaurant. How about Sollbie's?" Sollbie's was one of Atlanta's five star restaurants. It was too expensive for someone living on a policeman's salary. It was normally too expensive for a confidential investigator too, but I had the Sanderson check in the bank and I was ready to invest that ill-gotten fee on the lovely Amanda Halsell.

She left my invitation unanswered. She signaled Vigodsky with a slight nod and they drove off. She blew me a kiss and waved as they rounded the first curve.

---Fourteen---

I arrived at the Wellington's residence at seven twenty-nine, decked out in a dark gray suit with a freshly laundered white shirt and, as a power statement, a purple striped tie. If nothing else my outfit should impress the daughters, particularly Margaret. She might not be Mrs. Wellington's favorite, but she was mine.

I rang the doorbell and then waited for someone to answer it. It's always a little uncomfortable waiting on a doorstep. You never really know who will answer or what kind of reception you'll receive. That's why I'm not a door-to-door salesman.

A man answered the door. I recognized him as the man who had been with the Wellington family at the funeral. He wore khaki pants and a pastel blue button down shirt with - I swear I'm not making this up - a burgundy sweater tied around his neck. He must have stood in front of a mirror for hours practicing his broad smile. If he were running for the 'Mr. Preppy of the Century' award, I'd vote for him.

"Mr. Gaines?" he asked with a practiced accent that unsuccessfully added a continental European flare to his heavy southern drawl. If I had to guess, I'd pin him as being from deep in the heart of Mississippi.

"Yes," I replied.

"My name is Bradley Tucker. Welcome to our home. Mrs. Wellington and my wife are expecting you." He extended his hand. I took it and as expected his grip was unenthusiastic and weak.

"What about Margaret. Will she be joining us?" I asked.

He ignored my question and said, "This way."

He led me toward the left side of the hallway to a set of double pocket doors that ran from floor to ceiling. When he opened the doors, he stepped back to allow an unobstructed view of the room the door protected. The effect was spectacular. You can say what you want, but the really rich folks know how to get a jaw dropping reaction from us normal folks. A large round table was immediately in front of the door. The table was highly polished and made of a very dark, exotic wood that I couldn't identify without closer inspection. On the table was a massive flower arrangement that must have included more than one hundred stems. The arrangement was so large that it partially blocked the stone fireplace. Overstuffed leather sofa sat on each side of the fireplace. They were arranged at a forty-five degree angle, so anyone sitting on either of them would have a clear view of the large portrait suspended above the mantle.

The portrait showed a regal looking family group. Standing proudly in the rear of the portrait, but clearly in a dominant position, was a stern looking man. Although his face had the smoothness of a young man, his dark hair was littered with hints of gray and white that made him look older. On the man's right, an elegant bronze colored Afghan hound sat alertly, as if guarding the family. The lady sitting to his left was obviously Elizabeth Smythe Wellington when she was a younger woman. She held an infant in her arms and had two young girls in matching yellow dresses standing beside her. Everyone in the portrait was staring straight forward with a look of deadly sternness. Being excessively wealthy is very serious business, not to be trivialized by smiles.

Bradley led me around the flower table into an area on the left side of the room, where Mrs. Wellington and her two daughters were sitting around a small table. There was a tea service neatly arranged in the center of the table and a porcelain cup and saucer sat in front of each chair. Bradley took the empty chair next to his wife, leaving me a seat between Mrs. Wellington and Margaret. No one offered to shake my hand.

I smiled at Mrs. Wellington and took my assigned seat.

"Tea, Mr. Gaines?" Mrs. Wellington asked.

"Thank you, yes." I don't care for hot tea, but I didn't want to appear to be a common coffee lover.

"Margaret," she said in a tone that left no doubt that she was issuing an order.

Margaret sat forward in her chair and reached for the teapot. She poured the tea into my cup. "Would you like sugar and lemon or cream?" She made eye contact with me and smiled one of the sexiest smiles I had ever seen.

I allowed myself a few seconds to contemplate a life with such a wealthy woman. I decided it wouldn't be all that bad unless they made me dress like Bradley Tucker and run to the door to fetch callers.

"Just the tea, thank you," I said.

"A purist. I like that in my men," she purred.

Mrs. Wellington cleared her throat. "That will do Margaret." Margaret slipped back into her seat. "Now Mr. Gaines, are you in a position to take on an assignment for this family?" Mrs. Wellington asked after giving me time to sample the tea. I smiled as if it were the best tea I had ever had, but I would have preferred coffee.

"What did you have in mind?" I replied.

"We want you to find the fiend who murdered my son."

"I'm already committed to doing that," I said.

"I beg your pardon?"

"I plan to discover the murderer, or murderers, of your son."

"And just who retained you to perform this service?"

"Normally, Mrs. Wellington the identity of my clients is confidential, but in this case I'll make an exception and tell you, because I consider that I am working for your son. I take it very personally when someone is killed on my doorstep, so I'm not charging him a fee."

Bradley Tucker decided to enter the conversation. "Very commendable, Mr. Gaines," he said. Mrs. Wellington gave him a stare that let him know his opinion wasn't welcome.

"That's a very sophomoric gesture, Mr. Gaines. One should never be ashamed to seek a fee for providing a needed service."

"I'll try to remember that," I replied, attempting to counter her arrogance with sarcasm, but my efforts were wasted on her.

She ignored my quip and continued the conversation. "My son was a very wealthy man Mr. Gaines. Did you know that?"

"I surmised it," I replied.

"His final testament names his sister, Harriett, as his executor," she paused as if the group needed time to think about what she had said.

Harriet and Bradley looked down as if this little tidbit of information weighed heavily upon them. Mrs. Wellington turned to Harriett.

"Harriett, although it is most certainly your decision and not mine, I am of the opinion that the estate of my dear son should agree to compensate Mr. Gaines for his efforts to capture the monster who took sweet Berry's life." She paused again and raised her hand. Immediately, a uniformed servant appeared. "Amos, I'll have a gin and tonic. And you, Mr. Gaines?" she asked.

I turned to Amos and gave him my order, anxious to have something stronger than the tea to drink. Amos immediately left to fetch the drinks without taking orders from either of the daughters or from Bradley.

Mrs. Wellington sat back in her chair and we all waited for Amos to bring the drinks. A few minutes passed in silence before he returned with a tray and five drinks. He placed Mrs. Wellington's gin and tonic in front of her and waited while she took a sip. She smiled at him. That was his cue to deliver my drink. He did so but he didn't wait for my approval before placing the tray on the table and retreating to his hiding place. The daughters and Bradley reached for their individual drinks.

Now that each of us had a drink, Mrs. Wellington continued. "Mr. Gaines, will you be so kind as to instruct me on how someone in your profession is compensated."

I explained my billing practices and quoted my normal daily rate. Naturally, she didn't flinch at the amount.

"Harriett, as executor of my son's estate, do you agree to pay Mr. Gaines' modest fee?"

"Yes Mother, whatever you say," Harriett replied without looking at her mother.

"Well! That settles that. Now that this family has retained your services and assumed the responsibility for paying your fee and expenses, I'd like to know what the next step in your investigation will be."

Two days ago I had a corpse as a client, now I had a corporation and a socially elite family throwing money at me. I took my note pad from my pocket to double check a name. "The next step in my investigation will be finding and talking with a gentleman named Randall Kingsmore."

"He's a god-damned beast." Mrs. Wellington exclaimed almost before I had fully articulated his name She slammed her drink on the table to emphasize the statement.

"Mother!" Harriett gasped. Margaret smiled. Bradley kept his head down and nursed his empty glass.

"It's the truth. That son of a bitch gave my sweet, innocent Berry that awful disease."

Margaret made a noise and gulped her drink.

Mrs. Wellington's snapped her eyes to her daughter and they glared at each other with of mutual contempt.

"How long did they know each other?" I asked in an effort to break the tension.

Mrs. Wellington turned her glare to me and I felt cold run down my spine. "Mr. Gaines, if you feel it is important to your investigation to talk with that man, then talk to him, but this family does not want to discuss him at all. As far as we are concerned he does not even exist." She stated with the certainty of an executioner pulling the cord on a guillotine.

I quickly changed the topic. "There was a lady at Mr. Wellington's memorial service. She appeared to be very distraught. Who was she?"

A smile crept onto Mrs. Wellington's face. "Her name is Abigail Eddings Patrick. She is my son's second cousin once removed, on my side of the family." She added emphatically. "She and my son grew up together. Abigail is a remarkable woman. She is the main care giver for her invalid mother and a shrewd investor of money. She increased her family's net worth considerably after the death of her father who had the financial skills of a drunken sailor. She was the perfect match for my son and I intended for them to marry. A man like my son needed a wife who could understand the burden of his social position." She glanced disapprovingly at Bradley.

"Can you tell me how to contact her?" I asked.

"Harriett," she ordered.

Harriett recited Ms. Patrick's address and phone number. I wrote the information in my note pad.

I pulled the Confederate flag business card from my pocket and showed it to her. "Do you know anything about this card?"

"Put that thing away." She ordered. "Sometimes Berry could be influenced by the wrong people. I forbade him from being associated with that group, but he joined the organization without my approval. It's called *Our Heritage* or something like that. It's a very distasteful group and I'm embarrassed my son was affiliated with it. It is ridiculous that a man of Berry's social standing would be associated with such a pedestrian organization. Now do you need any additional information to begin your investigation?"

"Not at the moment, but I may have some questions later."

"Very well. Please contact Harriet if you need additional assistance." She turned to Harriet and said,

"Harriet will you be certain that Mr. Gaines has one of your card so he will know how to contact you?"

"Of course Mother," Harriet replied.

Mrs. Wellington snapped her gaze away from her daughter and raised her hand. Amos magically appeared again. She pointed and he walked toward a set of doors on the opposite side of the room and opened them. Mrs. Wellington stood up, followed immediately by Bradley and Harriet who almost fell over themselves trying to get from their seats quickly. Margaret was more controlled. She waited a moment before standing. I got up normally about the same time as Margaret, contemplating how nicely Margaret and I had timed the activity.

Mrs. Wellington grabbed my arm and placed her hand on it. "The dining room is to your right." She instructed. She guided me away and the two of us led the group into the dining room.

The dinner was acceptable. It started with an asparagus soup, to which the chef had added a hint of ginger that did not improve the dish. The Bibb lettuce and walnut salad that followed was lightly dressed with balsamic vinaigrette. There was nothing wrong with the salad, however a raspberry vinaigrette would have been a better choice. The main course was an individual Cornish hen, roasted, split and nestled on a bed of saffron rice with sliced and sautéed Brussels sprouts on the side. It was excellent and so well prepared that the spices blended perfectly, making identifying the individual components difficult. The desert, a scoop of vanilla ice cream with caramel sauce, was a nice finish to the meal. In a competition, I would have beaten the chef with my soup and salad, but he would have easily won with his main dish.

***

After the meal, Amos appeared with one glass of white wine on his serving tray. He placed it in front of Mrs. Wellington then he disappeared again. Mrs. Wellington emptied the glass, and then pushed back from the table. "It has been a pleasure having you with us Mr. Gaines. I pray that you can find my son's killer and I entrust you with protecting not only my son's reputation, but also the reputation of this family. Please keep us informed of your progress." Mrs. Wellington got up, turned and walked away.

"Thank you for your hospitality," I said to her back.

As she left the room she said in a commanding voice. "Amos!" Amos walked towards me and motioned toward the door. Mrs. Wellington's command indicated that my evening with the rich and famous was over. Harriet handed me her card, further emphasizing that it was time for me to go.

"Ladies, Bradley," I said and turned to follow the mysterious servant.

"Stop Amos!" Margaret said. Her voice didn't carry the imposing authority of her mother's, but you could tell she was accustomed to issuing order and to having people do what she told them. She jumped from her seat and grabbed my arm. "I'll show Mr. Gaines out personally."

Amos wasn't pleased with this development but he backed away and the two of us strolled from the room.

Once outside the front door Margaret pulled me closer to her. "Don't you believe everything my mother says."

"Don't worry about that, I'm a skeptic by nature," I replied.

"Randy Kingsmore didn't give my brother AIDS. It's more likely my brother gave the disease to Randy or even more likely they both contracted it from having sex with anything that breathed." She stopped and looked into my eyes. When she spoke the lightness was gone.

She was serious. "I loved my brother Mr. Gaines, but sometimes he was completely irresponsible. He knew he had the disease but he still didn't use the proper protection. My foolish brother just couldn't control his hormones. Such a pity!"

She didn't pause, but her tone changed instantly. Seriousness was gone from her voice. "I really can't fault my poor brother for having such a large sexual appetite. After all, the Wellington family is famous for its, shall we say, lust for life." The words purred from her mouth. "After all, my brother and I had a lot in common." She paused and turned to look me in the eye. "Both of us enjoyed playing with naked men."

There was something about hearing the words come from her beautiful mouth that gave me a start. I pulled away slightly. "Are you a prude Mr. Gaines?" She jerked me back and held me close to her side as we continued walking.

"I didn't used to think so, but you've made me question that belief."

"Would I like you naked, Mr. Gaines?"

"Do you want references?" I said. I was unaccustomed to being out-played in the snappy repartee game, but she was a true professional who made me ashamed of my amateur status.

"You'd like me naked, Mr. Gaines." The words sort of oozed from her mouth with a sensuality that made me feel slimed more than aroused.

"I'm certain of that."

"Do you think you could handle me, Mr. Gaines?"

"Probably not!"

"Modest too! That's a trait that's hard to find in a man." By this time we had reached the end of the walkway. She changed the tone in her voice and got serious. "Listen, Mr. Gaines, you really should talk with Randall Kingsmore. He owns a temporary employment agency. It is called Rent-a-Hand." She paused and switched on her seductive voice. "Randy specializes in finding, rugged, sweaty men with big, hard muscles for the construction industry."

She rubbed my shoulders as she spoke then she switched voice tone again and became serious. "You can find him at his office during the work day." She pulled a card from her purse and wrote a number on it. "There you go." She handed me the card. "I make a damned good assistant investigator, don't you agree?"

"I think you'd be a wonderful assistant, but what about Abigail Patrick?" I replied.

"A pure prude, but Berry banged her once or twice a week."

"I thought he liked boys?"

"Oh he did, Mr. Gaines. He preferred boys but he'd screw anyone." She looked up at me, pulled my head down to hers. "But enough about him. I'm interested in you."

She kissed me.

I tried not to kiss her back but it's difficult being indifferent when a tongue is rammed into your mouth. As she pulled away she grabbed my crotch and squeezed. Not finding me aroused, she said, "Oh, my, my, my, what a shame. I enjoyed that more than you did. Maybe next time."

She gently squeezed me again. "Ta-ta Mr. Gaines," she said. "See you later." She rushed away to the rear of the property and before I could get to my car Margaret sped out of the drive in a black BMW roadster convertible. She waved at me as she blew past so close that gravel pelted my leg and the exhaust smell filled the air. Off to search for another modest man no doubt.

In the event there are any women who are interested, I want them to know that I'm easy. I realize that the competition for the easiest guy to get into bed is keen, and while I may not win first place in the contest, I'm at least in the top twenty and on some days even higher. It's real easy to turn me on, sometimes I can even get hot and bothered just by the slightest possibility of interest from some attractive young lady or even a nice middle aged lady, oh hell, some days, even an old broad. But I would have to be terribly deprived before a seduction could succeed with any woman who addressed me as Mister Gaines.

---Fifteen---

My plan for the next day was to sleep late and then spend the remainder of the day repairing the damage to my front door and living room walls. Realizing that Chester would never allow me to sleep in, I cranked the old alarm clock to six o'clock so I could get up, feed Chester and Gort and then snuggle back in the bed to sleep away the morning.

When I awoke at eleven thirty, I was pleased at how well the plan had worked. It's always rewarding to outsmart that damned cat.

By two o'clock I was hard at work on the front door. It was a four-panel oak door, colored with a dark walnut stain that had faded from too many years of sunlight. Although bullets had damaged only two of the panels, the door would look better if all four were replaced, so I carefully pried the trim from around the panels and removed them. In the workshop, I ran some oak stock through the planer until it was the correct thickness and then cut them to size. To give them the raised look, I ran them through the shaper and beveled the edges. I mixed some stain to match the color of the stiles on the front door and applied it to the panels. While the stain dried, I mixed some joint compound and filled in the holes in the wall and applied a fiberglass patch over the hole and troweled on a coat of joint compound to embed the patch.

Around four fifteen, I was sanding the wall to blend the patch, when someone called my name. I looked around and found a young man staring at me through one of the spaces left in the front door by the missing panels.

"May I come in?" he asked.

I removed the mask that was keeping the plaster dust out of my lungs. "Sure come in. Do you know anything about sanding plaster?"

"Not me! But I'm a fast learner."

"Just kidding. What can I do for you? You aren't here to give me a religious tract are you?"

"I'm Randy Kingsmore, Mr. Gaines."

"I know. I was just kidding around. I recognize you from Berry Wellington's funeral. We shared a pew."

He smiled and looked at the front door. "Is this where it happened?"

"Yes." I gave him a few moments to look at the door and the wall. "Why don't you make yourself comfortable while I clean up and get this dust off me? Then we can talk."

"OK," he replied looking around for a place to sit.

"Through that door. We can sit at the kitchen counter," I instructed. "Make yourself a drink if you want. The booze is on the counter, beer and soft drinks are in the 'fridge."

"Can I fix you one too?" he asked.

"A scotch over some ice for me," I replied and headed for the garage to vacuum the dust from my clothes and hair and wash my hands and face.

I still felt dirty when I re-entered the kitchen, but at least white plaster dust wasn't decorating my body. Randy was sitting on one of the bar stools holding Chester in his lap and gently rubbing the cat's neck. That damned cat looked at me, then closed his eyes in ecstasy and melted into Randy's lap.

My drink was sitting across from Randy. I grabbed it and took a sip. "Just right," I commented. "I see you've met Chester."

"Yes I have. He's a wonderful cat."

"Not all the time. What can I do for you Mr. Kingsmore?"

"You can find the son-of-a-bitch who killed Berry," he replied.

"I'm already working on that."

"I can pay you."

"I've already got people paying me, but I'd be working on the case without pay. I take it personally when someone gets shot on my front porch."

"Berry was, such a wonderful man," Randy said. He sniffled back the pre tears moisture that was collecting in his nose.

"You call him Berry. Is that what most people called him?"

"That's a strange question. Why do you ask it?"

"Berry is an unusual name. Most people with unusual names have a nickname. My brother had the given name of Harold, but he preferred to be called Hal, although he did allow me to call him Buddy."

"No, Berry liked his name, and that is what

everyone called him. He didn't have a nickname. Is that important to finding his killer?"

"Probably not, but you never know what's important and what isn't. I like to poke around and ask lots of questions. Sooner or later I'll learn enough to make sense of the chaos."

"They say you're good. Are you?"

"Who is 'they' and why do they say I'm good?"

"Well, in this case 'they' is Andy Wilfield and he says you are the best investigator in the city."

"You know Andy Wilfield?" I asked as I downed the last of my drink.

"Everyone knows Andy," he replied. Chester opened his left eye to be certain I was watching. His purring grew louder.

"If the cat bothers you just put him on the floor."

"Chester could never be a bother, Mr. Gaines."

"Trust me, he can! Would you like another drink?" I asked as an excuse to freshen my own.

"No, thanks."

"What can you tell me about Andy Wilfield?" I added some ice to my glass and poured some scotch to replace what was missing.

"What do you need to know?"

"Why don't you just tell me what you think is important for me to know?"

"Berry was the most wonderful person I ever knew and the best thing that happened to me, Mr. Gaines."

"Are you avoiding my question about Andy Wilfield?" I asked.

"Oh no. I'll tell you anything you think you need to know. But I need to tell you about some other things before I tell you about Andy, Mr. Gaines."

"Do you think you could call me Art?"

"I'll try. I'd like that drink refill now, please."

I grabbed his glass and sniffed it. "Bourbon and Coke?" I asked.

He nodded affirmatively. It's hard to believe that anyone can drink such a concoction but I mixed the drink and placed it in front of him.

Randy's eyes were watering and he was stroking Chester. He turned his head and blotted his eyes on his shirtsleeve. Chester was alert now. He stretched himself onto Randy's chest and placed his head on Randy's shoulder. Randy took the drink from me. He rested his head against Chester's for a moment and continued with his story. When he started talking Chester returned to his lap, but he kept alert and watched Randy's eyes. "I begged Berry to move in with me and leave his family, but he wouldn't do it." He took a sip of his drink to fortify himself. "Berry rarely went home but he wouldn't make the formal break from his mother. She's a very demanding woman, Mr. Gaines ...ah ... I mean Art. Anyway Berry didn't want to take her on and he would never allow me to go with him when he went to visit his family. He said I didn't need to spend time with people like his family. Before Berry came into my life, I was accustomed to being alone so usually I didn't mind, but it was really hard during the holidays. His mother always insisted that he be at home for holidays. I spent most holidays, including Thanksgiving and Christmas, alone." He paused and sighed, "It looks like I'll have to get used to being alone again now."

"Did that make you angry?"

"What?"

"Being excluded from holidays with the Wellington family."

"You're damned right it did. But I wasn't angry with Berry. I was angry with his mother."

"Don't you think that, as an adult, Berry should have been responsible for his own behavior?"

"You make it sound worse than it was." His voice

was cracking.

"I don't make it sound worse than it was. I make it sound exactly like it was. From what you've said, Berry wanted to stay his mother's child. His personal behavior was abhorrent to Mrs. Wellington so he made it up to her by remaining her 'little Berry' in all other regards." I was making it up as I went, hoping to elicit a response.

"Are you some kind of a psychologist?"

"Nope, just a guy who can size up people."

"You can say whatever you want, but Berry was a kind and caring man. He wasn't a mama's boy!"

Chester nuzzled his head into Randy's stomach. Randy picked the cat up in his arms and raised him to his face and kissed him. Now let me make this perfectly clear, Chester's normal response to such displays of affection from humans would have been a terrifying hiss and a claws-out swat across the face. Who knew the damned cat had any sensitivity at all? They cuddled face to fur for a little while, and then Randy lowered the cat to his lap. Chester cut a quick glance at me, then assumed his supportive position attentively watching Randy's face.

"Are you HIV positive, Randy?"

"Yes, but it's under control with meds."

"Who gave the disease to whom?"

"Have you been talking with Mrs. Wellington?"

"I don't think anyone talks with Berry's mother. She is not adept at two way conversation," I said.

"AIDS was never an issue between Berry and me."

"But you didn't answer my question."

"And I won't, but I'll tell you anything else you want to know."

"It's a deal. Tell me about Abigail Patrick."

"There's really not much to tell. Mrs. Wellington wanted Berry to marry her. Mrs. Wellington kept trying to put them together, but Berry wasn't interested in marrying that girl."

"Why is that?"

"Because he loved me."

"I've heard that he saw Ms. Patrick regularly."

"And your point, Mr. Gaines?" He asked.

"Were they having sex?"

"Probably," he answered looking down at the cat.

"Did that bother you?"

"We had a very open relationship. Berry had more physical need than most people. I understood that."

"I see," I replied.

"You have a way of making things sound much

worse than they are."

"It's a gift," I said. "Let's change subjects. Tell me about a cabin Berry owned on Lake Alatoona and tell me about Andy Wilfield."

"I will, but please let me tell you some background information. You really need to understand what kind of man Berry was."

"OK, the floor is yours. Tell me what you think I need to know and I'll fix us a little something to eat."

He talked for close to an hour. I listened intently, but while he talked I heated some of my latest hot dog chili, cooked some franks and made the two of us hot dogs. He ate his without commenting on the quality of my chili. That lets you know his grief was intense.

Randy started his story by telling me about his business. He started it on a small nest egg and built it slowly. After five years of struggling to meet payroll, his hard work paid off and the business became profitable. Now his company was one of the largest temporary services agencies in the area and Randy was independently wealthy.

When he was starting the business, there wasn't enough time for both the business and personal relationships, so he suppressed his need for intimacy and companionship. After the business became successful, he continued to avoid personal relationships fearing that his money might be too attractive to a potential personal partner. Randy was terrified that his increasing wealth would make him a target for the unscrupulous, anything-for-a-buck crowd.

According to Randy, Berry Wellington also avoided personal relationship. Before they met, Berry spent time with Abigail Patrick. He also recklessly paid street prostitutes or picked up guys in clubs and bars, looking for a one-night stand. The inherent danger of these chance encounters was exciting to him.

He explained that Berry didn't have to build a fortune. He had one already. But, under the provisions of his father's will, he couldn't use the money. It was held in trust with very specific and rigid stipulations until his thirty-fifth birthday. One of the main provisions of the will required Berry to be continuously employed. As long as Berry had a job and proved to his father's administrator that he received a paycheck, he would receive a monthly stipend of five thousand dollars. But for each month he was not employed, he lost not only the stipend, but also he forfeited one percent of his inheritance which would be re-distributed in equal shares to his mother and his two sisters. Berry's first job out of college was with Wilfield Imports. He found that he enjoyed working and he continued even after his thirty-fifth birthday. When he gained control of his trust fund it was valued at twenty four million dollars. Due to his frugality and wise investments, at the time of his murder he had a net worth of over seventy five million dollars.

Randy and Berry met at a mid-town bar after attending a performance of the Atlanta Symphony orchestra. Randy said the concert was excellent. It's comforting to know that Annie Hamilton's viola player and his buddies put on a good show.

Randy and Berry became friends. Both of them felt comfortable enough with each other to allow their relationship to grow. Randy believed that whatever they felt for each other must be genuine since neither of them needed the other's money. Soon Berry was spending most of his time at Randy's house. It was during these early days when they discovered that each of them had an appreciation of sexually oriented pictures.

Their attraction to pornography became more and more important to them and soon they rented a downtown apartment, equipped it with the latest video cameras and hired a string of young men to prowl the streets for hustlers and prostitutes to bring back to the apartment where they videotaped the encounters.

Randy told this tale calmly and with little emotion, as if he were explaining how to bake a cake rather than how to gather a collection of pornographic smut.

For some reason, Berry told Andy Wilfield about the collection, and Andy became the first member of what would become a group of people focused on obtaining and viewing pornography. Randy was nervous about Andy's inclusion in the private 'ring of perversion' he and Berry had created, and when Andy began taping his own personal encounters, Randy's anxiety became panic. He was convinced that Andy's reckless behavior would expose him and Berry and endanger his business.

To reign in Andy, Randy took one of the most graphic videotapes Andy had made and stored it in a safe deposit box. He explained his concerns to Andy and promised to deliver the tape to Andy's father if Andy's exuberance endangered either Randy or Berry. Randy's threat worked, but it set a precedent for dealing with concerns that would haunt the group.

As the membership grew, Randy kept incriminating tape recordings that would damage each member if it were revealed. Randy felt he was protecting himself and Berry from the rest of the group.

"Now let me get this straight," I said interrupting his story. "You were prepared to use blackmail to keep the members of your little group of perverts from exposing either you or Berry?"

"We weren't perverts, Mr. Gaines." He made the statement in a calm steady voice.

"Regardless! Did it ever occur to you that some of the others in your group of 'honorable gentlemen' might have the same idea?"

He shrugged his shoulders and didn't answer my question, but he did continue with his story.

When Berry bought the cabin on Lake Alatoona, the group moved there. It was more private and discrete than the downtown apartment, but the cabin caused major concerns for Randy. He couldn't monitor it as closely as he had monitored the apartment. People could come and go without his knowledge. Randy became more vigilant in collecting incriminating information on each member of the group and hiding it securely.

When he finished his story, Randy sighed and slumped his shoulders as if he had just finished an exhausting task. I didn't give him any time to rest. "So you, Berry, Andy and some others were part of an exchange club for gay pornography?" I asked.

"It wasn't all gay; we had some straight guys, too."

"And that makes a difference?"

"You make it sound so....dirty," he protested.

"Well, isn't it?"

"No it wasn't like that at all. It was just some guys," he paused. "Haven't you ever looked at pictures of naked women?"

"Sure I have. If you have a picture of a beautiful woman with no clothes on, then your damned right I want to see it, but if all you have is a fuck flick, then hell no I'm not that interested in watching folks grunting and squealing and placing their bodies in contorted positions. And I have no interest in forming a secret club with my friends and hiding out in a secret cabin and using hidden cameras to get pictures of people having sex."

He bowed his head and his shoulders started shaking before his sobs became audible. "It wasn't dirty, Art. It was just a group of guys.... It wasn't dirty. We were all friends. We supported each other."

"Stop crying and stop deluding yourself!" I ordered. "It was dirty and perverted, but regardless it doesn't justify murder."

He nodded his head but he didn't verbally respond to my tirade.

"There are more questions you need to answer," I stated while handing him a paper towel. He dried his eyes and blotted his nose. Chester was staring at me with a 'what-did-you-do?' look. I ignored the damned cat.

Who was blackmailing whom?" Randy hadn't mentioned anyone blackmailing members of the group, but it seemed like an obvious motive. My question however was purely fishing for information.

"None of us would have done anything like that," he indignantly asserted.

"Damnation Randy, you run a business - you hire and fire people – stop acting like a naive high school boy. You've already told me you kept incriminating videotapes of the members of your little group hidden in a safety deposit box. Hell Randy, you've already admitted you were prepared to blackmail people. Do you honestly think that you were the only person in your group who realized that the risk of exposure made most of you vulnerable?"

"It wasn't like that," he snapped angrily. "I only kept the tapes to keep people from exposing Berry or me."

"OK, your motives were pure and noble, but

someone's weren't. Now I ask you again, who was blackmailing members of your group?"

"No one would, Art. You've got to believe me. No one would."

"Then what was Berry Wellington afraid of and what made him seek out my help, and most importantly, what did he know that caused someone to gun him down to stop him from talking with me?" I asked.

"Everyone liked Berry. No one who knew him would have done anything like that to him," he replied.

"If that is true, then why was he coming to see me?"

"We have asked ourselves that and no one has any idea."

"Who is this 'we' you refer to?"

"Me, Andy and Sammy Estes talked last night."

"Sammy Estes?" I asked.

"Sammy Estes is Andy's..ah...friend."

I rolled my eyes. "Does that mean lover?"

"Yes."

"Did they have a committed relationship?"

"I suppose."

"Describe him."

"About five feet ten. One hundred and eighty

pounds. Light brown hair, that's very curly."

"Was he a pall bearer at Berry's funeral?"

"Yes. Why?"

"Just curious," I replied.

"What can you tell me about the Keystone Land Development Company?

"What do you want to know?"

"Everything."

"There's nothing to tell. Berry and Sammy Estes formed a company to buy land. They sold some stock in the company. I bought some shares, but that's all I know."

"What kind of land did they invest in?"

"I don't really know. My only involvement was to cash my quarterly dividend checks."

"Do you really expect me to believe that a guy who built a staffing company from scratch would be so naive as to invest in a company without knowing everything about that company?"

"I trusted Berry. I didn't need to know anything else."

"True love?" I asked.

"You can call it whatever you like. I trusted Berry completely."

"Randy, I know you were secretary of the corporation. Do you really expect me to believe you didn't know anything else about it?"

"I told you already, I trusted Berry. My name was on the incorporation papers but I wasn't involved in the business."

"Surely you must have heard some talk. Didn't Berry discuss business with you?"

"No he didn't. I did overhear him and Sammy one night when they were arguing about the zoning of some of their property."

"What were they arguing about?"

"I couldn't really tell."

I gave up and let the subject drop. "Let me ask you about this card," I said pulling Berry Wellington's card with the group of flags from my pocket and handing it to Randy.

"What do you want to know?" he asked after glancing at the card and placing it on the counter.

"It seems a little strange to me."

"There's nothing strange about it. Berry was very proud of his family's history. On his mother's side, the Smythe family fought in the American Revolution. He's also related to the Edding's family who had one of the largest plantations in Georgia before the war. The Wellington family was from New Jersey. They moved to North Carolina after the War and were dirt poor farmers before Berry's great-grandfather moved to Georgia and made a fortune as a cotton broker."

"I recognize the Confederate flag, but what's the significance of the other flags?" I asked.

"Are you from the South, Mr. Gaines?"

"Born and raised right here in Margaret Mitchell's Atlanta."

"Have you ever studied the history of the Confederacy?" he asked.

"Just what they taught us in school."

"Southern schools are not a very good place to learn about Southern history. Would you like a little history lesson?" he asked.

I nodded and he continued, "Well, the center flag is the Confederate Battle Flag. Many people think the battle flag is the official flag of the Confederate States of America, but it's not. The Battle Flag is a combination of the cross of St. Andrew with thirteen stars representing the states of the Confederacy. It was popular on the battle field since it was distinctively different from the Union flag."

Randy looked up to confirm I was paying attention and pointed to another flag. "This flag is called the Stars and Bars. It is the first National Flag of the Confederacy. Then there is the Stainless Banner or the second National flag of the Confederacy. And this one is the third and final National flag of the Confederacy. The last flag is called the 'Bonnie Blue.' It was never an official flag, but the public loved the Bonnie Blue flag and considered it the true flag of the Confederacy."

"I see," I said, trying to pretend I cared. "So this card was just to indicate that Berry wanted all of us to 'save our Confederate money, cause the South's gonna rise again'." I did a fair impression of Yosemite Sam.

"It's not something to joke about, Mr. Gaines," he replied, "Berry believed that secession was constitutionally protected."

"So he was one of those state's rights revisionists, who try to re-write history."

"Not really. A large part of what he believed is historically accurate."

"Yeah," I said hoping to end this conversation.

About ten minutes later, Randy placed Chester on the floor.

I escorted him to my still unfinished front door.

"Where are the tapes now?" I asked.

"I destroyed them in the incinerator at the Hamilton Foundry. They are a client of mine and their security guard is my employee."

"Why did you do that?"

"With Berry gone..." he choked up.

"I understand."

"I hope I've helped you, Art," he said.

"You at least gave me lots to think about," I replied, and I meant it.

He extended his hand and we shook hands.

After he left Chester meowed at me and stalked away.

"You make me sick," I said.

Chester meowed again and walked away. Then I went to the back yard and played tennis ball chase with Gort before finishing my repair projects.

---Sixteen---

By the time morning rolled around I felt like Hank Aaron after hitting his seven hundred and fifteenth home run. I was on top of the world with reasons for feeling so good.

First of all, the repairs to my house were complete. Naturally, the project had turned out to be more complicated than expected. The new panels for the front door stood out on the faded portion of the door like a portrait of Franklin Roosevelt on the walls of the Piedmont Driving Club. So I re-sanded the entire door and applied fresh stain.

When I finished, the door looked better than new. The bullet holes in the wall were easy enough to patch, but matching the paint was impossible, so I repainted the whole living room. It's amazing what a coat of paint can do to make an old worn out room look revitalized. All in all, my house looked better now than it did before the Wellington murder.

Second, now that I had the papers Horace Wilfield hired me to find, I had one nice fee ready to collect and the potential of another nice fee from the Wellington family.

The pleasant feeling was much too wonderful to allow the morning traffic on Peachtree Street to ruin it, so I walked to the corner and caught the bus to my office building. I relaxed on the rear seat of the bus to read a review of the Bannister BTS thirty fifty table saw in the latest issue of Today's Science magazine. Let the bus driver yell at the incompetent drivers for a change.

At the office I found a pile of junk mail and two phone messages. One from a young lady who identified herself as Sandy Adams. Sandy promised that she could save me money on my phone service if I'd return her call. I hit '5' to delete the message. The other message was from Sammy Estes. "My name is Sammy Estes. I'm the founder of *Our Heritage* and I am responding to your request for information on my organization. *Our*

Heritage is an organization of patriots dedicated to fighting for our Southern heritage and reclaiming our stolen Southern history. To get more information on *Our Heritage*, email your request to newsletter@ourheritage.com. Thank you."

I hit '7' on the phone to save the message. Then I left my office and headed to the MARTA station and rode with a mob of morning commuters to the Five Point station and joined the herd of pedestrians – about a thousand strong and hoofed it to the McNamarra Building. It was almost nine o'clock when I opened the lobby door and pushed my way into the horde gathered to wait at the bank of elevators.

I felt out of place standing with my hands free. Everyone else in the lobby was carrying at least three things, some even more. The most common items being hauled around the lobby were an attaché case or a large purse, an oversized cup of coffee or a latte, and a bag with a bagel and a container of crème cheese. Almost half of the group also had a cell phone penned between their shoulder and their ear. If evolution continues, young professionals of the future will have three or maybe four arms and a hump on their shoulder to secure a cell phone.

It took more than ten minutes before I could squeeze into one of the elevator cars, but I didn't mind the wait. A clear majority of the working women at the McNamarra Building rated 8.5 and above.

I rode the elevator to the fifty-seventh floor, where the law firm of Handelman, Macek, Pickering, Brunstad and Deluca maintained their office. I've often wondered why lawyers with simple names never seem to form partnerships. You rarely see a firm named Jones, Smith, Wilson and Harris. I presented myself to the receptionist who was busy nibbling on a cinnamon-raisin bagel with crème cheese and cautiously sipping on a latte, being extra careful to not let any drip into her rather impressive cleavage.

"May I help you?" Her smile glowed brightly. She was nice looking, with light brown hair and a cute nose that turned up at the end, but without the smile she wouldn't have made the building attractiveness standard, even with the extra points she got for the "D" cup breasts.

"Mr. Macek, please."

"Your name, please."

"Art Gaines."

She glanced to her desktop and checked a book. "I don't find your name on his appointment log, Mr.

Gaines." Her fetching smile was replaced by a stern look of professionalism and she moved her latte and bagel to the side of her desk. I had moved from an invited guest to a potential gatecrasher who might require all of her attention.

I took one of my business cards from my pocket, turned it over and wrote 'Lake Alatoona cabin – Berry Wellington.' I handed her the card.

"Please deliver this card to Mr. Macek. He will want to see me." I emphasized the word will.

She frowned as she read the card, then got up and disappeared through a door behind her desk. I sat in one of the leather chairs and picked up a copy of Legal Review from the neat stack of magazines on the side table, and thumbed through the pages hoping it might be the 'Hot Babes of the Bar' issue. It wasn't. The wait was longer than expected, but fortunately the door to the inner offices opened before boredom forced me to read anything from the magazine. The latte drinking receptionist was standing in the door. "Please come with me Mr. Gaines." Her professionalism had been replaced by contempt. Obviously, I had moved from a gatecrasher to a trouble maker.

She marched me down a walnut paneled hallway

to the end office. The hallway was silent except for the click of her heels on the polished wood floor. She placed her hand on the door's handle of the end office and then paused. She looked directly into my eyes. "Mr. Gaines, there are only a few really decent human beings in this world. Bob Macek is one of them."

I started to tell her I was a decent human being too, but decided against it when I saw the wetness in her eyes. She opened the door for me and held it as I walked into the office. I smiled at her as she backed into the hall, quietly closing the door behind her.

The room was paneled with vertical cherry boards. Ornate crown molding framed the room and accentuated the antique tin ceiling. The room smelled of expensive leather with the lingering bouquet of a very fine bourbon. Bob Macek sat at the end of a massive walnut conference table that filled one side of his office. He twirled a glass with bourbon and ice cubes that rhythmically clanked on the glass.

"How long do I have, Mr. Gaines?" Macek looked up solemnly.

"I beg your pardon?"

"Before my wife and the police find out?" he asked.

"I don't know about your wife, but the police might not ever find out."

"But you did."

"Yes, but I'm better than the cops." I quipped and smiled.

"Can I hire you to keep my name out of this?"

"I already have two clients."

"Please Mr. Gaines. I've worked so hard. I have a political career, a wife and a family. Please."

"If I can I will, but no promises."

"Try hard Mr. Gaines, Please try hard. Whatever the cost I'll pay." His hand vibrated from fear and panic and the ice cubes clanged against the glass.

"I will but a lot depends on getting some information from you."

"What do you want to know?" He sniffed the bourbon then drank half the contents into his mouth where he swished it; savoring the hint of courage in the glass.

"Why would someone with a political career, a wife and a family, get involved with a bunch of pornographers?" He bowed his head and his body shook as he fought to keep from crying.

"I'm not gay," he said.

"I don't care," I said.

"But, it's important to me that you know that," he said.

"OK, now I know, but I still don't care. What I do care about is understanding why an intelligent, married politician would get involved with a group of men who are, or who were in the case of Berry Wellington, not only gay, but very gay and very proud of it. On top of that, Berry and some of the other members of the cabin group were associated with one of those 'the South was right' organizations that pop up and attract a lot of negative publicity to themselves."

He ignored most of what I had said. "It was only one time. Just one time," he replied, still fighting the urge to break down in tears.

"Yeah," I tried not to be sarcastic, but I failed. "Then, during your 'one time' who got enough on you to blackmail you?" I didn't really know that he was being blackmailed, but the odds were enough in my favor to justify a bluff.

"No one is blackmailing me." He attempted to look offended, but he failed. If we had been playing poker I would have called his look a 'tell.' "Would you like a drink, Mr. Gaines?" He said trying to change to subject and look more sincere with his 'one time' lie.

I looked at my watch. "Not this early in the morning. Now, let me ask you again. Who is blackmailing you?"

He got up and walked to a cabinet on the wall that contained a well stocked bar. He poured more bourbon into his glass. Macek's hand was shaking slightly and he grasped the glass of bourbon; holding it like a lifesaver. The courage from his first bourbon hadn't lasted long.

"I don't like being cross examined." He said returning to the conference table.

"This whole thing will go faster if you just answer my questions."

"My whole life is at stake here, Mr. Gaines."

"I can't help you if you refuse to answer my questions."

"No one is blackmailing me. Just keep my name out of all this. Please. I'll pay you. Just name your price. This is my life we're talking about."

"It is going to be damned hard to keep you out of this if you keep lying."

"I'm not lying."

I reached into the inside vest pocket of my sport coat and pulled out one of the pictures I had found at the cabin and tossed it to him.

"My god! Why are you carrying this around with you?" He grabbed the picture and placed it into a Gucci attaché case beside his chair. "What if you had had an accident? What if you had been mugged?"

"What if you'd never gotten naked in front of someone with a camera?" I said gently. "Now once more. Who is blackmailing you?" I said forcefully.

"Mr. Gaines, I resent the implications."

I cut him off. Being sympathetic and supportive wasn't helping, so I changed approaches and slapped my hand on the table. He gasped but sat still. "I don't give a damn what you resent," I said. "Let me lay it out for you. Berry Wellington and Randy Kingsmore started a gang for mostly gay guys, but some straight or bi-sexual guys, to have sex and record the experience. You were a member of, or somehow involved with, that group. Berry Wellington, Sammy Estes and Andy Wilfield, with some other members of this band of dangerous pornographers started a land investment company called Keystone Land Development. You, Mr. Macek, are treasurer of that company. I already know that Berry Wellington was involved in some questionable real estate schemes and it doesn't take a lot of imagination to conclude that the

Keystone Company was also involved in questionable real estate deals."

Macek turned pale. He sat motionless holding his glass of bourbon and ignoring the tears flowing on his face. "How did you find out all of this?" he said.

"Does it matter?" When he didn't respond I continued. "Somewhere along the line something happened that caused Berry Wellington to seek my assistance. At this point I don't know what it was, but I assume he was fearful that your little ring of pornographers and real estate crooks had gotten out of hand and that someone was using the private and confidential material the group horded to blackmail other members of the group."

"They are not dangerous men," he protested.

"At least one of them may be a murderer and I believe at least one of them is also a blackmailer. I'd classify that as dangerous, wouldn't you?"

"How dare you come in here and accuse me of being associated with such things. I'm a member of the county council and a happily married man. Get the hell out of my office." He stood up from his chair. This wasn't bourbon courage; it was desperation.

"Do you think the picture you took from me and

hid in your attaché case is the only one that exists?"

"Don't threaten me. You have no idea who I am or what I can do to you." The councilman tried to act assertive, but he failed.

I stood up, bent over the conference table and shoved him back into his chair. "Sit down and shut up, you idiot. I know exactly who you are. You're a man who gets turned on by naked guys. You're trying to keep that tidbit of information from a wife and the voters of this community. You're also a participant in some real estate schemes that probably couldn't stand the scrutiny of the legal system. And you're involved with a Southern separatists group that could ruin you politically. Now there's not a damned thing you can do to me. So just shut up." I was on a roll.

"The only chance you have of remaining in politics and keeping your wife from finding out about your extra curricular activities and the voters finding out that you're not worthy of their trust, is to talk to me and hope I can resolve this whole disgusting business before the police or the press gets wind of you and your little perverted group of dangerous men, who have invested their fortunes in a portfolio of deceit and lies."

Just the glimmer of hope that I could get him off

the hook calmed him. "Can you really get me out of this mess?" he asked.

"I don't know, but I can't see the up-side to having the Channel Five news team showing footage from the cabin on Lake Alatoona or from some news bimbo sticking a microphone in your face and asking you about your sexual practices. Also, Berry's mother expects me to protect his reputation. If I succeed, your reputation might be protected too."

We sat in silence while he contemplated his options. I looked at his face and watched him decide to talk to me.

"You're not a pleasant man Mr. Gaines and I don't like you very much, but I'll trust you. I don't see that I have a choice." He paused to let his insult sink in.

I shrugged my shoulders and waited. Too many people had insulted me to allow his mild rebuke to bother me.

"You're right; I am being blackmailed," he said when he continued.

"By whom?" I asked.

"I don't know and I have tried to discover his identity. Handelman, Macek, Pickering, Brunstad and Deluca is a very resourceful firm. We have a number of investigators we use from time to time. I retained one of them. You may know the investigator? His name is Zackery McMillen. He works for a firm called Phoenix Investigation."

He looked at me and waited for me to respond. I shook my head to confirm I did not know the man who shared my profession.

"Mr. McMillen is a clever man, but he was unsuccessful in discovering who was extorting money from me. My tormentor demanded that I place one thousand dollars cash in an envelope and mail it every Friday to an address he provided. Mr. McMillen took the address the bastard gave me and immediately determined that it was one of those private mailbox companies. You know the kind I'm talking about?"

He waited again for a response. This time I nodded to confirm that I was aware of such companies.

"Through bribery and guile, Mr. McMillen was able to determine that a lady had rented the box, but he was not able to determine her name. He did however discover that no one picked up mail from the box. From time to time, the owner of the service would receive written instructions to forward mail to yet another address. It seems that many of this company's box holders have their mail forwarded." He paused again and looked to me.

"Yes, I believe that is the way many of these mail box companies operate," I said, not knowing what kind of response he wanted this time and not knowing anything about how these companies operated.

Macek continued his story. "After a month with no new information, I terminated Mr. McMillen's services. Some people in your profession, Mr. Gaines, charge excessive fees for unimpressive results." He paused and looked at me again.

"I'm certain some do," I said.

"Then the demands changed from money to votes on zoning issues."

"What?"

"I would get notification of how to vote on various zoning issues before the county council."

"And how did you respond?"

"I voted like I was instructed to. No one could afford to keep sending all that money each week. I was going broke Mr. Gaines. I had no choice." He paused and looked to me for my understanding.

I maintained my best poker face and he continued. "Initially, the votes weren't particularly controversial, except the vote to change a large tract of land near the zoo from single family to multi-family use. That one got lots of press attention. The animal lovers were in an uproar."

"Did the Keystone Land Development Company benefit from your votes?"

"A couple of times it did, but not always," he stated.

"Give me some examples."

"Examples of what?"

"Examples of how Keystone was affected by your votes."

"Well let me see." He paused and thought for a few moments. "Keystone benefited from the re-zoning of a tract of land near the airport."

"How so?"

"We....I mean Keystone purchased an option on twenty-two and a half acres of undeveloped land. It had originally been zoned for industrial use, but there were no takers. When the council voted to change it to commercial, a bidding war ensued among a couple of national hotel chains that wanted the land. Keystone cleared over four hundred and sixty-eight thousand dollars by selling its option."

"Did the members of City Council know that you had an interest in a company that might benefit from the re-zoning action?"

"No."

I waited for him to add something to his declaration but he didn't.

"Shouldn't they have known?" I finally asked.

"It wasn't relevant. Many of the members have some stake in the matters council rules on. It's impossible to be on council unless you have some independent means of income, so almost every council member has business interests. It is very common for council to act on issues that impact other members' businesses or investments."

"Don't council members recuse themselves when a vote is taken on an issue where they have an interest?"

"Some do; some don't."

"But you didn't."

"That's right. I didn't."

"Give me an example of when your vote harmed Keystone."

The room was silent, except for the clinking of ice in his glass. "Well I really can't think of any that harmed Keystone, but there were some that didn't benefit them."

"Keep going," I ordered.

"Well, there was the parking garage near the new velodrome and a new high rise condo project off Butler Avenue."

"And those projects didn't impact Keystone?"

"No, they had no interest in either."

"Didn't you find that unusual?"

"Everything about this is unusual. I just did what they told me to do. What else could I do?" He paused and sipped the last drop of bourbon from the glass.

"I still don't understand why you got involved with Keystone."

"They made me do it. Don't you understand? They made me do it."

"Who is 'they'?"

"It's my life Mr. Gaines. It's my life. You've got to help me." He pulled a tissue from his bottom desk drawer and wiped his eyes.

"Cut it out. You've put yourself into a box and you can't get out by acting pitiful. Now answer my question. Who is the 'they' and what did 'they' make you do?"

"It was Andy Wilfield and Sammy Estes. They told me if I didn't let them put my name on the incorporation papers they would send those pictures to my wife. I had to do it Mr. Gaines. You can see that, can't you? Now I have to pay with my life."

"Stop being melodramatic! Why did they insist that you be an officer of the company?"

"They never said."

"You're a smart guy. Make a guess. Why was it so important to have you as an officer?"

"Maybe to make it easier to get loans from the bank. I don't know. Really I don't"

"Why would they need your name to borrow money?"

"How do I know, Mr. Gaines? How do I know?"

"Okay, let's assume for a minute that you were just an innocent victim."

He nodded his head enthusiastically at the suggestion.

"What did you do in your capacity as Treasurer of the corporation?"

"I had to sign some papers."

"What kind of papers."

"Just normal stuff. When we bought or sold property, I had to sign deeds and closing papers. That kind of thing."

"Did Keystone Development make money?"

"Lots of it. Berry Wellington, and to a lesser degree Andy Wilfield, had a knack for finding the right properties to invest in. When we first started the company we bought the Wilfield Importers and Distributors building, and then leased it back to the company. We got immediate cash flow and the Wilfields' got a substantial tax advantage. It was a sweet deal for both parties."

"For a guy who wasn't involved with the company, you seem to know a lot about its business."

"That's an uncalled for accusation. You don't have to be involved in the day to day operation of the business to know what property we bought and sold. Remember, I did have to sign deeds and closing papers."

"What other investments did they make?"

"The biggest was the purchase of the Highland Towers. We bought it at a distressed price to keep the owners out of bankruptcy. Spent a little to fix it up and now it's got an occupancy rate of ninety-five percent."

"Impressive."

"Then we bought the Magnum Building, where Sammy Estes lives. It's a small but upscale condominium building. That's now appraised for two hundred percent more than we paid for it."

"Wow!" I said, "Now let's get back to your blackmail situation. After you fired your investigator what did you do?"

"Well, when the blackmail demands changed from money to my vote on zoning issues, I made a list."

"Of whom?" I asked.

"Some people I thought might be capable of blackmailing me."

"Wouldn't that just be the principals in Keystone?"

"Of course not! They were wealthy and beyond suspicion. They would have never stooped to this kind of behavior."

"You're an idiot if you believe that," I said flatly, holding my voice in control.

"What?" he exclaimed.

"You just told me that Andy Wilfield and Sammy Estes threatened you with exposure if you didn't serve as treasurer of Keystone."

He got up from his seat and went to the credenza behind his desk and refreshed his glass of bourbon. Then he slowly returned to the table and sat down. He stared at the drink in his hand as if it would reveal the secret of living a life without making a complete mess of it.

"Do you still have the list?" I asked as much to break the silence as to get information.

He reached for a brief case on the floor and placed it in his lap. He thumbed the files and pulled one from the case. He handed me a sheet from the file. "Your question is insulting. I maintain extensive and accurate files." I shrugged my shoulders again and he continued. "I haven't known what to do with the list since I created it. I considered hiring Mr. McMillen again, but I realized he could be helpful only if I told him the details of the group and I wasn't willing to give him that much information."

Macek paused but this time he didn't look to me for a response. He was in deep thought. Finally he looked up and continued, "I find you to be a very disagreeable man, Mr. Gaines."

"You've said that once already," I declared.

"It's still true, but since you know about the group, it's not like having to let you in on a secret. Will you consider taking on the assignment of uncovering who is blackmailing me and recovering all the pictures and videos that might prove embarrassing if they were made public?"

"I already have clients"

"That wasn't what I asked." Negotiating was one of his skills and as he made me the offer his confidence increased. He was on familiar turf again.

"I think I can keep your sexual escapades out of this thing, but the cops are going to find out that you and Berry were involved in Keystone. That can't be kept quiet."

"That's a matter of public record. I can handle that. I still want to hire you to protect me," he said.

I quoted my daily rate and he nodded his agreement. Perhaps Mrs. Wellington was correct. Collecting fees was a noble endeavor.

"I'll draw up some papers," Macek stated.

"I don't need any papers Mr. Macek. I only work for people I can trust."

"But I need something for my files."

"Then you best hire someone like Mr. McMillan. I'm certain he will sign anything you want him to."

He pondered the situation for a few seconds then shrugged his shoulders. "Very well, Mr. Gaines. A contract based on trust." He extended his hand and we shook hands.

I quipped, "You do realize that if the Bar Association finds out about a lawyer taking a hand shake contract they might take your license away."

"If they did, that would be a fun case to handle," he said struggling to join in the joke.

"Why did you allow yourself to become involved with the *Our Heritage* organization?" I asked.

"I believe in their cause, Mr. Gaines." He cleared his throat and took another drink of bourbon. "I met Sammy Estes at a conference. We started chatting and soon discovered that we shared some common beliefs. It was so refreshing to find someone who agreed with me and understood the need for confidentiality. I understood that my beliefs were not shared by all the voters who had elected me and so did Sammy."

"And just what does this group believe?" I said.

He perked up invigorated by the prospect of giving the campaign speech he could never make to real voters.

"*Our Heritage* believes that our present form of government is more interested in gathering power for itself and has no real interest in protecting the rights of citizens. We believe that the citizens of this country are not motivated to change the government, nor are they concerned about the cancerous growth of government. We are convinced that the average citizen firmly believes that the government's primary concern is the safety and security of its citizens If the South withdraws from the Union and forms a separate Republic, Mr. Gaines, We believe civil liberties and individual freedom will be better protected than by the current government."

I interrupted him with a question. "Other than Sammy Estes, who were the active members of *Our Heritage*?" Normally, once you get a person talking, you let them go on as long as they want to. They longer they talk, the more you learn. However, I had had my fill of this Southern revisionist history.

"Basically, Sammy Estes and Berry Wellington ran the organization. Andy Wilfield was on the sidelines but wasn't an active member. Of course, Andy was always on the side lines."

"What do you mean?"

"Andy was always worried like hell that his old man would find out about his private life and his real estate investments."

"I can understand why Andy wouldn't want his father to know about his gay lifestyle, but why he would want to keep his real estate investments secret seems unusual."

"Why don't you ask Andy about that?"

I ignored his sarcasm. "I have one more question. Why did you join the Cabin Group? You don't seem to be the type who would be comfortable sharing a life you wanted to keep secret with those guys."

"I'm not gay. I'm a married man and I have a normal life with my wife and our children. It's just that sometimes....." He gulped the water from the melted ice and slammed the heavy crystal tumbler onto the table. "What the hell. You know what I mean." He picked up his glass and looked towards the bar before deciding against another drink. He slammed the glass down again. "I resent your implication. I resent it very much."

"I'm not implying anything. I just want to know why you joined the group and contributed to their collection of pornography."

There was a long pause. Finally he said, "I really don't know. But I can tell you one thing. I always felt safe with the group. That is, until I started getting the calls from the blackmailer."

"In other words, you engaged in behavior that would destroy your political career and your marriage for a fleeting feeling of safety."

He thought for a moment before shrugging his shoulders. I left him contemplating how to resolve the conflict between the reality of his life and the fantasy of his life. I didn't expect him to able to do it.

I smiled at the big boobed receptionist as I walked out. She didn't return my smile.

---Seventeen---

Outside the building, I stepped to a secluded spot on the side of the entrance and placed a call on my cell phone to Mrs. Wellington. Amos answered the phone and instructed me to wait.

When she finally took the call, Mrs. Wellington wasn't courteous, but she was, at least, civil. I requested a list of the men who served as pallbearers at Berry's funeral. She agreed to have a list prepared and although I agreed to stop by in the afternoon to pick it up, she told me she would have it delivered to my house. She was probably concerned about common folks like me being exposed to the high life at the Wellington estate.

Before disconnecting I asked, "Who selected the pallbearers?"

"How should I know? I leave such details to others. I believe that either Harriet or Margaret may have made the arrangements. Most probably it was Harriet since Margaret is so irresponsible." She wasn't using a cell phone so she abruptly slammed the receiver into its cradle and hung up. So much for civility.

Since there was no reason for me to be as rude as she had been, I said 'Thank you," into the dead phone and calmly pressed the 'end' button.

I also placed a call to Dr. Rudolph Kramer. He was a general practitioner who at one time had an office on the corner of Blossom and Peachtree within walking distance of my house. When the developers bought his building he moved to a high rise professional building in Buckhead. I took a four o'clock appointment. Kramer might be the last doctor in the country who worked late on Friday afternoon.

***

I hailed a cab and headed for a downtown address to visit with Sammy Estes. I knew he lived in the Magnum Building, a prestigious condominium building, between the old Fox Theatre and the Woodruff Art Center. From the information Bob Macek gave me I knew that Keystone owned the building. It was an eleven story structure with an engineered pre stressed concrete front that made it look ordinary. There was no doorman, so I marched confidently into the lobby. It was a dull, drab room. Its walls were painted a light gray color. The only decorations were a plastic floor plant beside the heavy glass doorway and an art print of a waterfall hanging on the wall beside the elevator.

The folks who lived in this building were trying to fool the bad guys into thinking the residents were just hard working people who couldn't afford any better. A guard desk, with two inexpensive chairs for visitors, covered most of the back wall. The guard sitting behind the security desk didn't bother to look up until I was standing in front of him. He glanced at me then barked, "Yes?" It was his attempt at courteous treatment of the public.

"Sammy Estes, please."

"What's your name?"

"Art Gaines," I replied calmly. Nothing much to be gained by getting angry with the hired help.

He picked up a phone and dialed a number. After a short wait he spoke into the phone. "There's a guy named...," he paused and looked up at me.

"Short attention span?" I quipped.

"Huh." he replied not understanding my humor.

"Art Gaines. My name is Art Gaines."

'Oh yeah. There's a guy named Art Gaines to see you." He listened to the instructions then hung up. "Eleven 'A,'" he said pointing to the elevator.

"Thanks," I said. He picked up a paperback novel and ignored me.

The exterior of the elevator fit with the décor of the reception room. The paint on the doors was scratched and there were visible dents. When the door opened however, I stepped into the real world of the building. The interior was polished stainless steel accented with walnut and bird's eye maple hand rubbed to a near perfect satin finish.

The car rose to the eleventh floor silently without giving you a feeling that it had moved at all. There were three units on the Eleventh floor so finding unit Eleven A was no problem. I pushed the doorbell and waited as it played the first few bars of Dixie.' "Come on in," a voice from inside called to me.

I turned the knob and opened the door. "Sammy Estes?" I asked before entering.

"I've been expecting you, Mr. Gaines." Sammy was standing behind a portable bar mixing drinks. "Make yourself at home. I'll be finished in a couple of minutes."

I punched the doorbell again. "Snappy little tune. 'Oh I wish I were in the land of cotton.'" I sang the words.

"Was, Mr. Gaines."

"Was?" I asked.

"'Oh I wish I was in the land of cotton," he said

"Nice to know. I'd hate to get something like that wrong."

I turned my attention to the room. It was nicely decorated but it was dominated by two large pictures. One was of Stonewall Jackson sitting proudly on his horse and holding his wounded hand in the air. The other was an ornately framed painting of Arlington House. Two flag staffs crossed over the painting, one held the Bonnie Blue flag and the other held the first flag of the Confederacy. I had paid attention to Randall Kingsmore's lesson.

Sammy saw me looking at the picture and said. "The tyrant stole it from Robert E. Lee." Sammy stated as he walked towards me with a drink in each hand.

"I beg your pardon?" I asked.

"Abraham Lincoln, the great dictator. He stole Arlington, Robert E. Lee's private property, and converted it into a cemetery."

"The great dictator?" I asked.

"Certainly. Dictator, Conniver, Schemer. There are not enough evil words to describe the sixteenth President of the United States."

"The war's over, Sammy. We lost. And here you are after all these years, an unreconstructed Southerner."

"I see you're a comic, Mr. Gaines. Very funny."

He still held the drinks in his hands so I reached for one of them and took it from his hand. I took a sip. "Different!" I said. "What is it?"

"A mint julep."

"A little too sweet, but not bad." I lifted my glass in a salute to General Lee and added. "Well slap me silly and pass the grits."

"Are you mocking the General or the South?"

"No Sammy. I'm mocking you."

"You don't know me that well. Why are you making fun of my beliefs?"

"You're right Sammy. I don't know you very well, but I've heard the noise from people waiting for the old South to rise again all my life. Maybe my prejudices are showing. I'll try to wait till I know you better before classifying you as part of the lunatic fringe."

"You sound like a Yankee."

"Born and raised right here in Atlanta. What about you?"

"I was born in Charleston, the cradle of the Southern way of life."

"How long have you been re-fighting the Civil War, Sammy?"

"You mean the War to Stop Southern Independence. Secession was legal and the Southern states had a perfect right to withdraw from the Union and form their own country."

"Sammy, the rightness or wrongness of secession was settled on the battlefield many years ago. It's ridiculous to fight that war again," I replied.

"You can say what you want but the country that Lincoln created is the United, by force, States of America."

"Bull shit," I replied.

"There are still too many people like you who do not understand the war and its tragic consequences on our constitution and on our culture – North and South. I consider it my patriotic duty to help people understand. That's why I founded *Our Heritage*."

I turned my free hand up in a 'who cares' gesture and took a sip of the mint julep with the other hand.

Estes continued talking, "I hope my response to the message you left with my answering service was helpful."

I shrugged my shoulders. "Was Berry Wellington affiliated with *Our Heritage*?" I asked.

"I wouldn't call Berry an active member, but he did contribute money to the organization and he believed in the morality of the new Confederacy and what *Our Heritage*' is trying to accomplish."

"Do you have any idea why anyone would want to kill Berry Wellington?" I asked not wanting to listen to his rant.

"Berry was a true friend and a fine Southern gentleman. There are too few Southern gentlemen left. He will be sorely missed. Everyone who knew him loved him and no one would ever do anything to harm him." His words were sincere but he delivered them with too little conviction.

"What is your relationship with Andy Wilfield?"

Sammy's face turned red and the veins on the side of his neck expanded. I watched as he fought for control. "My relationship with Andy has nothing to do with Berry's death."

"I'll be the judge of that," I replied with just a hint

of sarcasm.

He turned away and muttered something under his breath. "They warned me about you and they were right." He looked away and gathered his thoughts. "You're a piece of shit, Mr. Gaines," he said clearly. He walked to the bar and poured his drink into the sink, filled his glass with tap water and drank it. "Ok. Andy is more than a friend but less than a partner."

"Does that mean you're exclusive to each other?"

"That has never been important to either of us. But how is that fact significant or even relevant to your supposed investigation of Berry Wellington's murder?"

"I don't know. Maybe it won't be. I never know what's important and what's not until I put it all together."

"And you think you can put it all together Mr. Gaines?"

'You bet your Southern ass I can. And you can bet every Confederate dollar you can get your hands on, I will put it all together."

I took the list I had gotten from Councilman Macek. There were fourteen names on the list. I read all the names. "Do you know any of these young men?"

Estes studied the list, then said. "Most of them.

There are a couple of names I don't recognize, but if I saw them I'm sure I'd recognize them. Of course, take their clothes off and I'd recognize them for sure." He spoke the last sentence with an exaggerated Southern accent and he ended by making an embellished broken wrist gesture.

"That's disgusting," I said.

"You mean it's smart and witty when you mock me, but disgusting when I mock you."

"Let me tell you what is disgusting," I replied trying to make a come back. "It's beginning to look like Berry Wellington was killed by one of the people involved in a sex ring or in real estate scandals or a ridiculous Southern separatist group and I'm going to prove it and see that the murderer gets convicted and has his sweet butt put into the State of Georgia's penal system." Ok, I admit it was a childish response, but sometimes a childish response is appropriate.

"There are a couple of people I know who might enjoy being locked up with a whole bunch of bored, horny Neanderthals." Sammy joked back in response to my tirade.

I didn't have a comeback so I turned away from Sammy and looked at General Lee. "Tell me about Keystone, Sammy," I decided to change the subject.

"What's that got to do with the murder of Berry Wellington?"

"Who knows? Back to my question, what about Keystone?"

"There was nothing scandalous about Keystone Corporation. It's just a real estate company that buys and sells real estate and manages a few properties. It's all legitimate."

"Legitimate my ass. Keystone used blackmail to get favorable zoning ruling."

"Bullshit!" He took a sip of his drink

"Who owns Keystone?" I asked.

"Lots of guys own stock in the company. In fact, if you're interested, I'm sure we'd sell you some shares. It's a good investment. Would you like to buy some stock?"

"No thanks Sammy. I just don't see myself becoming a real estate tycoon."

He took another sip from his glass and smiled. "You've got your dogs barking up the wrong tree. You had better get your hounds chasing something that you can hunt."

"Might be. You never can tell. Do you own part of Keystone?"

"In addition to being rude and arrogant, you're

persistent."

"Just a few of my endearing traits. Are you an owner of Keystone?" I am, if nothing persistent.

"Yes. Now, does that get you any closer to finding the murderer of Berry Wellington?"

"Don't know whether it does or it doesn't."

"Go to hell!" he snapped. "Mr. Gaines, I have worked hard, invested wisely and chosen my friends carefully. In the process, I'm proud to say, I've become financially secure. So, yes, I do own part of Keystone in addition to other properties and personal investments. But that is none of your business."

"What about the property you own that is not part of Keystone."

"As I said before, that is none of your business."

"If you own property it's public information. I can go to the court house and find out for myself if you don't want to answer the question."

"Then that's exactly what you should do, because I'm tired of you. I'm tired of looking at you and I'm tired of talking with you. Now get out of my house."

"What about the cabin on Lake Alatoona? Have you ever been there?"

"Of course I have. So what?"

I took another sip of the mint julep I had been nursing and turned around and looked at a portrait of Stonewall Jackson on the wall. "Real estate and pornography seem to be at the core of this case," I said.

"You don't know what you're talking about. Don't turn your back on me," he said, but I ignored him. "Turn around you arrogant prick." Sammy yelled at my back. I still didn't respond and he grew angrier. "Get out of my house. Get the hell out of my house right now." Sammy moved toward the door to show me the way out. He walked behind me and attempted to push me aside, but I turned around, grabbed his shirt collar and jerked him back.

I slung the remainder of my mint julep into his face. Part of the drink splashed onto an expensive oriental rug. "Sit down Sammy." I ordered.

He remained standing. A piece of mint leaf stuck to his face. He fanned it away with the back of his hand. "Leave me alone. Just leave me alone."

I pressed him down into the overstuffed sofa facing the portrait of General Jackson and held him down with my knee on his chest.

"That hurts, damn it." I shrugged my shoulders and he continued. "None of this is any of your godamnned business."

"What's none of my business?" I asked.

"None of this, you bastard. I had nothing to do with Berry's murder and my real estate holdings have nothing to do with it either. You're wasting your time and mine."

"You remember Sherman don't you?"

"What are your talking about?"

"William Tecumseh Sherman. Remember what he did to Atlanta. Just connect the dots, Sammy. Do you get the picture? If you don't answer my questions, I can make Sherman look like a little blue haired lady having high tea at the Ritz Carlton."

I noticed Sammy's eyes cut to the right, before I heard a click of a revolver being cocked and felt cold steel against my temple.

"I told you I'd kill you. Now get up slowly." I recognized the voice of my overweight nemesis, James Andrews.

I pushed myself up, removed my knee from Sammy's chest and raised my hands. "Just stay calm James."

He patted me down and when he was convinced I didn't have a gun he said, "Turn around real slow."

"You mean slowly," I quipped.

"Just shut up and turn around." He pulled the gun back and I turned slowly.

"Been hiding in the bedroom James? How long have you been looking out for your boss's boy toys?" I said.

"I told you to shut up," he growled.

Sammy Estes slid over the sofa and moved away from us.

"Is that any way to treat a fellow employee?" I was facing James now, so I could look into his eyes. I smiled and said, "Wait a minute. I get it. How could I have been so stupid? It's not just your boss. It's you too. You like boys as much as he does."

Almost immediately the veins in his neck swelled and redness flooded across his face. The goon made the move I was expecting and when he moved his free hand into position to hit me, the hand holding the gun shifted enough so the cocked revolver wasn't pointed at me.

It was all I needed.

I plowed my head into his chin. His teeth crashed together before he stumbled backwards. The revolver fired and Sammy screamed in the background.

With James writhing on the floor, I took the

revolver from him and turned to Sammy. I expected that he had been hit by the stray bullet, but instead he was crying under the picture of Stonewall Jackson. The bullet had crashed into the portrait of Stonewall Jackson and ripped out the section showing his raised hand. Back in 1863, Stonewall's hand had been mutilated when his troops mistakenly fired at him, now his portrait had been mutilated by a stray bullet from an overweight moron who probably didn't even know who Stonewall Jackson was.

James was lying still on the floor. I bent down and checked his pulse. It was strong.

Sammy had removed the damaged portrait from the wall. He held it away from his body and, as tears rutted his face, he kept repeating. "It's an antique. I can't replace it."

I shrugged my shoulders, opened the cylinder of the revolver and shook the bullets into my hand. Then I dropped the gun onto James massive stomach.

"You might want to get some medical help, Jimmy. I didn't check the medical plan at Wilfield Importers. I hope your premiums are up to date."

"You son of a bitch," Sammy Estes said as I walked out the front door of his condominium.

---Eighteen---

It was around three thirty when I pulled into my driveway on Blossom Lane. The corner of a large manila envelope was visible under the welcome mat at the front entrance. It contained the list of pallbearers. Mrs. Wellington had done what she said she would do.

I compared the pallbearer list with the names I had gotten from Councilman Macek. All the pallbearers were on both lists. The pallbearers were: Sammy Estes, Troy Hanson, Terry Hanson, Richard Patrick, Bill Silverman and Jimmy Winsted.

I threw the package from Mrs. Wellington and the list from Councilman Macek onto the living room table and rushed off to freshen up before my appointment with

Dr. Kramer.

I arrived five minutes late for my appointment, but Dr. Kramers' receptionist still smiled at me and ushered me into the inner office where a nurse, whose name tag declared her to be Mary, was waiting for me. She had a huge head of hair that was a bright red color unlike any that existed in nature. Her uniform was stretched at the buttons and way too tight for her body. The uniform accentuated a ring of fat where her waist should have been. She directed me to the scales and recorded my weight.

"It's all muscle, Mary," I said. She gave me an 'un huh' reply and led me into an examination room.

"What seems to be your problem today?" she asked.

I wanted to talk with the doctor not his nurse, but I still answered the question. "I might have been exposed to the HIV virus."

"Well, tell me the story," she said, pulling a stool closer. "Unsafe sex, dirty drug needles, which is it?"

"None of the above," I replied.

"Thank God," she said, "I'd hate to think a good looking guy like you had been exposed in the traditional way."

"Never could happen while women as beautiful as you are around."

She snickered, "Now tell me the story of how you got exposed."

"There was an unfortunate event at my house and a man was shot."

"I think I saw something about that on the evening news. Some rich guy wasn't it?"

"Yep," I replied.

"And he was HIV positive?"

"Yep."

"And you got his blood on you?"

"Yep."

She wrote some notes in my chart and said, "There's not a whole lot of danger you'll get anything, but it's good you're getting yourself checked." She placed my chart in a box attached to the door. "Dr. Kramer will be with you in a minute."

After two short articles in a three month old magazine, Dr. Kramer came into the examination room. He had me remove all my clothes and examined my entire body for any open wounds. He asked if any blood had gotten into my mouth, eyes or nose. Then he drew some blood from a vein in my arm and said, "I wouldn't be too worried about getting infected by the blood from the poor man who was murdered at your home. It's more likely that a 747 will fall from the sky and land on you. However, I'll test this blood sample just to be safe. Speaking of safe, I want to remind you to use safe sex practices when you do have sex." The doctor opened the drawer under the supply cabinet and plundered through it until he found a pamphlet titled: *A Practical Guide of Safe Sex*.

"Is it illustrated? It's been so long for me that I might need a refresher course," I said.

I opened the book and parts of it were illustrated, but not the good parts.

---Nineteen---

The next day turned out to be dark and dreary. Clouds hung low over the city with rain misting most of the time. It was the kind of day made for staying indoors.

An idea for a corner table to go in Delia's bedroom had been floating in my head for a couple of months and this would be a perfect day to spend in the workshop turning that idea into a piece of furniture.

Working with wood is wonderful therapy. You have to concentrate on what you're doing, but it's the kind of concentration that clears your mind. Who knows, with a cleared brain, I might even fit some of the pieces of the Wellington murder together or maybe I could calculate how many invoices I needed to send and how much money I would be making.

A few years ago, while investigating the McManus embezzlement case, I'd found some old rough sawn cherry lumber in a farmer's barn. He sold it at a fair price and I hauled it home and left it standing in the corner gathering dust. I pulled some wide stock from the pile, ran it through the thickness planer and moved it to the table saw where I could cut it to size for the top. I then ripped some thicker boards to two and a half inches by two and a half inches for the legs. After cutting the legs to length, I cut the end of each leg into a tenon and chamfered the end grain. Then I put a mortise cut in each corner of the table top to allow the legs to go through and the top to rest securely on the tenon. I had calculated everything correctly and the legs passed through the top just enough to fully expose the chamfered edge of each leg. I added a center shelf to the table, and then declared it complete and ready for finishing.

I was sanding the table around six o'clock when the extension phone in the workshop rang. "Hello."

"Is this Art Gaines?" the caller asked.

"The one and only," I replied.

"You don't know me, Mr. Gaines. My name is Terry Hansen. I was a friend of Berry Wellington. He was a good friend." His voice cracked as he tried to control his emotions. He paused for a moment. "I have to talk with you."

"Were you one of the pallbearers at Berry Wellington's funeral?" I asked.

"Yes, I was and so was my twin brother, Troy."

"Come right over Terry. Do you know where I live?" I said.

"Not today and not at your place," he said with a hint of panic in his voice.

"Ok! Just tell me where and when."

"Tomorrow. In the Orchid House at the Botanical Gardens."

"I'll be there. What time?"

"One o'clock. This is important." He hung up abruptly before I could question him any further.

***

It was almost eight thirty in the evening when I turned out the lights in the workshop and headed for the shower to clean up. Around ten o'clock, I headed out for my regular Saturday night visit to Chez Monde for coffee and beignets. Chez Monde on Saturday night was a tradition Annie and I started when we were dating and it continued during all the years we were together. When she dumped me for that viola playing geek, she quit coming to the restaurant because the geek only drank organically grown teas. It was almost like getting Chez Monde as part of the separation agreement.

The restaurant is a wonderful find. They serve delicious sandwiches, fresh salads and restaurant-made soups, but they are most famous for their coffee and beignets. They serve two blends of coffee; one with chicory for casual customers and tourists who want the 'New Orleans' experience while they are in Atlanta and the other, a special blend custom roasted at the restaurant to a dark chocolate color, leaving the beans rich and oily with a spectacular fragrance. I prefer the custom roasted blend. They prepare their coffee a number of ways. Most customers are satisfied with a bland, drip brew. I prefer mine made in a French press. The beignets are made from scratch, cooked to order and served, too hot to eat, with a generous dusting of powered sugar.

Many Saturday nights, Ed Vigodsky would also show up at Chez Monde. He joked that he preferred beignets because he had a more sophisticated palate than a regular doughnut eating cop, but I think he was lonely and the company at Chez Monde was more pleasant than that at the Krispy Kreme.

Sometimes when Ed showed up, the two of us would take a corner booth, but when I was alone, I sat at the counter. Tonight all of the counter seats were empty, so I took one in the middle. A couple of minutes passed before Johnny came through the swinging doors. If Johnny had a last name no one ever spoke it, but he was in charge and everyone knew it. He was an average looking guy, about six feet tall, not too fat, not too slim and with a nice head of thinning dark brown hair. His face was dominated by a prominent hawk nose and dark almost black eyes. Making eye contact with him made you nervous, as if you were looking deep into the place where primitive rage is temporarily held in check. On those rare occasions when he got angry, his stare was frightening.

"Evening Art. Hope you didn't have to wait long." He didn't wait for an answer. "Want a cup of the good stuff ?" he asked

"The good stuff and half dozen hot ones," I ordered.

"Where's Delia?" Johnny asked.

"With her mother."

"Sure do like seeing that little darling."

"Me, too."

Occasionally I brought Delia to the café. She loved the beignets. Johnny always put an extra sprinkle of powered sugar on hers.

He scooped some coffee into a French press, filled it with steaming water and completed the assembly by placing the stainless steel plunger on the corner of the container. As he walked toward me, he yelled through the service window into the kitchen. "G'me a half."

He placed a coffee mug in front of me, pulled a spoon from under the counter and positioned it on a napkin beside the cup. He turned to the service window and impatiently drummed his fingers on the ledge on the kitchen service window. "Waiting!" He yelled at the window. It sounded more like an order than a statement. A few seconds later a plate with six steaming beignets appeared.

Johnny grabbed them and the French press and placed them both in front of me. "Your buddy Vigodsky coming?" he asked as he pressed the plunger down and poured my coffee.

"Don't know," I replied.

Johnny shrugged his shoulders and disappeared back into the kitchen. I lit into the plate of treasures while they were hot.

***

People who live in Atlanta aren't bothered by sirens, so when the sounds of a siren were in the distance no one even looked up. When the police car with flashing lights stopped in front of Chez Monde, however, everyone in the restaurant stopped and watched the uniformed officer hop out and run to the entrance. He stopped at the counter. Johnny had returned from the kitchen area and he walked up to the cop. "Can I help you officer?" Johnny was expecting an order.

"You know a guy named Art Gaines?"

"Sure do," Johnny replied.

"Can you point him out to me?"

"Sure can," Johnny pointed to me.

The officer walked over to me. "Got powdered sugar on the lip." He waited till I took a napkin and wiped my lips. "Lieutenant Vigodsky sent me to get you."

"Well, Officer Huff," I said glancing at the name bar on his chest. "Did the good Lieutenant know I'd be eating beignets and drinking the best coffee in the city?"

"Said if you weren't at your house, you'd be here. Also said you'd ask a lot of questions and he said to tell you that if you would keep your cell phone turned on and in your pocket, like every other civilized person on the face of the earth, you wouldn't have to ask so many questions and he wouldn't have to send someone to pick you up."

"Where are you taking me?" I asked.

"Valley Park Condos, down on Peachtree Circle."

"What's there?"

"A dead body."

Johnny had already gotten a couple of large Styrofoam cups from under the counter. He had them full of fresh coffee. He handed me the coffees and a box. "It's a half order of hot ones for Vigodsky." I grabbed Vigodsky's package and the coffee and started for the door. "Wait a minute. I need another coffee." Johnny fixed it and I ran after Officer Huff, balancing three cups of coffee on the box of beignets.

---Twenty---

Officer Huff held the yellow crime scene tape up so I could walk beneath it. The apartment was quiet, but a group of investigators was busily inspecting it with strong spot lights and tweezers to pick up any tidbit they might find. Another crew was silently dusting the area with brushes and black powder for fingerprints. Amanda Halsell stood by the front window. She wore cranberry colored pants and a tan jacket with a white blouse. She turned when I came in and smiled at me. Ed Vigodsky was pacing in front of the door into a bedroom.

"Get over here Gaines." Vigodsky yelled before I could enter the apartment.

"First things first," I said to Vigodsky while

walking towards Amanda. "I brought coffee for you. Just the way you like it." She took the coffee and gave me one of those smiles that could mean lots of different things. I took it to mean 'I want you to be my sex slave.' I gave her my 'I want to see you naked' smile in return.

Vigodsky walked over and reached across my shoulder to take the extra cup of coffee. "Johnny send these?" he asked, but he didn't wait for an answer. "Best damned coffee in the city," he reported to no one in particular as he took the plastic top from the cup and placed it into his pocket, so it wouldn't contaminate the crime scene. He took a sip of the coffee, grabbed the baker's box from my hand and took a beignet. "Best beignets, too." He handed the box to Amanda.

"Come with me Gaines," he barked, turning away and marching toward the bedroom, with coffee in one hand and the half eaten beignet in the other. I winked at Amanda before turning to follow him.

Vigodsky stepped into the bedroom, popped the rest of the beignet into his mouth and pointed to a body lying on the floor beside the neatly made bed. "Know that guy?" he asked.

I walked over and bent down to look at the body of the young man. His face was bloodied from a brutal beating, but his death was from a bullet wound in his chest. Blood had soaked into an expensive looking silk shirt he wore and been absorbed into the carpet. "He looks like one of the pall bearers from Barry Wellington's funeral," I said.

"Uh. Huh," Vigodsky replied.

"Who is he?"

"We'll get to that later. The medical examiner sets the time of death between Five and seven o'clock this evening. Based on the information we pulled from his cell phone, he called you twice. The last time was around six o'clock, so I place his time of death between six fifteen and seven o'clock. What did you talk about with him?"

"I don't know anything about two calls, but I did get a call this afternoon. I guess it was around six o'clock"

"And who called you?"

"He said his name was Terry Hansen."

"And you talked about what?" Vigodsky asked.

"Nothing! He just said he needed to talk with me, but that he didn't want to come to my house."

"And?" Vigodsky said as a question.

"He asked me to meet him at the Orchid House of the Botanical Gardens."

"When?"

"Tomorrow at one o'clock."

"Why is it everyone who tries to talk with you ends up getting themselves killed?"

"That's what I'm trying to find out."

"And he didn't tell you anything at all during this conversation."

"Just that he was a friend of Berry Wellington and that he needed to talk with me."

"And you expect me to believe that is all there was to your conversation?"

"To be completely honest, I don't give a damn what you believe, but that's exactly what happened. He said he needed to talk with me and he told me where and when to meet him." I turned away from Vigodsky and walked toward the bedroom door, when an idea hit me. "How long did we talk?"

"That's what I'm trying to get you to tell me, you prick," he responded.

"The cell phone will tell you. Just press....."

"Just shut your smart mouth. This is serious," he replied with a little embarrassment in his voice

"Go ahead. Look. How long did we talk?" I demanded.

Vigodsky's pulse became visible in his neck vein

and his face turned red. "Damn you Art, don't try to tell me how to run an investigation. Why don't you go do something useful like staking out some poor schmuck on worker's comp and trying to catch him cutting his grass? Just get out of the way and leave the real work to people who know what they are doing." He moved closer to me with his hand clinched tightly. I didn't budge. "Get the hell out of my way," he yelled and then pushed me aside with his arm with enough force to knock me firmly into the wall.

My muscles tensed and I started to react, but a hand on my shoulder held me back.

"Let it go," Amanda said. "Give me the room Ed," she said and Vigodsky stomped into the living room. When we were alone she asked, "Why do you goad him like that?"

"We've always goaded each other," I replied.

"What is it, some kind of a guy thing with you two?"

"I guess so."

"Never mind. I don't think I'll ever understand men. Did you tell Ed the truth Art?" she asked.

"Yes Amanda, I told the truth."

"It's hard to believe that your curiosity didn't force

you to ask more questions."

"It did, but Terry was insistent on meeting tomorrow in a public place and he hung up us as soon as we had agreed to a time and place. By the way, is that Terry Hansen on the floor."

"According to the driver's license in his wallet."

"Damn."

She squared her shoulders and asked, "Do you think he was trying to set you up?"

"You mean like a trap?"

"Sure"

"No I don't think so. He was scared. I could hear it in his voice."

"But the Botanical Gardens wouldn't be crowded on a week day at one o'clock. What about the second call he placed to you."

"Amanda, I swear, I only received one call from Mr. Hansen."

"Were you home all day?" she asked and I nodded affirmatively. "Did you run an errand or work in the yard?"

"Nope. I was home all day, but I was working in my shop."

"Maybe that's why you didn't hear the phone

ring," she commented.

"Could be, but there is a phone in the shop."

"Can you hear it above the noise of your shop machinery?"

"No. But there is a light on the phone that lets me know when someone leaves a message."

"And no one did?" she asked.

"And no one did," I repeated.

She walked to the door and yelled to Vigodsky. "He only talked to him one time."

Vigodsky slowly entered the room. "I know. I checked the cell phone. The first call was just a few seconds. He probably hung up as soon as the answering machine answered. The second call lasted eighty two seconds," he reported.

"Go on," I said.

"What do you mean?" Vigodsky asked.

"I mean, go on and tell me you're sorry for thinking I was lying to you."

"You know what I think, Art?" He walked over to me and leaned into my face. "I think you'll lie to me every chance you get and that pisses me off." He started to poke me in the chest with his finger but he stopped short and turned away and continued talking with his back to me. "I think you owe me. We've known each other too long and I've pulled your worthless ass out of the fire too many times. You owe me."

"Damn it Ed, don't pull this macho cop crap on me. I've pulled your worthless ass out of the fire too." I said to his back.

He turned around and the two of us were face to face; each of us waiting for the other to make the next move. Ed's face was red and both of us were breathing heavily.

"For God sake, cut it out," Amanda said. "You two are acting like school boys. There's too damned much testosterone flowing in this room! Now, both of you calm down." She pushed us apart.

"Alright!" Vigodsky said, "I shouldn't have flown off the handle like that, but I'm convinced you know something that could help us crack this case. I get my ass chewed every day by the Chief. He hates it when rich folks get shot in the city and now we have two murders and although Terry Hansen wasn't rich, the two murders seem to be connected."

"I think they're connected too, but I don't know how," I said.

"Keep talking," Amanda urged.

"Well, my working theory is that both Berry Wellington and Terry Hansen knew something they wanted to tell and someone was willing to kill them to keep them from telling. The problem is I don't know what that information was or who was willing to kill to keep them from telling."

He threw his hands into the air and yelled, "People pay you for this. Hell, I got rookies that could figure that much out. Tell me something that everyone doesn't already know." Vigodsky stormed from the room.

"Do we know where Terry's brother Troy is?" I asked Amanda.

"No, we don't. We sent a couple of officers to his apartment and he's not there. We have a crew trying to trace him down."

"I wonder if he knows about his brother."

"We think Troy placed the 911 call."

"You think Troy found his brother's body."

"That's our working theory."

"That puts a new wrinkle into things."

"Yes, it does," she replied as she stepped to the door. "Officer Huff, will you escort Mr. Gaines back to his home."

I turned to Amanda and said, "I'd be glad to wait

and let you drive me home."

"Maybe next time," she said.

"The offer for dinner at Solbies still stands."

"Make a reservation for eight o'clock Monday evening. I'll meet you there," she said.

"You got it," I said trying to keep my smile under control.

"Two rules," she said. "No talk about this case and..." she paused and looked me straight in the eyes. "Dinner only. Nothing else."

"You drive a hard bargain, but it's a deal," I replied.

She walked into the other room and left me with Officer Huff and my fantasies.

---Twenty one---

Abigail Eddings Patrick lived with her invalid mother three streets away from the Wellington mansion, and although the property value fell at least ten per cent for each block, the Patrick Residence was still elegant and imposing. It was a two-story brick structure, sitting on an oversized corner lot with a main circular drive to deliver visitors to the front entrance and a driveway on the side to carry the family's cars to a covered portico. Rich folks don't like to get wet when they have to run out for emergency supplies of pate and caviar. The portico was wide enough for three vehicles, but it only housed a single navy blue Lincoln.

I rang the door bell at nine fifty-five for a ten

o'clock appointment and the door was promptly opened by an older lady who was decked out in an immaculate nurse's outfit straight from the nineteen fifties, with a brilliantly white dress, white hose, white shoes and a starched and pressed white cap on her head.

"Are you Mr. Gaines?" she asked before I had the opportunity to announce my name.

"Yes," I replied.

She handed me a pair of paper shoe covers. "Please place these over your shoes." After they were snuggly over my shoes, she said, "Ms Patrick is expecting you." She backed into the house and pointed to her left. "That way please, into the study."

I walked over the highly polished hard wood floor and into a room paneled with knotty pine boards. Book cases lined three walls from floor to ceiling. The shelves were filled with books but they were grouped for appearance into matched sets by size and color. It was unlikely any of them had been read. Four elegant leather-covered chairs surrounded a square table in the center of the room. Abigail Patrick sat in the center one facing the door. She stood as I entered the room.

She was taller than I remembered and more self assured than the crying mourner she had been at Berry's funeral. She wore a dark grey dress that was more appropriate for a sixty year old school teacher. Her hair was pulled back from her forehead with a bow, in an obvious attempt to accentuate the elderly matron look. I walked over and extending my hand which she took in both of hers. When she released my hand she invited me to sit in the chair beside her. "How may I help you, Mr. Gaines?"

"Please call me Art," I said and gave her one of my best smiles.

"I'm sorry I can't do that. Mother would never allow me to address someone I have just met by a familiar name."

"Then may I call you Abigail?"

"You may, and in the event we become friends, I will tell you the name I prefer."

"You could tell me now and save us both some time. That is unless you think it unlikely that we become friends?" I responded.

"Surely you don't think an investigator is in the same social circles as I am?"

"I guess not." I replied.

"You guess correctly," she said. Her voice had a condescending tone that would have made Mrs.

Wellington proud.

"Now that that's settled. May I ask you some questions, Abigail?"

"Yes, you may Mr. Gaines. But, first please close the study doors?" she asked, more as an order rather than a request.

I stood and complied while she reached under the table and opened a drawer. She removed a heavy glass ash tray and placed it on the table then she pulled a pack of cigarettes and a lighter from a pocket on the side of her chair. She lit the cigarette as I returned to my seat.

"Mother doesn't approve of smoking," she said, taking a draw on the cigarette and inhaling the smoke deeply into her lungs. She let the smoke come out as she spoke. "I do believe I've told the police investigators everything I know, but I'm more than willing to do anything I can to assist you. It's my understanding that the Wellington family has retained your services to investigate the death of my fiancé."

"Yes they have, but I also have a personal reason for engaging in this investigation. Someone shot Berry at my home and I feel obligated to find out who did it."

"I see," she said, "And if I recall the information I received from the Wellington family, your house if off

Peachtree Street."

"Yes it is. It's a very comfortable place to have a home." Here I was again, having a verbal battle with a wealthy snob to determine if someone with a modest income could have a home.

"If you say so. But tell me, why would my fiancé be in such a neighborhood?"

I decided to ignore her remark and our` game of one-upmanship.

"I'm no longer just investigating the death of your fiancé. Last night there was another murder. Someone beat up, shot and killed Terry Hansen."

"I beg you pardon?" she asked, taking another deep puff from her cigarette.

"It was in the paper this morning and reported on all the local TV morning shows."

"We don't take the newspaper and I never watch local news so, I didn't know....Why would anyone kill Terry?" Wetness formed in her eyes and she blotted them with a lace handkerchief from her blouse pocket.

"I assume you knew Mr. Hansen?"

"I know many of Berry's friends," she replied as she crushed her cigarette into the ashtray and removed another from the pack to replace it. "Berry kept no secrets from me, Mr. Gaines."

"Do you have any idea where his brother, Troy might be?"

"Have you checked his apartment and his place of employment?"

I ignored her response. "Can you think of any reason why Troy Hansen would disappear after his brother's murder?"

"How should I know that?"

"OK. Then do you know Randall Kingsmore?"

"Yes, I know Randy."

"Did you know he and Berry were homosexual lovers?"

"I did."

"Just what kind of relationship did you and Mr. Wellington have?"

"We, too, were lovers," she said, while exhaling a cloud of smoke. She spoke matter of factly, as if it had the same significance as a statement about the color of wall paint. "Does that bother you Mr. Gaines."

"Many things about this case bother me," I said, before changing the subject. "Mr. Wellington was HIV positive," I said.

"Yes, I know."

"And you were lovers."

"Mr. Gaines, we used safe sex practices. Berry was very careful when he was with me."

"Do you know about the Keystone Investing Company?

"Certainly! As I told you, Berry and I had no secrets."

"Do you own any stock in the company?"

"Oh no. Berry trusted other people too much. I prefer to make my own decisions about what I buy or don't buy. I don't rely on other people making those decisions for me."

"Then you own property Ms. Parker?" I asked.

"Why are you interested in my investments?" She asked in return.

"I'm interested in lots of things. Do you object to answering the questions?"

"Not at all." She cleared her throat and coughed lightly. "As caretaker of my family's finances, I own some real estate and various other investments. Mother has been an invalid for over ten years now. She requires around the clock medical care and this house requires a large staff to maintain. When my father died over sixteen years ago, he left us only a modest amount of money.

Mother never had a head for money. She was on the way to spending all of what little we had before she became ill and I took over the management of our family's financial affairs. I have grown the money she didn't squander into enough to meet my family's needs and to prepare for my future needs." She stubbed out yet another cigarette into the ashtray and immediately lit a replacement. "Will that information help with your investigation?"

"It might."

"Well then, continue with your questions," she said.

"Berry knew many people. Who would you say he trusted most?"

"Me of course," she stated assertively.

"Who else?"

After a pause, she replied, "I'd have to say the Hansen twins."

"Not Randall Kingsmore?"

"Berry was very fond of Randy, but Randy was just too protective. Berry felt smothered. He sometimes said Randy was just like his mother. Randy also had a tendency to overreact to personal situations. He was too emotion for a rational man, like my Berry."

"So Berry kept things from Randy?"

"Yes he did."

"Such as?"

"Oh my! Let me think. Well for one thing, holidays. Randy got really upset that Berry didn't spend holidays with him. Berry blamed it on his mother but he didn't spend all holidays with his family. Many times he was with me. Once he and I went to Vegas for Thanksgiving. Berry told Randy he was visiting his mother's family in Savannah."

Our conversation was interrupted by a gentle knock on the door and the nurse slowly opened the door. "What is it Lois?" Ms. Parker asked.

"She's awake and calling for you"

"Can't you do anything without me?" she snapped and took a last puff on her cigarette before throwing it still lit into the ashtray. "You'll have to leave now. Mr. Gaines. I must attend to my mother. If you have additional questions you may call for another appointment." She turned to the nurse, "Lois, show Mr. Gaines out and get one of the girls to empty this ashtray and spray some air freshener."

---Twenty two---

Back at the house, I pulled my navy suit from the back of the closet, dusted it off and tried it on. It fit loosely. I congratulated myself on loosing weight since the last time I wore it, then I matched it up with a freshly laundered white shirt and a blue and red regimental stripped tie and dressed myself for the Colvin retirement luncheon.

When I entered the banquet hall, I still had no idea what I would say. An usher greeted me and escorted me to a table in front of the podium. There was a paper tent with my name and I took my seat between the mayor and Brian Colvin. The other people at the table were one of the mayor's assistants, the police chief, one of his assistants, Ed Vigodsky and Cynthia Colvin, a stunningly attractive young lady who was Sergeant Colvin's daughter.

After lunch, the chief got up and stepped to the podium to welcome all of us and thank us for attending. The mayor followed next. She thanked Sergeant Colvin for his dedicated service and since the election was coming up soon, she reminded us of the new hospital and renovations to the library she had sponsored. Ed Vigodsky was next. He recounted a couple of notable achievements from Brian Colvin's career and stated how proud he was to have worked with such a fine officer. Then it was my turn. A few ideas were floating in my head but I still didn't have any prepared remarks. The crowd courteously applauded as I walked to the podium.

"Thank you." My voice shook with nervousness. "I'm here today to honor service to the Atlanta Police Department. Being a cop is hard and frequently thankless work and those people who dedicate their career to police work deserve our thanks and respect." A few people starting applauding and more joined in. I almost lost my concentration while I waited for them to stop. "Our police spend their working life in a world the rest of us like to pretend doesn't exist. Their working lives are spent with people who ignore the principles of law the rest of us try to follow. They deal with good people who find themselves in tragic situations and they deal with people who are purely evil. It would be understandable if police work left the cop depressed and cynical but at the end of the work day, most cops do something that is wonderful and heroic; they disassociate themselves from the depravity they deal with every day and return to the real world and their friends and families."

I talked for another five minutes and received an enthusiastic ovation from the audience. During my speech, I never once mentioned Brian Colvin's name or said anything either favorable or unfavorable about him.

When I sat back at the table, Ed Vigodsky gave me a thumbs up signal and the mayor took my hand and told me she enjoyed my remarks, and then Colvin leaned over and whispered in my ear. "Feel better, now?"

"Yes, I do," I replied.

"You should get yourself a relationship coach," he said.

We smiled at each other and shook hands.

***

I spent the remainder of the afternoon at the

Fulton and Dekalb counties courthouse digging through land and corporate records. I had a hunch rattling around in my head and I needed to see if there was anything to contradict it. The police have to keep digging until they find enough evidence to convict someone of a crime, but I could play my hunch. If I was wrong, then it would be back to investigating, but if I was right I could start sending invoices.

By the end of the day, although I still couldn't prove a thing, I was ready to goad some people into making stupid mistakes. The ploy was dangerous because there were already two corpses and I didn't want to be the third.

---Twenty-three---

I arrived at the restaurant for my date with Amanda Halsell at seven forty-five. The maitre d sat me at a table with a view of the entrance and I sipped on water while I nervously waited for her.

She arrived fashionably late at ten minutes after eight. As she walked towards me there was no doubt about it. She had the look. It wasn't her clothes or her hair or her makeup or how she moved. It was the total package. It communicated sensuality without the slightest trace of vulnerability. She was wearing a little red dress. It wasn't a tailored outfit, but it had been altered by a perfectionist and it hung to her body exactly as it was supposed to. The business clothes she wore when on duty were designed to hide the revolver she carried, but they also masked her figure. The dress didn't. As she moved to the table, the dress swished from side to side further accenting her body.

Immediately I turned into an awkward high school boy and stumbled over my feet getting up to greet her. To make matters worst, I almost fell while pulling her chair from under the table. I held on to the table and maneuvered myself back into my seat without bumbling too badly.

When I first started flirting with her, the most I was considering was companionship and sex. As she sat down, I was struck with the realization that whatever relationship we would have would be more than a one night stand.

"Hi," I said

"Hi."

"You look spectacular."

"So do you," she replied.

I felt like an elementary school boy with a crush on the prettiest girl in the class. I desperately wanted to start a conversation, but I couldn't put the words together. Fortunately, the waiter interrupted before I resorted to passing a note. You remember those school yard notes: -- I like you!! Do you like me?   Check yes or no.

The waiter introduced himself, recited the specials and took our drink orders. Amanda ordered a cosmopolitan and I ordered iced Stolichnaya Vodka.

I fumbled with the menu while trying to start a conversation.

Amanda broke the ice. "How did you get into the investigation business?" she asked. The damsel rushing to the rescue of the hero.

"It was really my brother's business, but he was killed and I took it over from him. He was really good at the detective business. He taught me a lot, but I'll never be as good as he was."

"Don't sell yourself short. I hear you're pretty good" she said.

I could feel the heat of a flush on my face. "Thank you. I have to admit I've had a pretty good run since I started on my own, but Buddy had a way about him. He was really good." I said, buying some time for the redness to fade.

"How was he killed?" she asked.

"Let's talk about you first. Tell me about Amanda Halsell."

"There's really not much to tell. I'm a cop and I love my job. What else do you want to know?" she replied.

"Everything! Start at the beginning where were you born?"

"In rural South Carolina in a small community called Hallsellville."

"Named for your family?"

"That's right. It seems they built a post office and made one of my relatives the postmaster. Then they named the community after him."

The waiter delivered our drinks and offered to tell us about the specials again. We listened, or more accurately, she listened and I watched her listen. When he finished his recitation he disappeared. I took the mini bottle of vodka that was encased in a small block of ice from the saucer and poured half of it into the shot glass that accompanied it.

"Keep on," I said, after taking a sip.

"Well let's see. I was an only child. My parents were older when I was born. The doctor had told them they couldn't have children. My father was fifty-one and my mother was forty-five when I was born. You'd think that being an only child of an elderly couple in rural

South Carolina would be a lonely way to grow up, but it wasn't. There were always lots of people around. Cousins, other relatives, friends." She paused and gazed into the air content with her memories and with a slight smile on her face.

"Why'd you leave?" I asked.

"I wanted to be a cop."

The waiter returned to ask if we were ready to order. Neither of us had looked at the menu, but Amanda ordered the baked Salmon special and I ordered a small filet. It was a four star restaurant and I should have ordered something that challenged the chef's ability, but a steak was good enough since I would have been content to be with Amanda at a diner eating cheese burgers.

"So you came to Atlanta to be a cop."

"Yes. You see my Uncle Moses was the sheriff back home and every time he came to our house I would sit in his lap and listen to his tales of law enforcement. There wasn't much crime in the county - domestic violence, the occasional robbery, and every once in a while there would be a murder. Still, I loved hearing Uncle Moses' stories, but I knew I wanted to do more than arrest husbands who beat their wives, catch shoplifters and direct traffic for funeral processions. My parents died while I was in college so when I graduated I moved to Atlanta and the rest is history."

The waiter delivered our salads. She took a bite, then added some salt and pepper and sampled it again. The taste must have suited her, because she loaded her fork full and stuffed the next bite into her mouth. We ate in silence. When she finished she turned her fork over and placed it across her salad plate. I had already pushed my half eaten salad to the side. The waiter appeared and removed the salad dishes, the service plates and the salad flatware.

She continued the story. "I never sold the house where I grew up. For some reason, I just can't think about parting with the place. It's still the only place I think of as home."

"Sounds like the kind of place you should hold on to," I replied.

"OK. Your turn," she said.

"What's Vigodsky told you about me?"

"You wouldn't want to know," she said with a mischievous smile.

"Whatever he's told you. It's not true."

"Not all of it was bad. He has some good things to say about you."

"Well those things are true," I said and she laughed. "I was born right here in Atlanta. Went to school here and this is the place I feel most at home."

"And?" she asked.

"Well that's about it. You know where I live. You've met Chester and Gort. There's not much else."

"Flag on that play. Twenty yard penalty," she said.

"Are you into football?" I asked.

"Don't try to change the subject. Now cough it up. Tell me about the real Art Gaines."

"After high school I went to the Georgia State University. I'd been into wrestling in high school but I just didn't want to do college level sports, so, I limped along academically, drank a lot of beer, played a lot of poker and managed to cram four years of college education into six years." I paused hoping this would be enough information. I wanted to know about her more than I wanted to recite my history.

"Go on," she ordered.

"After I graduated, I didn't have any trouble finding a job, but I did have trouble finding a job I liked. Finally I landed a job with a consulting firm. I traveled all over the country, had a great time and did some good for troubled companies, but I never really fit in with Corporate America. When Buddy got shot, I quit the job to take care of him."

"And that's when you became an investigator?"

"Yep, now you know the whole story."

The waiter had returned to serve our entrees. He placed them if front of us and poured me a sample of the wine I had ordered. I took a sip and nodded to him and he filled both our glasses. Amanda cut into her salmon and took a small bite. She added some salt and pepper, and then cut a bigger piece. I cut into my steak. It was cooked exactly as I had ordered.

"Do you like being a private investigator?" she asked between bites of her steamed vegetables.

"Yes I do. I didn't at first, but now I do. As I said, my brother Buddy was in the business first and he was a genius at it. He made a pile of money and became a celebrity. He was always trying to get me to come into the business with him, but I wasn't interested in it. Then he got shot. He was driving on a rural road late at night. We believe he was chasing someone since the bullets that hit him broke through the windshield. He lost consciousness and his car ran off the road and rammed into a tree."

"Oh my God, how awful," she said.

"We think it was over an hour before a passing driver found him and called for help," I paused and took a deep breath.

"Don't forget your steak," she remarked, nodding toward my plate.

I cut a bite, chewed it and then continued, "Buddy came close to dying and, in fact, he never fully recovered from his injuries. He died less than two years after he left the hospital." She reached over the table and grabbed my hand. She held it for a moment then gently released it.

"When they discharged Buddy from the hospital, he moved in with me and my ..ah.. roommate." I paused to think about how I would talk about Annie.

"Ed Vigodsky mentioned your roommate."

"What did he say?"

"He said you hadn't gotten over her yet. He said you were one of those guys who love too deeply and hold on too long. He said that you deserved better."

I shrugged my shoulders.

"Do you?" she asked.

"Do I what?"

"Do you deserve someone better?"

I shrugged my shoulders again. How do you

answer a question like that?

"Go on with your story. You moved Buddy in with you and your lover, then what."

There was something about her calling Annie my lover that bothered me, but I continued the story.

"Her name was Annie and I helped Buddy with his rehabilitation. As he got better, he sent me on errands and both Annie and I kept getting more and more involved in his business. After a few months, I took on my first client. It was a simple case involving an employee who embezzled money from a brokerage firm. I followed Buddy's instructions and we proved the guy's guilt after only four days on the case. The client was impressed and paid their bill on time, which was good because Buddy's medical expenses were eating up his money. I didn't enjoy the business, but we needed the money so I kept taking on clients and using Buddy as a resource. We were doing pretty well until Buddy told me it was time to bring his attacker to justice. I did what he told me, but it didn't work out like he planned."

"Most things never do," she said.

"What?"

"Work like they're planned," Amanda said clarifying her comment. "Anyway, I'm sorry for interrupting. Please continue with your story."

"Well, we caught the guy who shot Buddy and we caught the guy who ordered the killing, but in the process I almost got killed," I paused, "and I had to shoot a guy." I choked up a little. "He died."

She took my hand again and held it tightly. "They're all hard to deal with," she said.

"Vigodsky got me through it. He and Buddy had been close in high school. Buddy called him and he came over and we talked long into the night."

"He's really a nice guy."

"Who?"

"Abe," she replied.

"Yeah, I think deep down he really is," I said.

"What about your daughter?"

"Vidogsky told you about her too."

"Yes."

"She's wonderful. Her name is Delia. She's a beautiful nine-year-old genius. I don't get to see her as often as I would like. Her mother..." I paused something about telling Amanda about my previous relationship was difficult.

"Go on," she said.

"Well, her mother thinks that my work puts Delia

in danger."

"That's sad."

We both skipped dessert but ordered coffee. We drank coffee and kept talking until the waiter came by the table and advised us it was closing time. I paid the check and we walked outside. "Where are you parked?" I asked.

"I took a cab," she replied.

I took her arm and escorted her toward the garage where I had parked my car. Coming out of the garage, I turned left out of the lot.

"I live to the right," she said.

"I know," I replied.

"Did you forget the rules? Just dinner, nothing else."

"No, but I was hoping you did," I said as I made a U-turn.

---Twenty-four---

The following morning, I settled behind my office desk with a large cup of coffee and a sausage and egg sandwich on an onion bagel from Frank's Deli. One of the fire safe boxes from the Lake Alatoona cabin sat beside the desk. I killed a little time working a sudoku puzzle while slowly eating my breakfast. Anything to put off the task of looking at the smutty materials in the box and making some phone calls on the chance I might goad someone into taking some action.

The police would consider the box, and everything in it, evidence in a murder investigation. It was unlikely the tapes would contain any new information about the killing of either Berry Wellington or Terry Hansen, but I had to be certain.

Keeping evidence from the police is not only foolish, it's illegal, and if I weren't careful I could end up spending lots of time locked in a twelve-by-twelve cell with a guy named 'Brutus.' If there was any evidence on the tapes I'd find a way to get them to the police. If there wasn't, I'd risk the obstruction of justice charge.

***

Around nine o'clock, I decided to put my plan into action. It was a simple plan. I'd make a couple of phone calls, plant a hint that I could identify Berry Wellington's murderer and then wait while the rumor mill did its work. If things worked out like they should, one or more people would be contacting me in an effort to find out what I really knew.

I dialed the first number and a cheerful voice answered the phone. "Good Morning Wilfield Importers and Distributors. How may I help you?"

"Good morning Emily," I replied in my most cheerful voice. "This is Art Gaines. May I speak with Horace Wilfield?"

"You certainly may, but first you need to talk with me."

"That would be wonderful Emily; I love talking

with you."

"I heard you beat up James Andrews again?"

"That's a fact," I replied, "But Jimmy's too fat and not very coordinated so beating him up isn't much of an accomplishment."

"He hates being called Jimmy."

"All the more reason to do it."

"Heard you beat up the bosses SUV too?"

"That's a fact too, but beating up the car was easier than beating up Jimmy. The car didn't fight back at all."

She snickered, "Let me get Mr. Wilfield for you. I'm certain he'll be glad to talk with you." She added, making no effort to hide the sarcasm.

Horace Wilfield answered the phone angrily. "Mr. Gaines!" he snapped. "You will pay for all the damages to my vehicle."

"And I will bill you double, maybe even triple, for having Little Jimmy Andrews interfere with my investigation."

That seemed to calm him down or perhaps the anger was just an act to intimidate me. "We can argue about that later. Now why are you calling?" He was talking in his 'I'm the boss – I'm important! – Why are you interrupting me' tone of voice.

"I have a report," I replied in my 'I don't give a damn' tone of voice.

"Very well. I'm listening."

"I'll be able to identify the murderer of Berry Wellington, without disclosing the documents Mr. Wellington created to hide the illegal financial transactions necessary to purchase property for you, your son and himself."

"Then you have the papers?" he asked excitedly, loosing all pretenses of authority.

"I do."

"Then you have satisfied your obligation to me and I expect you to deliver the papers to me immediately," he ordered. "I'll forgive the damages to my vehicle and if you'll tell me how much your fee is, I'll have a check cut and waiting for you when you bring the documents."

"I appreciate the offer but that'll have to wait. There are a few more details to confirm before giving the police the information they need to make an arrest, so I'll be spending my time converting all my notes and observations into a written report. The police prefer things like this to be written." I added the last part to make a direct attack on me less likely. The killers couldn't just wait for me in some secluded place and put a bullet in my head. They would need to talk with me to see what I really knew and to be certain they could get control of all of my 'written evidence.' I placed my feet on my desk and took a sip of the warm coffee.

"Mr. Gaines, you are being obstinate. You've already told me that the documents will not be necessary to your main objective, the identification of the person who murdered Mr. Wellington. Therefore, these documents only have value to me and I demand that you deliver them to me today." He paused, but before I could respond he continued. "And just what are you writing for the police? Will my name, my company's name or my son's name be a part of whatever you are preparing to give to the police?" He was trying to maintain his in command tone of voice, but his concern made his words sound desperate and pitiful.

"Certainly not, but as I said, Horace, I have a few things to resolve. I expect to deliver my evidence about the murder of Berry Wellington to the police tomorrow."

"Where are you? I'll send someone to pick up my documents. And you must promise that you will not include anything about us in your report." Again, there was panic in his voice.

I had accomplished what I wanted. I said, "Thank you, Horace, but I'll be much too busy today," and hung up the phone.

Before he could call back and make more demands, I placed a second call.

"The Wellington Residence." I recognized the voice of the mysterious Amos.

"Good morning Amos. This is Art Gaines. I hope you remember me. May I speak with Mrs. Wellington?"

"Yes, I remember you. Hold please." Amos was a man of few words.

It was close to five minutes before she picked up the phone. "How may I help you, Mr. Gaines?" she asked.

"I have a report on my investigation into the murder of your son."

"Well!" she said, as an order to tell her.

"There are a few details I need to confirm. I'll get that done today and meet with the police tomorrow morning. They should be able to make an arrest after that."

She demanded to know who had killed Berry, but I held my ground and ignored her attempt at intimidation, but I was careful to let her know about my 'written report.' "I'll call you tomorrow with more information," I said before hanging up the receiver.

***

I sat back and congratulated myself on putting my plan into motion and prepared to view the video tapes. There's a walnut armoire on the wall in front of my desk that I built about ten years ago. It was the first piece of furniture I made with dove tail joints and although it wasn't a showpiece, it was functional as office furniture. Behind one of its doors was a wet bar with a small ice machine. Behind the other door was a shelf holding a TV and a VCR – I hadn't upgraded the office to a DVD player. There was a locked drawer under the TV shelf where I kept a bottle of Laphroaig scotch for a special occasion. If everything worked out like it should, the scotch wouldn't be locked away much longer.

I slipped the first tape into the VCR and started my smut viewing marathon. There was very little erotic value in any of the tapes and after ten minutes it was a chore to continue paying attention. The ordeal took over four hours. At lunch time, I ordered in and continued watching the tapes. I did stop the player when a scruffy looking kid delivered my coke and corned beef sandwich. He had a tattoo of Satan on his left arm and a stud pierced through his tongue and another through his right nostril. Just another one of the city's youth heading for a career in the fast food industry.

When I finally watched every tape in the box, I had seen every conceivable combination of males and/or females involved in every conceivable sexual act imaginable and some I would have never imagined. I recognized some of the participants, including Bob Macek who was actively having sex with a number of women and two different men. Now that I knew he was a liar, I would feel much better about sending him an invoice.

There was nothing on any of the tapes that would help identify the murderer of either Berry Wellington or Terry Hansen. Of course the police wouldn't agree with me on that but knowing it made me feel better about withholding evidence.

---Twenty five---

Around four o'clock I gave up on The New York Times crossword puzzle and on my plan. I had expected either Horace Wilfield or Mrs. Wellington to spread the word that I could identify who had killed Berry Wellington. I expected someone to make an effort to get their hands on my 'written report' or to keep me from meeting with the police, but nothing had happened. No one had visited the office and the only calls I had received were from a telemarketer trying to sell me office supplies and a headhunter trying to help me with my staffing needs.

When a plan fails, it's time to rethink things and come up with a new plan. So about fifteen minutes later I was heading for the garage to pick up the car and head home. Some scotch and a good cigar would make my brain work better while figuring out why my plan failed and deciding what to do next.

Everything looked normal in the garage. At this time of day, it was full of cars and there were lots of places for an attacker to hide, but I wasn't expecting a sneak attack. Foolish me.

I heard the pop first. It sounded like an air rifle. Then I felt two quick pricks one in the arm and one on the side before fifty-five thousand volts of electricity shot through my body, dropping me instantly. I had been shot by a taser weapon. A taser has a range of fifteen to thirty feet, depending on how much money you want to spend. It was an excellent weapon for incapacitating someone without doing permanent damage or without getting too close. I was sprawled on the floor in a semiconscious state but I was aware that my legs were spastically jerking. The pain which was initially unbearable had lessened to excruciating. My brain tried to scream but my body couldn't. I had no control of my muscles and could not change positions or stop the muscles in my arms and legs from twitching. I felt a prick in my right forearm. I willed my left hand to swat it away but all it did was twitch. A burning sensation sprang into my right forearm as a cold liquid was pushed into it from a hypodermic needle.

***

I woke up in the trunk of a car hog tied with my hands secured behind me and attached to my bound feet, forcing me into a cramped reversed 'C' position. I don't know how long I had been out, or how long I'd been in the trunk but I was sure we had been traveling long enough to be beyond the stop and go traffic of the central city. Although country music blared from the radio speakers, the traffic noise was still easy to hear. We must have been outside the perimeter highway on one of the expressways that web the metropolitan Atlanta area because the traffic noise was constant and vehicles were passing us on both sides.

Whoever had tied me knew what they were doing, but there was enough slack in the ropes to allow limited movement. I remembered the little pocket knife I had taken from James Andrews. It took a while to move it inside my pocket so it would fall on the floor. It took a while longer to maneuver myself into position so I could pick it up. By the time I had the knife in my hand, the traffic noise was less and the road was becoming bumpy.

We must have left the expressway and turned onto a secondary road.

I worked the knife behind my trousers and belt. If I cut myself free now, I would only have one option and that would be to pull the emergency release lever, open the trunk, jump out and run like hell. If I could be patient, I might have more options.

The road kept getting rougher and whoever was driving didn't seem to be making an effort to miss any of the bumps. When we slowed down, I heard branches scraping on the car, I was certain we were pulling into the cabin on Lake Alatoona.

After the car stopped, the heat in the trunk began climbing quickly. The driver side door opened and the driver got out of the car. The outside noises were muffled but there must have been another vehicle nearby because another car door opened and then closed. I could hear the muttering of at least two men, but couldn't make out any words. Sweat began stinging my eyes, but all I could do was wait for my captor to get me out of the trunk.

A few minutes later the trunk latch popped open and someone yanked me out and threw me to the ground. It was evening and starting to get dark, but my eyes were still adjusting to the light slowly. Both men were behind me working on the ropes. They freed my legs, and then one of the guys jerked me to a standing position. My legs buckled under me and it was difficult to stand.

One of my capturers grabbed me under my arms and said, "Stand up you ass." I recognized the voice of James Andrews.

James grabbed one of my arms and held me upright. The second man was behind me. I turned and looked into the face of Sammy Estes. He grabbed my other arm and they forced me to move with them. We climbed a step and were on the cabin's porch.

The three of us could not fit through the entrance door together so they released my arms and James Andrews pushed me forward. My hands were still tied and without them to stabilize me I crashed into the wall and fell to the floor.

"Damn it Jimmy that hurt," I said.

"Just shut the hell up, you son of a bitch." James was trying to sound tough and for the first time since he and I had been interacting he was succeeding.

James forced me into a straight back wooden chair. I looked around the cabin. Someone had straightened it up. The furniture was back in position and the mattress was on the bed. I fidgeted in the chair to confirm that the knife was still securely lodged behind my trousers and my belt.

Sammy pulled a chair in front of me and sat down. He looked me in the eye with a smirk on his face. "Looks like the table has turned now," Sammy said. He placed one hand on each of my legs and as he spoke he leaned closer and closer. Finally, he kissed me on my forehead and leaned back in his chair laughing.

"I hope you enjoyed that Sammy, but it didn't do much for me," I said.

"Didn't do much for me either. I guess you're just not my type," Sammy replied.

"That happens to me a lot. Heard any good Yankee jokes lately, Sammy?" I asked.

"No, the only joke I know is the one about the private investigator who ran his smart ass mouth one time too many." Sammy Estes said.

"What's the punch line?" I asked.

"He gets himself killed," Sammy replied.

"I haven't heard that one. Are you going to tell it to me?"

"You can count on that. You know something Gaines, we've got you figured out," Sammy said.

"I'm easy to figure out," I replied. "Even people

who aren't very smart can do that."

"We don't think you can prove a damned thing. We think you are bluffing and we think you are too damned much trouble"

"Just who is 'we'?" I asked.

"You don't need to worry about that. But let me tell you what else we believe. We don't think you have any written report for the police."

"And if you're wrong about that, you and your 'we' will go to jail," I said.

"Mr. Gaines, there is nothing you can say that will concern us. We know you are bluffing and we are calling your bluff"

"Again can you tell me who the 'we' is? I know it couldn't be you and little Jimmy. He's not smart enough to figure anything out."

James was standing behind me. I turned towards him and winked. One thing is certain, the big lug was predictable. The anger built up quickly and he swung his fist and hit me across the face. I fell down and felt the warmness of blood dripping from my nose.

"You fool. You damned idiot," Sammy yelled. "Now his blood will be in the cabin. Quick get some paper towels." Sammy helped me to get upright into the chair again and then took the paper towels from James and cleaned my face. "Get some toilet paper," he ordered. James lumbered off to the bathroom.

When he returned, Sammy gently packed my nostril with the paper. "There's only a little blood on the floor. Clean it up with soap and water. Put all the paper towels you use into a plastic bag and be sure you put the bag in the back of your car when you leave." James scurried off to comply.

"Damned fool," he said to James' receding bulk. We sat in silence until James returned and maneuvered himself into a kneeling position and began attempting to remove my blood stains from the floor. While Sammy watched to be certain James got all my visible blood from the floor, he said, "Now, Mr. Gaines I want to tell you what is going to happen to you. Would you like to know?"

"You know what they say about curiosity," I said. My voice sounded strange with the toilet paper stuffed in my nose.

"Won't be curiosity that kills you," Sammy stated.

"Nice to know. So what will?"

Sammy just smiled and continued talking. "We are going to put you into that little aluminum fishing boat at the dock." He turned in his seat and pointed through the picture window. There was a single light bulb suspended from a cord over the dock area. It provided just enough light so I could see an old flat bottom boat tied to the dock. "We'll use some duct tape to keep your mouth shut and some more to hold your ankles together. Then we're going to tie a rope to your legs." He pulled a pack of cigarettes from his pocket, tapped one out and lit it. "Do you want to know more?"

"Sure I want to know more. We've already determined that I'm a curious type guy," I said.

Sammy's smile turned to a frown as James grunted from the exertion of scrubbing the floor. "Don't scrub so hard. You're just spreading the blood more. Blot it up with some dry towels," Sammy ordered.

"OK, OK. But you ain't paying me to be no janitor," James protested.

"I'm paying you to do what needs to be done and I'm paying you a hell of lot to do it," Sammy replied angrily.

James pulled some dry towels from the roll and continued working on the blood smears. His breathing was heavy and became labored with the little bit of effort he was spending on his cleaning task.

Sammy lit another cigarette and blew smoke into

my face. "They say second hand smoke is dangerous, but you won't be living long enough to find out if it is or isn't. Now where were we?" he asked rhetorically.

"I was in the boat with my feet duct taped together," I replied.

"Oh yes. Now the rope that is tied around your feet will be tied to a concrete block. We'll tie another longer rope around the block too. Then James will get into the boat with his fishing gear and the two of you will go out into the lake. It'll be dark by then, but that won't matter much since we are in a little cove and there's not a lot of boat traffic. After a while James will stop the boat, pick you up and throw you overboard. He'll try not to make a lot of noise but it really won't matter much, either." Sammy leaned back in the chair and drew smoke from the cigarette deep into his lungs, held it a few seconds and blew it back out. "I regret I won't be able to see you struggle, but by then I'll be heading back to the city."

"Got a 'South will rise again' rally to attend?"

"Still a joker, I see. Of course, you'll quit joking when that concrete block slowly pulls you under the water." He took another long drag on his cigarette. "You weigh about a hundred and seventy-five to a hundred and eighty pounds?" he asked.

"Close enough," I replied.

"And the block weighs around twenty-five pounds, maybe thirty, when it gets saturated with water. Doesn't seem like enough, but it is."

He got up and walked to the bathroom and threw his cigarette into the toilet. "You'll struggle very, very hard, but in the end the concrete block will win. Its' weight will pull you down to the bottom of the lake. You'll fight it, but eventually your body's instincts will take over and you'll gasp for air and fill your lungs with water. They say that when you drown you are conscious long enough to panic with the realization you are dying. I hope so. I hope your last thought is about me and what I did to you."

Sammy walked back to his chair, pulled it close to me and when he was beside me he whispered into my ear. "Now here's the good part. You'll be dead and it won't matter to you, but let me tell you what will happen to your corpse." He pushed his chair back and continued in a normal voice. "After you're in the water, James will take out his fishing gear, put a lure on it and cast it out into the lake. He'll keep doing this for a while. Hell, who knows he might even get lucky and catch a fish, but I doubt it. After thirty minutes or so when he's absolutely sure you're dead, he'll use the second rope tied to the concrete block to pull your body up from the bottom of the lake. He'll remove the duct tape and all the rope, and then he'll put you back into the lake. Do you know what happens to a dead body in water?"

I shrugged my shoulders.

"You'll sink back to the bottom of the lake. You'll bounce around with the current for a few days while you start rotting. Some of the fish will nibble on you but they probably won't do a lot of damage. The current will take you into the main part of the lake. After you've been under the water for about a week the carbon dioxide gas will build up in what's left of your body. It will make you bloat up like a balloon and you'll begin to float to the top of the water." Sammy lit another cigarette and smiled as he blew smoke into the air.

"Enjoying this fantasy?" I asked.

"Oh most definitely, but this is no fantasy. Now to continue, you'll be floating and you'll end up in the main part of the lake, which is usually full of frustrated executives from the city, running their speedboats too fast for the crowded conditions but what the hell?" He took another drag on the cigarette. "Now this is the part I like the best. You'll probably be hit by between ten and twenty boats and their propellers will probably tear you to pieces." He blew smoke into my face. "Eventually someone will find you, or parts of you, and they'll be able to do some DNA analysis to determine your identity."

He took the cigarette to the bathroom and flushed it down the toilet. "Do you have anything to say about all of this?" he asked as he returned.

"Just some questions."

"Sure why not."

"Why did you kill Berry Wellington?"

"You're not very smart if you think I did that. It took someone more cruel and diabolical than I to kill Berry."

"But you know who killed him."

"Mr. Gaines, I've already told you I know and understand many things."

"Ok, then did you kill Terry Hansen."

"You're a foolish man. I don't kill people. I have people who kill people." he smiled, proud at his comeback. "For a man who is about to die, you ask a lot of questions."

"It's better for my health than eating a last meal full of saturated fats."

"Terry Hansen knew too much and he couldn't keep his mouth shut. You, in fact, are responsible for Mr. Hansen's demise. You see, he made the mistake of telling the wrong person that he planned to talk with you. We couldn't have that." He paused and took his cigarette pack from his pocket. "I don't need to smoke another cigarette." He replaced the pack in his pocket. "It's time to send you to the bottom of the lake."

"You've wasted a lot of time developing this plan, but it won't do you any good," I said.

"Why is that Mr. Gaines?" he asked.

"Because I'm going to kill you and I'm going to kill your big buddy too," I said pointing with my head to James Andrews who was standing in the kitchen door drinking a beer.

"I doubt it Mr. Gaines," Sammy said and nodded to James Andrews.

James walked over and zapped me with a stun gun. They may not be lethal but they hurt like hell. The hand-held tazers don't seem to carry the zap of the traditional fired dart models, but it was enough to instantly turn all my muscles into Jell-O.

When I regained control of my body my feet were bound tightly with duct tape and a piece of tape covered my mouth. They had removed the toilet paper from my nose. James was holding my arms and Sammy my legs and they were carrying me towards the dock.

---Twenty six---

They placed me on the dock. James was remarkably gentle and he supported my head so it didn't slam into the dock. Sammy however, dropped my legs and let them fall. James attempted to get his bulk into the flat-bottomed boat. It swayed violently and he almost lost his balance, but he stabilized himself by holding onto the dock. He fidgeted in the boat trying to find a way to lift me into it with out capsizing it.

In a disgusted tone Sammy ordered; "Sit on the deck with your feet in the boat."

"You could help," James protested. "Make this whole thing a lot easier."

Sammy ignored him.

From the sitting position, James pulled, slid and lifted me from the dock. He grunted and strained as he placed me into the boat and he gently propped me against the bow as if I were a prize rather than a victim.

"Pull the tape off his mouth." Sammy ordered.

James was gasping for breath but he leaned down and yanked the tape from my mouth.

"Still think you're going to kill me?" Sammy asked.

"You can count on it," I replied.

Sammy laughed and nodded at James. James wrapped rope around my ankles and tied a knot. He pulled the rope and it tightened around my feet.

"You've cut off the circulation." I protested.

"Won't matter. All your circulation will be cut off in a few minutes." Sammy motioned James to the end of the pier.

James forced himself onto the pier. He was on his knees and had to struggle to stand. He paused to gain his breath before joining Sammy at the end of the pier where they talked quietly for a few moments. I couldn't hear what they were saying; but it didn't matter because I was intent on getting the pocket knife freed from my belt. I needed to cut my hands free long before James threw me

317

into the water if I was going to have a fighting chance of getting out of this situation. I had the knife in my hand when James got back into the boat, but I hadn't been able to get the blade opened.

Again, he almost capsized the boat as he got his bulk in place, but I was able to hold on to the knife. When the boat stabilized, Sammy handed James a fishing rod with a bait casting reel attached and a small tackle box. James Carefully placed them on the floor of the boat. He turned to the stern and started pulling the starter cord of the small motor. The boat rocked with each pull. It took close to ten tries before the motor coughed to life. It sputtered and tried to quit running, but James maneuvered the choke lever in and out and kept it running. James sat down on the rear bench seat exhausted from the effort and allowed the engine to chug along at idle speed. As the engine warmed up it started running smoothly. He pushed us away from the dock and turned the throttle on the steering handle. The little boat moved slowly through the water. The ride was smooth and stable as James guided us toward the center of the cove.

I finally got the knife blade opened and started sawing on my ropes. I was working with my hands in an awkward position and when James stopped the engine I hadn't cut through the ropes. He waited for the boat to drift to a stop, and then he started working his way towards me. He had difficulty moving without loosing his balance and that gave me some extra time. I needed all I could get.

"Why are you doing what Sammy tells you to do?" I asked in an effort to buy more time.

"He pays me. Pays me damned good too."

"Don't the Wilfield's pay you too?"

"Yeah, but not enough."

"They mind you freelancing?"

"Andy don't care and old man Horace don't know. He's happy as long as I do what he wants done, when he wants it done."

"I'll pay you lots of money to turn this boat around and take me back to the shore."

He made an effort to move towards me. "Hell, no," he said stopping to get his balance.

"How about a hundred thousand dollars," I offered.

"No deal. Don't like killin' people, but I'd kill you even if Sammy wasn't paying me. I'd kill you just for the fun of it." He took another tentative step and was close enough to bend over and grab my shoulders, but the movement of the boat when he attempted to lift me was too much. He sat down on the plank seat and pulled my legs to get me closer to him. From a sitting position, he was more secure and he grabbed my legs and threw them over the side of the boat. Then he started lifting my torso to get me into position.

All the movement made it more difficult to cut the rope, but I was frantically trying to complete the cut. He had pulled me up to his chest level. He paused gasping to get his breath. It gave me enough time. Although I had not cut completely through the rope, I had cut them enough that I was able to force my hands free. I dropped the knife onto the floor of the boat. James was holding me under my arms so I brought both hands around and hit him simultaneously on both sides of his head. He dropped me and I crashed into the bow of the boat. James stumbled and crashed into the rear bench seat in front of the motor. I got my legs back into the boat and managed to get myself into a kneeling position. When James got himself upright I clamped both hands together and clubbed him on the side of his face. The blow knocked him to the side of the boat and when he braced against the side to control the fall the boat tipped enough that water poured over the side. James overreacted and leaned in the opposite direction too much and lost his balance. He tumbled into the lake and I scrambled to find the knife.

"I can't swim," he yelled.

"I don't care," I yelled, continuing my search of the bottom of the boat for the pocket knife. I found the knife and cut through the tape holding my feet and with my hands free, I easily cut the rope that connected my leg to the concrete block.

James thrashed about in the water and managed to move himself toward the boat. When he was close enough he grabbed its side and attempted to hoist himself back into the boat. His efforts caused the boat to tip below the water level. He was going to sink us if I didn't do something, so I stabbed the knife into his hand and he lost his hold on the boat.

"Let me in!" he pleaded as his bloody hand grabbed the side of the boat more tightly this time.

"Not a chance," I said. I braced myself on the opposite side of the boat and kicked him as hard as I could in his face. He fell from the boat and silently drifted away.

I grabbed for the motor's starter rope and pulled.

It started on the second pull. I turned the throttle to full open. The five horsepower motor responded quickly and I turned the boat toward shore with the throttle full open. A gun shot vibrated in the confined space of the cove and a bullet slammed into the water beside the boat. Sammy Estes stood on the dock with a gun in his hand. It was pointed in my direction and he was pulling the trigger as fast as possible. One shot hit the boat above the water line. Then a bullet hit me in my right forearm. I ignored the pain and kept the boat aimed at the shore.

Silence descended when Sammy ran out of bullets. He turned and ran for his car, a bright red Mercedes coupe. He started the car and spun his tires as he headed for the exit. I held the throttle full open as the little boat neared land and ran it onto the ground. The propeller hit a tree root and the motor locked up and shut down. I jumped from the boat and ran for the cabin. My arm was bleeding heavily. I needed to stem the flow of blood. I kicked the door open and ran for the bathroom, pulled a clean towel from under the vanity and tied it around my arm.

That accomplished, I ran for the car that had brought me to the cabin. The keys weren't in the ignition. They weren't in any of the normal hiding places – above the visor, under the floor mat or under the front seat. I glanced out at the lake. The water was calm and the full moon reflected serenely off the water. Could the keys be in James' pocket on the bottom of the lake? I sat in the driver's seat. I had no cell phone and it was a long, long walk to a road that would have traffic or a convenience store with a phone. I needed a plan. Then I noticed the keys sitting in the passenger seat.

I started the car and pulled away from the cabin slowly since all chances of following Sammy Estes were gone. I drove James' car to the commuter parking lot at the Doraville MARTA station and left the keys in the ignition. I didn't want anyone to find the car near my house. I took MARTA into town and then a bus to the corner of Peachtree and Blossom. The few people who noticed the bloody towel wrapped around my upper arm didn't seem to find it unusual.

---Twenty seven---

By midnight, I had fed Gort and Chester and showered. Then I started the task of dressing my wound. The bullet had passed through the muscle at the top of my shoulder and it was difficult to fit the dressing so it didn't interfere with the movement of my arm. When I finished, the wound was throbbing, but otherwise I felt good. However, barely escaping being killed and leaving James to drown had left me too alert to sleep. I put on a pair of jeans and a tee shirt, then poured a scotch straight up and went to the sun room to unwind and determine how I was going to deal with Sammy Estes and uncover the identity of his unnamed accomplice.

After couple of sips into my second scotch I was

totally unwound and all the tension had left my body. I was drifting between awake and asleep when Gort's barking snapped me back to alertness. I noticed a shadow moving in my yard. I might have ignored it as part of a waking dream, except Gort doesn't bark at dream figures.

I slipped from the lounge chair and crawled to the desk in the living room. From the center drawer I took a nine millimeter Sig Sauer P226 pistol. It carried fifteen rounds and had a four point four inch barrel and was small enough to fit on my back behind my belt. As a backup, I also grabbed the gun I had taken from James Andrews when he broke into my office. I wasn't wearing shoes but there was a pair of running shoes by the door. I took time to put them on; then I grabbed a light jacket, gently opened the front door and slipped out using my foot to keep Gort from following. There was no where to hide on my front stoop so I quickly ran down the steps.

"That's far enough." A voice said as I stepped onto the lawn. "Just stay where you are smart ass and don't move," the voice ordered. "Get his gun, Dick." A hand reached from behind me and took the light weight expensive pistol from my hand. "Pat him down." The voice kept giving orders.

"I got his gun in my hand." Dick said.

"Pat him down anyway. Sammy says he's a tricky son of a bitch."

From behind, Dick patted my legs and under my arms. He was an amateur who had learned from watching TV and reading detective novels. "He's clean," he said. He had not detected the gun on my back.

I hadn't seen either man's face, so I decided to turn around. No one stopped me. To the guy nearest me I said, "Hi, Dick, I'm Art Gaines." I stuck out my hand. I recognized him as one of the pall bearers from Berry Wellington's funeral. His name must have been Dick Patrick. Dick recoiled as if I was holding a rattlesnake in my hand.

The other guy came over and slapped me on the face. I recognized him as a pall bearer too, but I didn't know his name yet.

"Tie the son of a bitch's hands behind him, you idiot," he said to his partner.

Dick Patrick was a slightly built guy but he grabbed my hands and jerked them behind my back with the force of a body builder.

I held my hands away from my body hoping to keep him from feeling the gun under my windbreaker. Again, he was an easy-to-fool amateur.

Behind me, I heard the guy who was issuing all the orders pressing numbers into a cell phone. "It's me," he said. "Yeah, went just like you said it would. The fool just walked out his door and we got him." He paused. "Okay, should take us about thirty minutes to get there. Maybe ten or fifteen minutes more to get to the top." Another pause. "Don't worry; he ain't gonna get away from us." He snapped the phone shut.

"Sammy worried I might get away from you two guys?" I asked

"Sammy ain't worried asshole, but you should be." Then he issued an order to Dick. "Duct tape the bastard's mouth."

I heard the tape being torn and then Dick spun me around and placed tape over my mouth.

They placed me in the back seat of their car and buckled my seat belt. The car was one of those vehicles that look like a box and is so ugly it passes into the cute area. The guy giving the orders got into the driver's seat and Dick Patrick rode in the passenger seat. He turned sideways so he could keep his gun pointed at me.

We worked our way to the Perimeter Highway and merged in with the traffic. It was around two o'clock and the traffic was light by Atlanta Standards. Dick had been fidgeting since we left my house. Finally he turned his attention to the driver. "What's going to happen, Bill?"

Now I knew that my other captor was Bill Silverman.

"I don't know a damn thing more than you do. Now, just keep quiet," Bill said.

"If he's planning to kill him, I don't want a thing to do with it," Dick said.

"Too damned late to back out now," Bill said.

"I didn't sign up to kill nobody. I don't want to get in any trouble," Dick said.

"We done kidnapped that bastard in the back seat. You're already in trouble. If Sammy can't find a way out of this mess, it's gonna be bad for all of us. All of us could end up in jail. Sammy's right this bastard has caused us too much trouble." Bill said.

Dick turned toward me again. His expression showed fear.

***

We parked in an isolated area on the back side of historic Stone Mountain. Sammy Estes' red Mercedes was in the parking area, along with a Toyota SUV and a Ford Ranger pickup truck. With his gun, Bill pointed me toward a partially hidden foot trail. Dick led the way, shining a small flashlight that just barely provided enough light to keep us on the path. The trail ended in a grassy area where service vehicles were parked. The grass was worn thin and the ground was rutted from parking on it when the lot was wet from rainfall. With Bill's gun pressed into my back, we crossed the parking lot and ended at a service road leading to the top of the mountain. I grunted in protest as Bill forced me to start the climb to the top, which would probably take from forty five minutes to an hour. I was too tired to make the climb, but the gun in my back motivated me.

About five minutes into the trail there is a small recessed area. Sitting in the middle of the area was a battery powered four-wheel All Terrain Vehicle. Dick got into the driver's seat and Bill forced me into the passenger seat. He clamored into the rear bench seat and turned sideways to hold his gun firmly against my neck.

Dick drove the vehicle onto the road. The machine climbed the incline effortlessly and in less than ten minutes we emerged at the trail end just as the clouds moved from the moon and lit the area. It was a spectacular view of the top of the mountain. Well, actually it isn't a mountain. It is only six hundred and fifty feet above the surrounding ground, but it's the largest exposed piece of granite in the world and it is spectacular.

Georgians are proud of modern Stone Mountain, but it has a tarnished history that most of us try to ignore. In nineteen fifteen it was the site for the formation of the second Ku Klux Klan. The new KKK members were administered the oath required for membership by Nathan Bedford Forrest, II, grandson of the Grand Master of the original Klan. One of the early owners of the mountain granted the Klan a perpetual easement to use the land as a site for rallies. When the state acquired the land and the mountain, they condemned the land they had just purchased in order to void the Klan's claim on the use of the land.

The Mountain is famous for the bas relief carving on its granite face. The carving was completed in nineteen seventy. It shows three heroes of the Confederacy, Stonewall Jackson, Robert E. Lee and Jefferson Davis, on horseback. They are bare-headed and holding their hats over their chest. In warm weather there is a spectacular laser light show. The climax of the show is the illumination of the three Confederate heroes who are animated and made to move off as if they are circling the mountain.

***

Dick drove to a large flat area and stopped the vehicle. We sat in the ATV for a moment or so then Bill ordered, "Get out." He jammed his gun into my side to motivate me and then he got out of the vehicle and pushed me. I stumbled a few feet.

Dick turned the vehicle around, drove it about a hundred feet away and parked it. He stood beside it as two men emerged from the wooded area beside the trail. The three of them walked toward me and Bill.

With the moon shining brightly, I recognized Sammy Estes, but I had to wait for them to get closer before I recognized the other man as yet another pallbearers from Berry Wellington's funeral.

"Get that tape off the bastard's mouth. I want to talk to him." Sammy Estes said.

Dick Patrick walked to me and yanked the tape.

"Damn that hurt," I said. "Could you get one of your goons to untie my hands? My nose itches."

"You are the dumbest son of a bitch in the world. You're standing here with four guys with guns and you're still joking."

"If I didn't joke I'd be terrified by you four vicious looking Southern gentlemen who have kidnapped me, and hauled me to Stone Mountain, but my nose still itches."

Sammy nodded to Dick Patrick who walked over and cut my hands free from the ropes.

"I know Dick and Bill and I certainly know you Sammy but who is the fourth guy?" I asked.

"Meet Jimmy Winsted," Sammy said.

I moved toward Jimmy and stuck out me hand.

"Just stay where you are, damn it. Don't none of us want to shake your hand," Sammy said.

"Did one of these guys kill Terry Hansen?" I asked.

"You forgot to scratch your nose." Sammy said.

Truthfully, my nose did itch, but I didn't scratch it. "Itch seemed to have gone away, Sammy. Did you forget my question?"

"Well, Art. I see you're still as curious as ever, but once again you're off base. Although any of them would have done it, if I had asked them to, it was James Andrews who had the distinction of sending Terry Hansen to his reward. By the way, did you kill James?"

"I'm sure you boys have heard that old Southern saying, 'he needed killin'." I waited for a response but the group remained silent. "Well, James really did need killing, but I suspect it was the fact that he was fat and out of shape and couldn't swim that really got him. Of course I didn't help any when I kicked him in the head and drove the boat away."

"You won't be so lucky with this group." He motioned to Dick Patrick. "Did you pat him down? Dick nodded. "He's clean," he said.

"Check him again. He's a tricky bastard. Be sure you didn't miss anything." Sammy demanded.

Bill Silverman and Jimmy Winsted held their pistols on me while Dick Patrick walked over and ran his hands down my legs and under my arms. I thought I had gotten lucky and Dick had missed the pistol in my belt, but then he patted on my back. He jerked my jacket up and pulled the pistol out. He showed it to the group.

"You damned incompetent bastard. I thought you had searched him already. Do I have to do everything? Can't you do anything by yourself?" Sammy growled at Dick Patrick.

Dick had his hand on my shoulder as he tried to respond. "I....I...," he stammered, then he became determined and angry. "Go to hell, Sammy. It's as much your damned fault as anyone else's that we're in this mess. In fact, you're a hell of a lot more responsible than

I am for messing things up so much. If you'd just...."

Sammy didn't let him finish. He yelled "Just shut up Dick. Just shut the fuck up. We're in this together and we're going to fix it right here and right now."

"Why don't both of you shut up and let's get this damned thing over with," Bill Silverman said.

I decided it was time for me to jump in and goad Sammy and his little group a little more. I needed to make them angry in order to get even a small advantage. "Have you guys come up with some elaborate scheme to kill me? You'll aren't much better than those movie villains in James Bond films. Why not just shoot me in the back? Stab me with a knife? Sit me front of a TV running a continuous loop of The Jerry Springer Show?" I said.

"We want you dead, but we don't want to become the subject of another murder investigation. You see Art, you are about to have a terrible, tragic and fatal accident." Sammy nodded and his three helpers started circling me.

"Just what kind of accident am I about the have?" I asked.

"You are going to fall down the face of the mountain. You see that chain link fence behind you?" he pointed and I turned around to look, which gave me the opportunity to see where each of the three men was standing. Jimmy Winsted was behind me. Dick Patrick was on my left with his hand still on my shoulder and Bill Silverman was on my right. When I turned back to Sammy he continued, "There's a place where the fence has been pushed down by folks leaning on it hoping for a better view. You're going to 'fall' over the fence and tumble down the mountain at that point. Anyone who might investigate your accident will assume you tripped and fell into the weak section of fencing."

"You've seen way too many movies. Don't you think the police will be interested to know why I was on Stone Mountain at...," I looked at my watch, "Four-thirty-seven in the morning?"

"That will be a mystery for a while," Sammy answered nonchalantly. "One of the rangers, the one on the night shift, is a friend of ours. He'll swear that he didn't see anyone on the mountain. But the detectives will find a gallon can of red enamel paint. I'll let them know that in a fit of rage you pulled your gun in my house and shot at a priceless painting of Stonewall Jackson. I'll tell them that you were angry that our group *Our Heritage* was trying to educate the public on true Confederate history. The police will assume that the great detective was a paranoid Unionist who sought to deface the monument to our Southern heroes."

"The police know that I'm investigating the murder of Berry Wellington and Terry Hansen."

"Sure. They'll wonder if there is any connection between the murders you were investigating and your 'accident,' but they won't be able to find the connection and in a couple of days they'll forget about it and move on to more pressing business. They'll forget about you."

"That's a stupid plan Sammy. No one will believe I turned into a vandal. Does the person you work for know what you plan to do to me?"

As expected, Sammy's face flushed red and he took a step in my direction. He stopped, reining his anger back into check. Sammy nodded and Jimmy Winstead, the largest of the three, grabbed me from behind and wrapped his arms around my chest, pinning my arms down. Bill Silverman stepped in front of me and spread his feet apart. He checked to be certain he had solid footing then he rammed his fist solidly into my stomach. All the air went out of me and light flashed in my head as the pain shot through my body. I gasped opened mouthed for air.

Dick Patrick then walked up behind me and gave me a round house punch in the kidney. It was as if I had no bones in my body. I collapsed into the grasp of Jimmy Winsted unable to hold my self upright.

"Take him to the side," Sammy ordered.

Although I was barely conscious, I realized I had to do something. Desperation and the certainty of death dulled the pain and adrenaline rushed through my body. I took a deep breath and willed my body into action. I raised my left foot and kicked back as hard as I could. I caught Jimmy Winstead in the shin. He grabbed for his leg and dropped me onto the granite. As I fell I grasped for Dick Patrick and pulled him down with me. I landed on my wounded shoulder with Patrick on top of me. The pain was unbearable and I gasped loudly, but no one could hear me above the screams of rage coming from Sammy Estes.

History says that during the Civil War the Confederate soldiers yelled when they charged into battle. If it was anything like the screech coming from Sammy, I can understand why Union soldiers were terrified by the Rebel Yell.

Two shots rang out as Sammy continued to rage. "You God-damned bastard. You ruined everything."

Dick jerked as one of the shots hit him in his back. Blood splattered over my face, but I didn't have time to let it bother me. I grabbed for his loose arm and reached for the pistol he held. Even in death he held it tightly.

I threw him off me with enough force that I could yank the pistol loose. I rolled to the side and found myself sliding out of control down the granite. I tried to grasp the rock but couldn't find a hold. I turned over and sat on the rock and planted my feet in front of me and let the heels of my shoes stop the slide.

Sammy and his remaining men were carefully moving toward me. I fired the gun. My first shot hit Jimmy Winstead in the stomach. He dropped to the ground and the group stopped. I fired again but the shot missed and ricocheted off the granite. My next shot wiped out Jimmy Winsted's knee cap. His pistol flew from his hand and landed solidly on the granite. Sammy fired repeatedly without aiming. His shots bounced all around me.

Then Bill Silverman fired at me. His bullet slammed into the underside of my arm below the wound Sammy had given me at the lake. I was knocked backward by the force of the shot and slid down the granite incline on my back. It was an impossible shot from my back and sliding down the mountain but I aimed for Bill's shoulder and pulled the trigger. I missed his shoulder but the bullet hit him solidly in the chest. Just then I rammed into the chain link fence that keeps the tourists from getting to close to the edge.

Pain shot through my body and the urge to lie down and wait for help was overwhelming, but Sammy Estes was rushing at me. He raised his gun and pulled the trigger but nothing happened. He threw the gun at me and it hit the fence beside my head. He continued towards me, but he stopped long enough to pick up the pistol Bill Silverman had dropped. He pointed it at me and pulled the trigger, but the fall had jammed its mechanisms and it wouldn't fire. He threw the weapon at me in anger. It bounced on the rock in front of me and continued down the face of the mountain. Sammy started running at me and I forced myself into a crouching position. As the incline increased he moved faster and more reckless. I braced myself and as he dove toward me I leaned back against the fence and caught him on his chest with my feet and vaulted him over the fencing. He tumbled down the mountain.

Later, I discovered he hit the carving of Traveler, General Lee's horse, before impaling himself on a stake used to hold fireworks for the climax of the nightly laser show.

Silence descended on the mountain as darkness overtook me and I passed out.

---Twenty eight---

I re-entered the world of consciousness slowly; disturbed from my stupor by the annoying sound of a steady beep... beep... beep. I convinced myself that it was an alarm clock. I wanted to shut it off or at least press the snooze alarm, but my body just wouldn't respond. I couldn't even open my eyes to find the source of the damned noise so I could throw it against the wall.

A soft comforting voice broke through the haze in my brain. "Just relax you're safe." Then she talked to someone else in a tone that was still soft but the comfort part was gone. "It looks like he's coming around. Run down to the nurses' station and call that policeman who left his card." A door opened and someone left the room.

I willed my eyes to open, and was immediately blinded by a bright light. I tried to shade my eyes with my hand but it was restrained to my bed.

"Where am I?" It took a great effort to form the words. Something was restricting my throat and making it difficult to talk.

"Hold on a minute. Just lie still. I need to finish checking your stitches and re-dress your wound," she said.

"The light," I struggled to form the words.

"Just keep your eyes shut," she ordered; all the comforting tone was out of her voice now.

"You're hurting me," I said. The more I talked the easier it became, but it was still difficult.

"Quit being a weenie. We have you pumped full of sedatives and pain killers. Nothing I'm doing can be hurting you too much. Men patients are a pain in the butt. You ought to have a baby then you'd know what real pain is."

I kept quiet and after a few minutes, when she completed her tasks, she announced, "There all done." She clicked off the light. "You can open your eyes now."

I opened my eyes and as they slowly adjusted to the room's light, she came into view.

"You're beautiful," I slurred.

"And you're full of drugs," she replied.

"Where am I?" I asked again.

"Grady Hospital," she replied. Grady is a teaching hospital and a major trauma center. It's located near downtown and right beside one of the busiest expressways on the East Coast. The hospital provides indigent care to those who need it. The people who rely on its emergency room as their treatment center call it "The Gradys." It's debatable if the term is favorable or not.

"How long have I been here?"

"Four days. Lots of folks have been up here to check on you. The police are also anxious to talk with you. There have been two cops who've been here every day. One of them is a scruffy looking guy, but the girl cop who comes with him is cute as a button. I think she likes you."

"Are you jealous?" I asked.

"Damned right I am," she pressed a button on one of the machines and a blood pressure cuff tightened around my unwounded arm. "Now close those eyes and go back to sleep. The doctors should be here soon and those cops will be here too. You'll need your rest." My angel of mercy fluffed my pillow and placed her hand on my forehead. I didn't want to sleep but somehow with her hand on my forehead the beeping of the monitors turned into a lullaby.

***

It could have been a few minutes, or a few hours, or even a few days but slowly the real world came back into focus. There was a large number of people standing around in my room. Some of them were just looking at me and some of them seemed to be engaged in some important activity. The nurse I had previously classified as beautiful was standing beside my bed. She was holding my wrist and looking at her watch. It was a wasteful activity since there were monitors measuring everything, but I was thankful to have another human being touching me. The nurse later told me that monitors never replace the human touch. She was right.

With the limited motion my condition allowed, I tried to identify the people standing around in my room, but the only people I recognized were Ed Vigodsky and Amanda Halsell. They walked over. Ed stood beside my nurse and Amanda stood behind. I tried to turn to her but couldn't.

"Welcome back, chump," Vigodsky said.

I wanted to say 'I'm not your chump,' but for some reason I couldn't make words come out of my mouth. Finally, I nodded my head to indicate that I recognized him.

"Looks like you wrapped up this one," he said.

That was just like Vigodsky to jump to conclusions. I screamed 'NO' in my head but again I couldn't form words. I shook my head.

"What do you mean?" Vigodsky asked.

I tried to speak, but my throat was dry and when I tried to speak the sound that I made was garbled. I said, "Not done yet," but no one could understand me.

My attractive nurse pushed him aside. "You've got him upset. Now, get out of the way." Vigodsky moved aside. I watched my nurse push the plunger on a hypodermic syringe and deliver its contents into one of the tubes that carried fluids into my body. As darkness once again replaced my brief encounter with the real world, I felt Amanda brush her fingers through my hair. I wanted her to hold me. I knew she could make me feel better.

**

Time passed again. This time when I started coming around it was night, my room was dimly lit and I was alone. The monitors still chirped away recording data and monitoring what went into and out of my body, but the noise had become such a part of my life that I no longer noticed it. What I did notice was an urgent need for water. There had to be some nearby. If I could just get some water I knew I would be better. I tried to sit up in the bed but just didn't have the energy to do it.

My activity level must have alerted the nursing staff because there was running down the hallway and the door to my room burst open. A nurse and an assistant ran to my bedside.

"I need water." I forced the words out and realized that although the words came from my body, it was an alien voice that spoke them. The assistant produced a cup of crushed ice and placed a piece of it on my tongue. My body soaked it up and I looked to her for more. While she rationed the ice, the nurse checked the tubes and monitors and straightened my bed. As I lay in the bed waiting for more ice the world became clearer and I became aware of a tube inserted into my nose. I hadn't noticed it before but now that I knew it was there it was a constant irritant.

For breakfast I had a cup of bouillon and a bowl of jell-o. It was a huge feast to my body. I begged the nurses to remove the tube in my nose, but they ignored me. When the liquids I had consumed worked through my body and I found out they were being drained by a catheter, I demanded that it be removed too, but that demand was also ignored.

By mid-morning, no fewer than twenty doctors, interns, residents and medical students had checked my condition. They came in groups of three to four with an older doctor serving as their mentor and critic. Each group poked and prodded my body and looked at parts of my anatomy that I normally reserve for special people only. The whole process was demeaning and insulting. As each group came into the room I started my demands that the nasal tube and catheter be removed and the lead physician in each group explained that the tubes were part of my treatment and would help me improve and heal faster. The explanations did little to lessen my desire to have the nasal tube and the catheter removed. Finally, I raised so much hell that one of the teaching physicians ordered a student standing in the back of the room to remove them. The rest of the students smiled. That should have been a clue, but I missed it. Too much pain killer was still in my body and it must have dulled my senses.

Let me pause a moment to give you a word of advice. If you are ever in a teaching hospital, don't make too many demands and don't make an ass of yourself, because they can let the "C" students work on you.

I yelled a number of times as he removed the nasal tube and I'm not even going to go into what happened when he removed the catheter. When it was over sweat was beaded up all over me. One of the students placed a cool cloth on my forehead.

"Is there anything else we can do for you?" the professor asked.

"Just glad I could play a small role in the education of future healers," I replied.

Soon after they left, one of the nursing assistants brought me a plate with some grits and scrambled eggs that were left over from breakfast. The grits were cold and lumpy and the eggs were hard and leathery, but it was a welcome treat for a man who hadn't eaten solid food in many, many days. For lunch I had mashed potatoes, green beans and a bowl of soup with microscopic pieces of chicken and a few noodles. Naturally, there was more Jell-O for dessert.

***

The television in the room received only three stations. The hospital claimed they had cable service, but the other channels came in with snow and hissing sounds. By mid-afternoon, I had given up finding anything to entertain me and settled for yelling obscenities at Dr. Phil as he played tough with some damaged soul desperately seeking fifteen minutes of fame. Just as they were getting ready to bring on the good doctor's next victim, Ed Vigodsky came into the room. I willingly clicked the TV off.

"Feeling better?" he asked.

"Don't you knock? What if one of these pretty nurses had been giving me a sponge bath and I didn't want to be disturbed?"

"I'd disturb you anyway, because we need to talk. And if the nurse was really pretty, she'd be more interested in talking with me than giving you a bath."

"Speaking about pretty, where is Amanda?" I asked.

"Paperwork," he replied, "One of us has to feed the bureaucrats."

"Too bad, I feel good enough to ask her to dance with me. Catch me up. What have I missed?"

"Not too much! We have four dead bodies and one guy in ICU. He's crippled with a busted knee cap and he has, what the doctor's call, a septic stomach. They don't expect him to make it."

"Four dead bodies?" I asked.

"Yep, four. First there is Sammy Estes. You know about him. He's the guy you threw over the mountain." He cut his eyes to me. I didn't react. "Then, there's a guy named Dick Patrick. He was shot in the back. We don't figure you for that one. Then there's Bill Silverman. He was shot through his heart. I told folks you weren't that good a shot. And last there's a guy we found floating in Lake Alatoona. Turns out his name is - oops, excuse me his name was - James Andrews, who coincidentally was an employee of the same company as Berry Wellington. We don't know if you had anything to do with his death or not, but I suspect you did." He paused and looked at me, expecting me to respond. When I didn't he said, "Ok! Now it's your turn. Tell me everything."

I rang the nurses' station and requested a Coke and an extra cup of ice. When it arrived I told Vigodsky some of the story, starting with being kidnapped by Dick Patrick and Bill Silverman. I left out the part about being disabled by a tazer in my parking garage and the events at the cabin and skipped over those parts that would violate my commitment to any of my clients.

"I don't believe you've told me everything, but we'll deal with that later," he said after I finished my tale.

"Come off it Ed. I've handed you a hell of a lot more than you knew and I've given you the murderer of Terry Hansen and the person who ordered the murder."

"I know, I know, but you're holding out on me."

"No I'm not," I lied.

"What about the murder of Berry Wellington? Was Sammy Estes tied into that one too?"

"No, I don't believe he was directly involved, but I do think he knew about it," I said. "I don't have any theories on who killed Berry." I lied again, but since I really couldn't prove anything yet, I felt it was a justifiable lie. "I am, however, going to find out who did it."

"That's our job."

"I know."

"Let me tell you something. You need to keep out of this thing and let us do our job. You're already in enough trouble. You know there will be an investigation into the deaths of Sammy Estes and Bill Silverman. This is real life, it's not some detective novel where you can go around and wreck havoc on things and never even fill out a report. He was getting agitated and I knew his emotions would continue to escalate if I didn't divert him. Ed continued talking. "I'll do everything I can to cut through the red tape, but you'll have to answer for what happened."

"I know. Listen Ed, will you do something else for me?"

"What?"

"Check the autopsy report on Berry Wellington and see if he was beaten before he was killed." Ed calmed down and began thinking about the new direction I had given him.

"The coroner's running behind. We should get his report soon. I'll check it. You think the same guys who beat you up, roughed him up too?"

"It's a starting place and maybe another piece of the puzzle."

We chatted for a few more minutes before Ed glanced at his watch and said. "Sorry, but we've got to cut this short I have an....appointment."

"You have a date?" I asked.

"Could be," he said.

"Looking for number four?" I asked, referring to his three previous marriages.

"Nope, I'm not looking, but a potential number four is looking for me."

"Has she got a chance?"

"You never can tell. She's prettier than number two; the sex is better than with number three; and she can cook better than number one."

"What about Peggy Fulton?" I asked.

"I'm saving her for number five. She and I can grow old together."

I gave him a thumbs up as he walked towards the door and said, "Good luck."

"Thanks!" he said.

"I meant it for the lady."

"Yeah! See you tomorrow. We have lots more to discuss. I'll bring Amanda."

---Twenty nine---

I was beginning to feel better and discovered I could entertain myself by playing with the bed's control without causing my wounds to hurt. As a bonus playing with the bed was more fun than watching television. I had the head of the bed as high as it would go when there was a gentle knock on my room door. I quickly lowered the bed.

"Come in," I said.

Annie Hamilton entered the room. She stopped at the foot of my bed, looked at me for a moment and then smiled.

"You look better than I expected you to," she said.

"Thanks, I guess."

"I had to come and see for myself. Are you really alright?" she said.

`"Sure I'm fine. Thanks for checking on me."

"Delia wanted to come with me, but I needed to be sure you were alright before letting her visit."

"I'll be out soon. She doesn't need to visit me at this hospital. Just tell Delia I'm doing great and I'll see her in a few days."

"It was in the paper. On the TV, too. You could have been killed Art."

"But I wasn't. We're not going to have that discussion again are we?"

"No Art. I'm just glad you're going to be OK."

She stood silently for a moment as moisture formed in her eyes. "I can't do it Art. I just can't." She started to cry.

"Can't do what?" I said.

Normally, I would have made an effort to comfort a crying lady, but with the argument we had recently and my dread of yet another session in Family Court defending my visitation rights, I didn't really want to comfort her.

She grabbed a tissue from the service table beside the bed and blotted her eyes. "At one time Art, we had a wonderful relationship. In fact, it might have been as good as any two people have ever had."

I nodded my head in agreement, but otherwise remained neutral.

She continued, softly "I don't know what happened to change things. Sometimes, I wish we could go back to how things use to be, but we can't. Too much has happened between us."

A nursing assistant came into the room without knocking. She pushed a small cart with a computer station. Annie and I remained silent while the young aide took my temperature with an electronic thermometer and my blood pressure with some computerized gizmo while a plastic clip stuck on the end of a finger measured the oxygen level of my blood. The she recorded some of the monitor readings.

When she left the room Annie said, "I can't marry Zackary."

Zackary was the viola player she had been living with since she left me.

"Why?" I said.

"Does it matter?" she said.

"Probably not."

"I told Delia." She paused as if she expected me to

respond, but I didn't have anything to say. "She got all excited. She thought you and I were going to get back together." Annie paused yet again but I still didn't have anything to say. "I told her that was never going to happen."

"Why not," I said.

"We've done too much damage to each other."

"Given enough time we could repair the damage," I said.

"Maybe, but things could never be the same. We've changed too much. We aren't the same people we were back then. Things can never be like they were back then. But they don't have to be as bad as we've made them. Art, if we both work on it, we can learn to be friends. We have to try Art. We have to because of Delia."

I nodded my head in agreement, but I really didn't agree with her. I believed that Annie had precipitated most of the conflict between us. She was the one who left me. She was the one who fought me in family court trying to revoke or limit my visitation rights. I was more of a victim than an equal partner in our troubles. But I didn't say what I felt. Nothing could be gained by escalating her visit into another argument.

"You need to help me Art. I can't do it by myself. I need you to talk with Delia. I need you to help her understand that we can all be friends but we can't live together. I need you to help her understand that her mother and father love her but they don't love each other anymore. We can learn to be friend, Art."

Annie always did have a flair for the dramatic. I nodded.

"Call Delia when you get out of the hospital." She had spoken it as an order, and then to soften things she added. "Will you?"

"I will, but I think Delia understand already."

"Talk to her anyway."

"You're a dangerous man, Art. Doesn't this prove it?" She motioned to the hospital room. "I'm concerned for Delia's safety." She sniffed and wiped her eyes. "Our daughter is pig headed stubborn. She loves you and I've learned that I might end up her adversary if I try to keep her away from you." She wiped her eyes again. "We have to find a way for you to be part of her life."

She walked beside my bed, bent down and kissed me on the forehead and left the room.

---Thirty---

About an hour after she left, I removed the clip from my finger, the monitors attached to my chest and the blood pressure cuff on my arm. Then I carefully removed the tape covering the IV catheter in a vein on my hand and slowly withdrew it. My clothes were stored in a wall unit. My trousers and shirt were neatly hung on hangers and my underwear, socks and shoes were in a plastic bag. The trousers were torn at both knees and the shirt was dirty with visible blood stains. The shirt fit tightly over the bandages that covered my chest area and midriff.

The door to the room flew open and one of the assistants looked at me. "What are you doing?" she asked.

"I'm checking out,"

"Get yourself back in that bed," she ordered.

"Nope!" I replied. The assistant turned and ran from the room.

I started to open all the drawers looking for my wallet, cell phone and keys. Before I found them, my nurse entered the room.

"Get back in the bed Mr. Gaines." she said taking my arm to assist me.

"No, I'm leaving." I said, gently removing her hand from my arm. "Where are my personal belongings?" I asked.

"Mr. Gaines, you have two cracked ribs, and a bruised kidney. More importantly, we have no idea how much damage was done to your liver and spleen. You are under the care of three physicians. None of them has released you. Now get back in bed."

"Where are my personal belongings?" I repeated hoping I sounded more emphatic.

"You realize you are leaving against medical advice."

"Yes ma'am I do, but I'm a big boy and I can make my own decisions. I'm responsible for my health and well being. I pay the bill so you guys work for me. I'm the damned customer here. Now where are my personal belongings?"

"They're in the safe in the business office. I'll call them and let them know you're on your way." she stormed from my room.

***

A security guard was waiting when the elevator opened on the first floor. "Mr. Gaines?" he asked and I nodded. "This way to the business office."

"A personal escort?" I asked

"Just part of our service for patients who check themselves out of the hospital against medical advice or who try to slip out without paying their bill."

"Or both?"

"Yeah, or both." He led the way, keeping a close watch on me. I couldn't move as fast as usual, but my pace seemed perfect for the security guard.

In the business office, he sat me in the side chair beside the desk of Tanika Smith according to the name plate on the office door. "I'll be right outside," he announced as he backed from the room. A few minutes later the door opened and a grossly overweight woman entered. She had professionally styled hair and perfect makeup but she must have weighed more than three hundred pounds. "I'm Betty Compton," she announced as she extended her hand to me.

I shook her hand. "I was expecting Ms. Smith." I replied.

She plopped into the desk chair. "I'm Ms. Smith's supervisor," she stated, and then she flipped through papers on a clip board and extracted one sheet. "Sign this. It acknowledges that you are leaving this facility without being released by a physician. We call it Release Against Medical Advice. You're a very foolish man, Mr. Gaines."

"I'm a man who's smart enough to weigh the risks and determine what needs to be done." I took the form and signed it.

"Thank you," she took the form and placed it back on the clipboard and removed a stack of papers held together by a spring clip. "This is a copy of your bill. How do plan to take care of these financial obligations?"

"I plan on taking care of this obligation like I take care of all my financial obligations, by paying it. I'll be pleased to either write you a check or provide you with a debit card, whichever you prefer."

"We prefer payment by a debit card. May I see

your card?"

"As soon as you return my personal belongs I can give you my debit card."

"Mr. Gaines, we can't release your personal belongings until your obligation to this hospital is met."

It took close to fifteen minutes for Ms Compton, the supervisor, to understand that I could only pay if she gave me my wallet. Eventually it sunk into her head and she hoisted herself from the chair and went to the safe. She returned with my wallet, keys, cell phone and some loose change and I paid my bill, which ate up all of the fee from the Sanderson affair and a chunk of my savings.

Outside I hailed a cab and gave the driver an address. I had to see Abigail Eddings Patrick. If my theory was correct, I could end this thing tonight. I turned on the cell phone and found it still had some battery time left. Fortunately, they had turned it off before storing it. I called the Patrick residence and Ms. Patrick answered the phone.

"Hello"

"Ms Patrick this is Art Gaines."

"How dare you call here? I was very close to both Sammy Estes and Bill Sanderson. You have some nerve disturbing me after what you did to them."

"I thought you never read the papers or watched the local news."

We argued for a few minutes, but when I explained I would kick down her door and let myself in, she agreed to see me.

"Very well then, I'll see you at nine thirty tomorrow morning," she said

"You'll see me when I get to your residence and I'm on the way now." I replied and hit the END button.

Before I could place the phone in my pocket it vibrated with an incoming call. I pressed the SEND button and said, "Hello."

"Just what do you think you're doing and where the hell are you?" It was Amanda Halsell. She was angry and she was making no attempt to hide it.

"There's one more thing I need to take care of," I replied.

"Damn it Art, taking care of one more things is our job. Your job is to heal your body. The doctors are convinced you should still be in the hospital. In fact they are convinced you are in danger of doing irreversible damage to yourself."

"To tell the truth, I think they might be right, but I have to do this," I said.

"Just what is it you're doing?"

"Visiting with Abigail Patrick"

"Is she involved?"

"Yes, she is very much involved."

"Then Ed and I will prove it and she'll pay."

"I'm not sure you can prove it. She might just get by with a murder."

"You're being foolish. I'll meet you at her house."

"No, I need to do this alone," I said.

"Like hell you do, but regardless I need to be there too."

"Okay but plain clothes and an unmarked car."

"I'm off duty and in my personal car," she said.

"I'll wait for you, but remember Berry Wellington was killed trying to get help from me and that trumps any obligation I might have to the Atlanta police."

"I'm no more than ten minutes behind you."

"How did you arrange that?"

"I called the taxi company dispatcher and found out where you were going."

"Resourceful."

"Damn right," she said.

---Thirty one---

The cab driver parked at the curb in front of the Patrick residence and in less than three minutes Amanda pulled her car in behind us. She was driving a bright red roadster which was a perfect car for her – sleek and sexy, but unique and allusive and just a little bit rebellious.

"You must have broken the speed limit," I said after paying the driver and exiting the cab.

"I'll give myself a ticket later. By the way you look awful," she asserted.

"And you're beautiful," I replied.

She was dressed in a pair of jeans with simple pink blouse that clung to her body in all the right places. Her hair was loose and bounced around her head when she moved. There was a single curl that hung in front of her left ear as an invitation to nibble gently on the ear lobe. If I felt just a little better, I would have had a strong reaction to how she looked, but all I could do was appreciate her and hope for better days.

We walked to the entrance together. I knocked on the door and it was quickly opened by a different nurse than the one I had meet on my first visit. This one too was dressed in an old fashioned all white uniform. When she saw me, she gasped for breath. "You can't come into this house looking like that," she said.

She attempted to close the door but I jammed my foot into the path of the door and leaned on it. The effort hurt like hell but it was enough to cause the nurse's foot to slip on the highly polished floor and allow the door to fly open.

"Don't worry, I know the way," I said to the nurse, who was sprawled on the floor.

Amanda stooped and helped her get to her feet. The nurse straightened her uniform and confirmed that the heavily starched white cap was properly placed on her head. "Thank you young lady" she said to Amanda, and then to me she yelled. "Your shoes. You must have shoe covers."

"I think it will be alright this time," Amanda said.

I waited for Amanda to join me and we walked into the room together. The same four chairs were placed around the square table and Abigail Patrick sat in the chair facing the doorway. She was still dressed for the old lady look. This time she had on a black dress and had her hair pulled back and shaped into a bun.

"My god, Mr. Gaines, you look terrible. You could have at least changed your clothes before visiting." She shifted her gaze to Amanda then back to me. "I see you brought a friend with you."

I resisted the urge to comment on her appearance. "This is Amanda Halsell. She's my..." I stopped, stunned that I couldn't think of the correct word to complete the sentence.

Abigail broke the awkward silence. "I believe I've already met Ms. Halsell when she, and a man who I found to be more disagreeable than you, visited with me and interrogated me regarding the death of my beloved fiancé. But tell me Mr. Gaines, why did you feel it necessary to bring a ... ah...police person with you?"

Before I could respond Amanda said. "Let me make one thing perfectly clear Ms. Patrick, I'm here as a private citizen and as Mr. Gaines' friend. He's been the victim of a serious attack and he has physical injuries that need medical attention. I am concerned that he will over extend himself and exacerbate his injuries," Amanda replied.

"How very touching! But as a result of your so-called friend's actions, two of my friends are dead and two have been seriously injured." She stared directly at Amanda. "I feel no sympathy for your ... friend," she reached into the pocket beside the chair and pulled out a pack of cigarettes, then opened the drawer under the table and removed the ash tray. "Would one of you please close the door? I anticipate this discussion to be disagreeable and I will need to smoke."

Amanda went to the door and closed it. When she returned Abigail was inhaling cigarette smoke deeply into her lungs. I took the chair immediately in front of Abigail and Amanda took the chair to my right.

"Now, why are you here at this late hour in clothes that are torn and dirty and in the company of a police person?" Abigail said police person snidely.

"I'm here to tell you that I have satisfied my obligation to my client and to his family."

"And just what does that mean?" Abigail asked.

Amanda gave me a shocked look, but I continued

talking to Abigail. "As I explained to Ms. Wellington and her daughters, I consider Berry Wellington to be my primary client in this case. I was personally offended that someone would shoot and kill him on the front stoop to my home." I paused to give her time to comment and wrapped my arm around my chest in an attempt to control the pain.

"Please continue." Abigail said, letting the smoke exhale with her words, then immediately taking another deep draw on the cigarette re-inhaling part of the smoke.

"It is obvious that Berry had someone he trusted drive him to my home to solicit my assistance."

Again I paused, but Abigail did not react.

"When I got to him Berry was still alive. His last words were difficult to understand, but what I heard him say was: 'We weren't evil, but we set it in motion and it got out of control.' Then he uttered what sounded like the word 'key'. As I got deeper into my investigation I came across Keystone Land Development Company and I was convinced for a while that Berry's last words were intended to guide me to a deeper investigation into Keystone." I took a deep breath and winced as my chest expanded. Then I continued. "But he wasn't trying to say anything about Keystone. He was trying to start a sentence with the word 'she'."

"What an interesting theory? And just what was that sentence my sweet Berry was trying to say?" Abigail asked.

"Oh, I don't know exactly what he was going to say, but I do believe he was about to tell me that you shot him."

"How utterly preposterous. In addition to being rude and arrogant, you're also a lunatic. Berry was the love of my life."

"Then why were you screwing Sammy Estes?"

"How dare you insinuate such a thing? And Sammy would never be interested in me. Sammy was queer."

"So was Berry, but you were screwing him too," I said

"You son of a bitch." She stood up and raised her hand to slap me, but Amanda grabbed her arm.

"Don't even think about hitting him. Now sit down," she ordered.

Abigail sat down, pulled yet another cigarette from the pack and lit it. Then she forced a calm façade over her body and in a mild controlled voice said. "Mr. Gaines, you are speculating and you can't prove a thing. I am offended that you would make this ridiculous attempt to connect me with the murder of Berry Wellington and I find your presence and that of your companion annoying. So, will you and Ms. Halsell get the hell out of my house?"

"You're right about one thing. At this point I can't prove a thing and that's why I haven't told the police everything I know." I cut my eyes to Amanda quickly and found she was smiling at me. "But as for as leaving, there's not a chance that's going to happen," I said.

"I'll call the police," she threatened.

"You do that. Amanda could you give her the phone number."

"Be glad to. Would you like to use my cell phone?" Amanda replied as she reached into her purse.

"No thanks," she said realizing her bluff didn't work. "It appears I have no choice but to sit here and allow you to abuse me; however, be aware that I will be contacting my attorney." Abigail stated. Amanda hadn't removed her hand from her purse. I hoped Abigail hadn't noticed.

"Let me tell you how this whole mess started," I said.

"Please do." Abigail responded contemptuously.

"Berry Wellington and Randall Kingsmore

gathered together a ... how do you describe it? ...a small group of men to collect pictures of themselves having sex with other people."

"That's disgusting."

"But you knew about it."

"Of course I knew about it. I told you before Berry and I had no secrets from each other."

"That's a lie," I stated.

"Are you calling me a liar?"

"Yes ma'am, I most certainly am, but let's save that discussion for later. Now to continue. Berry and Randall expanded their group and involved some straight guys who wanted to mess around on their wives and a few who could swing either way.

I continued, "As the number of people involved in this little group of perverts grew..."

"I resent your referring to my friends as perverts," she said

"Ms Patrick, I could give a damn less what you resent," I replied.

She inhaled deeply and puffed out her chest. "You will not use profanity in my home."

"You remarkable bitch," I said. "We're not playing around here. Do you not understand what's happening?"

She shifted in her chair then puffed herself into a stiff upright position. "You can rest assured, Mr. Gaines, you will be hearing from my attorney and as for you Ms. Halsell, I have many friends in city government and they will hear about your participation in this brutality." She took another cigarette from the pack and lit it, leaving her previous one smoldering on the lip of the ashtray. "You've been warned." She was trying to sound menacing, but it came off as pitiful. "Go ahead continue your ridiculous performance."

I resumed my summary, "As I was saying, as the number of perverts grew Randall, became convinced that there was a possibility one of his over-sexed friends could use their activities to blackmail either Berry or Randall for money or special favors. In an effort to protect Berry and himself from this possibility, he made certain that he had copies of incriminating photographs and video tapes of each of the guys involved in this little porn ring. If any of them tried to blackmail either him or Berry, he could reverse blackmail them."

"I knew that too, Mr. Gaines," Abigail said, as if having that knowledge was an accomplishment.

"Oh, I know you knew that. In fact, you were empowered to lure Sammy Estes into your plot based on your knowledge of Randall's stash of photos and video tapes." I stood up and moved to the chair beside Abigail and in front of Amanda. With Amanda on one side and me on the other, she fidgeted and attempted to push her chair back, but it didn't move.

"Get back in the other chair. I don't want you near me," she ordered.

"No ma'am. This is where I'm sitting now," I said. My plan was to focus her attention on me. I anticipated she would have a violent reaction as I continued goading her and I wanted Amanda to have an advantage if she had to intervene.

"You're filthy and disgusting."

"I do apologize for my blood stained shirt," I said pointing to the spots on my shirt.

"That's blood?" she asked.

"Yes."

"Whose?" she asked with dread in her voice.

"Some of it is mine, but most of it is from Jimmy Winstead and a guy named Dick Patrick, who I believe is not related to you."

"You're mistaken Dick is my second cousin. Our families weren't very close but he is my friend."

"Then you'll be sad to know that he is dead. He

was shot in the back by Sammy Estes."

She gasped and sat back in the chair. After a moment she took a deep breath and started puffing on her cigarette again.

I continued by pointing at my shirt. "Of course, some of this blood is from Bill Silverman, who made an effort to kill me and some of it is from Sammy Estes, who was the ring leader of the group and your partner in blackmail, real estate deals, sex and murder."

Wetness formed in her eyes. "You're a cruel man."

"That may be true, but I want you to look at the blood on this shirt and acknowledge that it was your conniving and scheming and greed that was the root cause for three of your friends loosing their life and one more being permanently disabled."

Her body began shaking and tears started flowing from her eyes. I had anticipated a violent reaction, but I was unprepared for her to breakdown in tears. Amanda produced a packet of tissues and handed them to the sobbing woman. She wiped her face and the room grew silent while she regained control.

"You'll never prove any of this," she said.

"I believe we will and let me tell you how. First,

the public records will reveal that Sammy Estes' rise from poverty to wealth directly corresponds with your elevation from barely subsisting to being financially comfortable. The cops will dig and dig into real estate transactions and they'll find out that you and Sammy were involved in some kind of shady real estate transactions together. They'll discover that you and he were using the pictures and video tapes to blackmail various people to give you more favorable interest rates or zoning rulings."

"That doesn't prove a thing about my involvement in my sweet Berry's murder."

"I'm getting to that. The police will initiate a national search for Troy Hansen. I believe Troy fled after his brother was killed, but the police will find him. I believe that Berry told Terry and Troy his concerns. After Berry was killed, I believe Terry's conscience forced him to decide he was going to tell me the secrets Berry was prepared to reveal.

"But the real proof will come from this house. In a few minutes, Officer Halsell will place you under arrest. She'll call for a squad car to take you away; then a horde of police will descend on this place and search every inch of it. They'll look in the heating vents and light fixtures and underwear drawers. They'll look everywhere and they'll keep looking till they find the gun you used to kill Berry Wellington."

She sat up in the chair supporting herself on the chair arms. "You're a worthless piece of....."

I interrupted her. "Now, now Ms. Patrick, let's not use profanity."

She settled back in her chair and lit yet another cigarette, leaving her previous one smoldering in the ashtray.

I continued talking. "At some point, Berry came to you with his concerns that someone was blackmailing local officials to give favorable zoning and other considerations to various properties. That was when you told Sammy that Berry was becoming a problem and then Sammy had his henchmen, James Andrews, beat Berry. The police have conducted an autopsy on Berry's body and it will confirm that he was beaten before you shot him. After the beating, Berry came to you believing you to be his friend and someone he could trust. He asked you to drive him to my home - a tragic mistake." I paused to allow her time to react, but she sat passively listening and weighing her options. "I imagine you sat in your car watching him walk up to my door and trying to determine what to do. You waited as long as possible, but when I turned on the light you realized you had to do something so you grabbed your gun and shot Berry Wellington in his back as he stood at my door." Tears were flowing down her face. "You're not a professional, so you probably didn't dispose of the gun. The police will find it and if we're lucky your finger prints will still be on the gun, but at a minimum ballistic test will reveal that it was the murder weapon." I paused to watch Abigail. Her hand was shaking and the ash from her newly lit cigarette was almost ready to fall onto the rug.

"What about mother?"

"I don't understand," I replied.

"Who will take care of her? What will she do without me?"

"I'm certain your ill gotten properties can be liquidated and placed into a trust for her care."

"Mother will never tolerate police running over her home."

"Ms. Patrick, she will have no choice," I said.

"It will kill her."

"The police will not interfere with her medical care, but the house will be searched, including your mother's room."

She sat quietly for a while weighing her options. Then she took another cigarette from the now wrinkled pack and lit it. "Mother didn't know anything about money. Her family always had money and she just assumed money would always be available to her. When Father died he left us very little money. We didn't even have enough to care for the house much less for Mother's care. I had to do something. You can understand that can't you." She looked from me to Amanda seeking validation. "Mother had no skills to deal with being poor. If I hadn't done what I did she would have died." Again she looked from me to Amanda. When she continued talking she had turned in her chair and was facing Amanda. "Ms Halsell, do you have a family?"

"Yes, I do," Amanda stated.

"Are your parents still alive?"

"My parents were elderly when I was born. They died when I was in college."

"Wouldn't you have done anything to protect your parents?"

"Not murder," Amanda replied.

Abigail sniffed back more tears, got up from her seat and started walking to one of the bookshelves. Amanda immediately got up and followed her. She had pulled her gun from her purse and she held it in her hand.

Abigail turned to Amanda. "If I give you the gun I used will you stop the search of the house?"

"The only thing I can promise is that I will try," Amanda said.

"Very well, then I'll get the gun for you." Abigail said.

"Stop! Just tell me where it is," Amanda ordered sharply.

Abigail stopped and pointed to a group of book bound in red leather. There was a normally bound book in the middle of the group. "There's a copy of Rex Stout's *In the Best Families* in the middle of the Sinclair Lewis books. My father was a big Nero Wolfe fan. He had the book altered so it could conceal the pistol he used for target practice."

Amanda pulled the book from the shelf and opened it to confirm the gun was inside. She closed the book without touching the gun.

---Thirty two---

Thankfully, Amanda took charge of the situation because I had reached the end of my endurance. Somehow, I found a semi-comfortable position in the chair and managed to doze off. I was vaguely aware of what was going on at the Patrick house, but I didn't really wake up until two of Atlanta's finest lifted me from the chair and guided me to Amanda's roadster.

Getting into a low car with an injured arm and cracked ribs was a challenge. I would later find out that getting out of the car would be even more difficult. Amanda got into the driver's seat and started the engine.

"I'm taking you to a hospital," she stated.

"Hell no! Take me home."

"You need medical attention."

"I need a little rest and some pain killers." I wanted to ask questions about what had happened at the Patrick residence, but the need for rest trumped my need for information.

Amanda shook her head in disgust but headed the little car toward Blossom Lane.

***

The next day, the heat from the sun woke me, I was confused and my body was covered with sweat. It took a few minutes to realize that I was in my own bed. It must have been mid-afternoon, which is the time of day when the sun is low enough in the sky to shine directly into my bedroom. I tried to piece together what happened after leaving the Patrick residence, but my mind was a blank. All I could remember was the pain of getting into and out of Amanda's roadster.

Chester was lying on the pillow beside my head, but as soon as he realized I was awake he jumped to the other side of the bed. He certainly wouldn't want me to think he was this close to me on purpose.

My stomach was growling and I needed food, but my bladder was screaming and needed immediate attention, so I got up to solve that problem and I realized two things: first, my chest and arm didn't hurt as badly as I remembered and secondly, I was naked. I didn't mind being naked but in my last memories I was clothed in a pair of torn trousers and a blood stained shirt. I wondered who had undressed me.

I took a quick shower, shaved and brushed my teeth and was starting to feel almost normal. I pulled on a bath robe and walked out. The bed clothes had been straightened, the pillows fluffed and the bed neatly turned down. A voice came from the kitchen. "Climb back in the bed, I'll have you something to eat in less than five minutes."

I wandered into the kitchen and found Amanda Halsell tending a couple of pots on the stovetop. She was wearing a white tee shirt with blue shorts. The shirt was tied in the front exposing her hips and midriff.

"There must be a law against looking that good in front of a sick man."

"Hush! Stop flirting and get back into bed. You have a bunch of pain killers in your system and you need to be in bed. I'll bring you something to eat in a few minutes."

"I need to move around and get some exercise," I protested.

"You do not. You need rest and lots of it."

"I need to check on Gort and Chester."

"You do not. They've both been fed and they are perfectly content. Of course Chester still thinks I'm the wicked witch of the west, but Gort is in love with me."

"Smart dog."

"Now get in bed."

"You have no idea how many times I've dreamed of you saying those words to me."

"Get out of here."

I went back to the bedroom and climbed into the bed.

When Amanda came into the room she had a tray with two plates and two glasses. She placed the tray beside me then gently sat on the bed.

"Now eat something." She took one of the plates and pointed to the other. "Eat up," she ordered. The plate was full of rice topped with a meat hash with two thin biscuits resting on the plate rim. I scooped a small bit of the hash on my fork and ate it.

"Spectacular! What is it?"

"It's a beef hash, made from an old family recipe. It's one of those dishes you either love or hate."

"I could never hate anything you made," I said.

"Will you stop flirting and get some food into your body?"

"Yes ma'am," I replied.

"Let me give you just a little advice. When a lady spends the night in your house, you're past the need for flirting," she smiled at me.

"Even if nothing happened?" I asked.

"We both got a good night's sleep. That counts, too."

My mind immediately jumped to a night with very little sleep. "Does that mean...."

She interrupted me, "That means you need to get better. Now drink some tea."

The tea was strong and sweet. "Tea's great too," I said.

"Back home we learn to make sweet tea shortly after we learn to walk."

"Thank you for this."

"For what."

"For taking care of me. For feeding me. For being you," I said and meant it.

"You're welcome. I know we haven't known each other that long and I certainly don't want to rush things, but I enjoy doing things for you. I'm comfortable being around you. I feel a strange closeness to you."

"I understand."

"It's a nice feeling," she said.

"I know."

We chatted and ate. The hash really was excellent but that didn't matter much because Ramen noodles with Amanda would have been a feast. When we finished Amanda carried the tray and dirty dishes away. She returned with a fresh glass of tea in one hand and two pills in the other.

"Take these," she said handing me the pills.

"What are they?" I asked.

"A double dose of pain killers. They'll knock you out and give your body a chance to heal itself. Last night when I pulled into the driveway, your next door neighbor, Mr. Grainger, helped me get you into bed and he called Dr. Kramer who made a house call at two o'clock in the morning. You certainly have some amazing friends. Anyway, he dressed your wounds, gave you a couple of shots and left these pills with specific instructions to give them to you. He's the only doctor in the City of Atlanta, and maybe in the State of Georgia, who makes house calls in the middle of the night. He said he owed you."

"Dr. Kramer is a good man who needed a little help one time," I replied.

"He said you were a stubborn patient and I was to hold you down and force you to take these pills if I had to. Your doctor says you need three more days of rest but he insisted on at least one more."

"I don't want to rest anymore."

"Quit whining. You're going to do what the doctor says."

I swallowed the pills. She fluffed my pillow and I placed my head on it. She bent down and kissed my forehead.

***

When I awoke the next morning, even before I opened my eyes, I could smell just a hint of Amanda's perfume. It was a wonderful way to start the day. The bedside clock read seven thirty three AM. I turned over and saw that the other side of the bed had been slept in but was now empty. Amanda had spent another night in the bed with me and I had slept through it.

---Thirty three---

The next week was a blur. Most of it was spent fighting off requests for interviews from the media and meeting with various members of the Atlanta police force and assorted state police and lawyers. True to his word, Ed Vigodsky helped make the process move smoothly, but when you're involved in the death of two people and the serious injury of another one, you have to contend with piles of red tape and loads of bureaucrats.   I recounted the night on Stone Mountain so many times it felt more like giving a performance than telling a story.

James Andrews' death was ruled accidental and none of the investigating authorities implicated me in it. If they had, it would have been even more red tape and a whole new group of cops and lawyers, since his death occurred in another county.

By the end of that week however, I was feeling fine. I was working out at the Vuitton Gym every day and was slowly overcoming the effect of my injuries and a couple of weeks of inactivity. My cracked ribs only hurt when I coughed and there didn't seem to be any serious damage to my internal organs. The stitches in my arm had dissolved and although the wound still itched I no longer carried my arm in a sling. I would have a nasty scar from one of the bullet wounds and it would take a lot of exercise, but I would have full use of the arm again.

During the week the police located Troy Hansen. He had fled to a friend's condominium at Myrtle Beach after discovering his brother's body. Berry Wellington had told both brothers that he suspected one of the members of the Lake Alatoona cabin group was using information about the group's secret activities to gain inside knowledge about real estate as well as to gain favorable zoning variances and bank loans. Berry confided to the brothers that he planned to hire me to investigate the situation. After Berry was killed, Terry had announced that he would carry on Berry's crusade and hire me to investigate. Troy was convinced that Sammy Estes orchestrated his brother's death and that his life too was in jeopardy.

During that same week, Abigail Patrick confessed to the murder of Berry Wellington. According to Ms. Patrick, Berry trusted her completely and shared his most intimate secrets with her. Berry never suspected that she was involved with Sammy Estes, either sexually or as a partner in real estate transactions. Berry told her he planned to hire me to investigate the Lake Alatoona cabin group. She realized that an investigation would most certainly uncover Sammy Estes' involvement and possibly hers too. Abigail asked Sammy to stop Berry from hiring me and Sammy paid James Andrews to threaten Berry and use force if necessary to deter him from continuing with his plan. James, as usual, became overly enthusiastic, and beat Berry severely, but instead of stopping him, the beating encouraged Berry to continue. Berry managed to get himself to the Patrick's residence and one of the nurses gave him first aid. Then he asked Abigail to drive him to my house.

After the police arrested Abigail Patrick, they also discovered that her mother wasn't an invalid at all, but a victim of over medication by her daughter. Although it would take extensive rehabilitation, the elder Mrs. Patrick was expected to recover and be able to care for herself.

***

I sat at my desk and ignored the messages waiting light on the phone. It was more important to finish the Wellington/Hansen murder investigation than conduct normal business. My first call was to Councilman Macek. I got through easily.

"Mr. Gaines," he said instead of "Hello."

"Good morning Councilman. I assume you have been following the news."

"With great concern. Since no police have yet called on me I assume you have been able to keep my name out of this affair."

"I have not mentioned your name, but the police are aware that Sammy Estes and Abigail Patrick were blackmailing people. It's possible the police will dig deeper and uncover you were one of those people and it's possible that they will uncover your role in this disgusting affair, but I doubt it. Now that the murderers have been identified the police have very little incentive to spend great amounts of time on follow up.

"I do not believe your sexual activities will be revealed. However, I recommend that you resign from the city council and be an extra attentive husband and father."

"I will Mr. Gaines and I can never thank you enough."

"Sure you can. Pay the invoice I will be sending you on time."

"You can count on it." He took a deep breath. "One more thing, what about the ah...pictures."

"I believe I have them all in my possession."

"I'll double your fee if you'll give me all of them that ah ... relate to me."

"Can't do that. I'm keeping them until Ms. Patrick's trial. I don't anticipate I'll need them, but you never know. After she's convicted, I'll destroy all of them."

He argued with me for a few more minutes, but finally gave up when he realized I wasn't budging.

My next call was to Mrs. Wellington, and as expected, getting her on the phone was difficult. Amos, the mysterious servant, answered the call and instructed me to wait. It took another five minutes for her to come to the phone. Based on my experience she doesn't answer her calls any faster than five minutes.

I reviewed the investigation and let her ask questions for close to fifteen minutes. When she had gathered all the information she wanted, I told her I would send her an invoice.

"You certainly will not," she exclaimed. "It was not I who retained your services; it was the estate of my son and Harriet Wellington Tucker is the executor of his estate." She gave me Harriet's address. "How dare you even insinuate that I would engage in such pedantic activities as paying the invoice for a ....private investigator?" I could hear the derision in her voice. Then she abruptly hung up the phone.

I said "You're welcome," into the dead phone. "It's been a pleasure doing business with you, too." I hung up the phone.

My last call was to the Wilfield's. Emily answered the phone.

"May I speak with Horace Wilfield please?" I asked.

"Who may I say is calling?"

"I hate it when beautiful women forget me."

"Ah, yes Mr. Gaines! I could never forget a man like you. You've become a celebrity. They talk about you on the news all the time. The photo they printed of you didn't do you justice, but I cut it out of the paper and have it taped on my desk."

"Thank you, but I wouldn't believe everything you hear on the news."

"I hear other things too. For example, I hear that James Andrews is dead and there's a rumor floating around the company that you might have been involved in his death. Is there any truth to that?"

"Emily, shame on you for even suggesting such a thing," I jokingly rebuked her.

"Everybody here hates that James got himself drowned, but there's not a single soul here who will miss that fat slob."

"Any other rumors floating around the company?" I said trying to change the subject.

"Just the one that says you have the hots for me."

"That's no rumor and I'm sure that's true for every guy who's ever seen you," I replied.

"You're sweet to say it," she blew me a kiss over the phone line. "Is it true that you killed two men and seriously wounded one other?"

"I've never been very proud about having to kill anyone."

"From what I read in the paper and heard on the news, those two deserved to be killed."

"People shouldn't always get what they deserve."

"I don't know about that Mr. Gaines, but I'm glad you didn't get killed."

"Thank you, but can you call me Art?"

"Certainly, Art. One more little tidbit of information that has everyone here talking." She paused for dramatic effect before continuing. "This is Andy Wilfield's first day back at work since the death of his...friend." She paused and snickered like a school girl, who was in on a special secret. "Now, let me get Mr. Wilfield for you." She placed me on HOLD before I could respond. It seemed as if calling me by my first name excited her so much she couldn't continue the conversation.

Horace Wilfield picked up the phone quickly. "Mr. Gaines!" he barked as a greeting. "You told me that you have the documents I retained you to recover. Is there any plausible explanation for why you have not delivered them to me?"

"You arrogant prick," I responded angrily. "During this investigation I had to kill people and people have tried to kill me, including one of your company's employees. So delivering documents that could be used to confirm that you're a crook who's involved in deceptive and illegal real estate transaction is not that damned high on my priority list."

"Are you referring to James Andrews?"

"Yes."

"And you say he tried to kill you?"

"Yes. That's exactly what I'm saying."

"Mr. Gaines, if that is true, and I don't know that it is, then James Andrews was acting independently and not as a representative of this company. However, I apologize for my earlier remarks; they were uncalled for. I read about what happened on Stone Mountain and I realize how difficult all of it must have been, but those documents could not only ruin me; they could destroy this company and I have to be concerned for the wellbeing of my employees and stock holders."

"How noble of you," I quipped.

"There's no need for sarcasm," he replied.

"Like hell there's not. Everything about this whole disgusting affair warrants sarcasm," I responded. "Now here's the deal. The documents you are so anxious to get are packed and sealed and ready to be delivered to you. I can send them by messenger or you may send someone to my office to pick them up."

"I'll send someone," he responded. He yelled instructions to someone, but he must have had his hand over the phone since the sound was muffled. "My man will be there within the hour."

"I'll also include my invoice with the package. When may I expect payment?"

"Just how much is your fee and my man will bring a check?" I gave him the amount. "That's considerably more than I expected," he protested.

"Horace, are we going to quibble about money?"

He paused for a moment. "No, we're not going to argue about money. My man will have a check when he arrives at your office. Good day, Mr. Gaines."

"Whoa! We're not through yet."

"What else could we possibly have to discuss." He spoke as if he were addressing an entry level employee.

"I need to speak with Andy," I said.

"My son is not available for a conversation with you," he quickly replied. "I have only recently learned of his...ahh...lifestyle choices and I recognize that he has experienced a personal loss and because of his...relationship with.....that man.....he has been hounded by the police." Horace's voice cracked slightly as he spoke.

"Horace quit arguing with me and put your son on the line. I still have the documents in my possession and

I can change my mind about turning them over to you."

The line went silent, while the two of them debated my request.

After a few minutes Andy picked up the phone. "This is Andy. I'm sorry for keeping you waiting. How may I help you?" He was trying to sound cheerful and nonchalant, but there was a little bit of grief and a whole lot of fear in his voice.

"I want you to know that you should be in jail or even at the bottom of Stone Mountain along with Sammy Estes." He gasped for breath. "Everywhere I turned in this investigation I uncovered your influence."

"How dare you?" His voice quivered as he tried to sound assertive and failed in the attempt.

"Just shut up and listen. You're guilty as hell and it looks like you're going to get away without getting caught. People like you make me sick. You hang around in the background and manipulate people. You live by deception. I don't have enough information to convict you of a crime, but I have enough to get the police interested in investigating you more deeply. If they do I'm certain they will find enough to put you in jail for a long time. I'm fed up with you and your band of swindlers and perverts and I'll use the information I have if I see your ugly face anywhere near me or anyone I care for." I took a deep breath. "Before I go, I want to give you one piece of advice. You need to take some time and learn to control both your greed and your zipper."

I hung up the phone, leaned back in my chair and let the contempt I felt flow through me. After a few minutes I cranked up the computer and got busy creating invoices. I collected the first one without even spending postage when the Wilfield's courier arrived and we exchanged the packet of documents for a nice check. I put the others in the mail chute.

When I returned the phone was ringing. I answered it. It was Ed Vigodsky.

"You owe me for this one," he said.

"I know."

"I stuck my neck out and convinced my boss that solving the Wellington and Hansen murders was more important than getting you to admit what else you might know."

"I hope you know what you're doing. Let's hope Abigail Patrick pleads guilty and we won't have to fool with a long drawn out trial."

Ed paused for me to say something, but I realized this wasn't the time for a flippant remark. "I can't help you when you're sitting in the witness chair committing perjury." He paused again and again I stayed silent. "Whatever you're hiding I hope it's worth the risk."

The line was silent.

"Thank you, Ed," I said.

"You're welcome, chump," he replied and hung up.

While I was talking with Vigodsky the call waiting feature had beeped indicating that someone else was calling. The blinking message light said the caller had left a message. I dialed the message line and punched in my password. It was Tim Mangram, my attorney. Art. I just got a call from Ms Hamilton's attorney. She is dropping her petition to alter your visitation rights. Looks like you avoided another battle in the family court. Talk to you soon. By the way, I didn't spend a lot of time on this matter but I'll get my invoice to you in a couple of days."

Later that afternoon, the phone rang again.

"Good afternoon. Art Gaines." I answered, anticipating a call that might bring a new client, but it was something better.

"Hi, big boy."

"Hi pretty lady," I said to Amanda Halsell.

"How are you feeling?"

"Couldn't be better, now that I'm talking with you."

"My shift just ended and I'm off duty for a couple of days. I'm thinking about throwing a couple of thick cut pork chops on the grill, nuking some sweet potatoes in the microwave and drinking a bottle of wine. You interested?"

"You bet I am," I said trying to sound eager but not overly enthusiastic. "Can I bring any thing?"

"No, it's all taken care of."

"Okay. What time?"

"How about seven o'clock?"

"I'll be there."

"Art. On second thought there is something you can bring."

"Sure anything."

"Bring your toothbrush. See you around seven." She hung up quickly.

I went to the armoire and opened the locked drawer where the bottle of single malt scotch sat undisturbed and waiting. I took it out, broke the seal and poured a generous shot into a glass. I had reason to celebrate.

Made in the USA
Charleston, SC
11 December 2010